PRAISE FOR MARIEKE NIJKAMP

"A compelling story of terror, betrayal, and heroism... This brutal, emotionally charged novel will grip readers and leave them brokenhearted."

—*KIRKUS REVIEWS* ON *THIS IS WHERE IT ENDS*

"Love, loyalty, bravery, and loss meld into a chaotic, heart-wrenching mélange of issues that unite some and divide others. A highly diverse cast of characters, paired with vivid imagery and close attention to detail, set the stage for an engrossing, unrelenting tale."

—*PUBLISHERS WEEKLY* ON *THIS IS WHERE IT ENDS*

★ "With exceptional handling of everything from mental illness to guilt and a riveting, magic realist narrative, this well-wrought, haunting novel will stick with readers long after the final page."

—*BOOKLIST* ON *BEFORE I LET GO*, STARRED REVIEW

"Immersive and captivating. Thrilling in every sense of the word."

—KAREN M. MCMANUS, #1 *NEW YORK TIMES* BESTSELLING AUTHOR OF *ONE OF US IS LYING* ON *EVEN IF WE BREAK*

"The darkly twisted ode to self-discovery briskly whisks an intersectionally inclusive group through a reasonably stormy, emotionally charged scenario that considers the sometimes-steep price of growing up and growing apart."

—*PUBLISHERS WEEKLY* ON *EVEN IF WE BREAK*

ALSO BY MARIEKE NIJKAMP

This Is Where It Ends

Before I Let Go

Even If We Break

At the eND of EVERYTHING

THE WORLD
NEVER WANTED THEM.
THEY
REFUSE TO BE FORGOTTEN.

MARIEKE NIJKAMP

sourcebooks
fire

Published by Sourcebooks Fire, an imprint of Sourcebooks
P.O. Box 4410, Naperville, Illinois 60567-4410
(630) 961-3900
sourcebooks.com

Cataloging-in-Publication data is on file with the Library of Congress.

Printed and bound in the United States of America.
VP 10 9 8 7 6 5 4 3 2 1

CONTENT WARNING

This book deals with ableism, abuse, death,
illness and implied eugenics, imprisonment, and
transphobia. In addition, it includes mentions of assault,
blood, gunshots, racial profiling, and sexual violence.

one
LOGAN

WE ARE THE LAST ONES.

Leah and I squeeze into the hallway just in time for movement line. There's eight of us to a wing, and the six others are already standing in front of their doors underneath the fluorescent light, all in various stages of awake. Thankfully, there are no guards in sight yet.

Next to me, Leah yawns. "So early," she whispers.

I elbow her. It's always early.

Life at the Hope Juvenile Treatment Center follows a routine. That's a good thing. Lights go on at six. The day starts at seven with movement line, a head count, and breakfast. Our cohort—the east and the south wings—starts school at eight, while the other two wings have school in the afternoon. Lunch is at noon. Half an hour of recreation time. Twice a week, it's followed by PE. And therapy or group therapy or work in the communal garden.

Then another count. Dinner. Recreation. Lights out at nine.

It's the schedule Leah and I were given when we got here nine months ago. It's never changed.

Leah runs her fingers through her brown hair and braids it so she won't get in trouble for not following dress code. Her hair is darker than mine, but not by much. Her hazel eyes are lighter, but they mostly look red and tired now. We're not identical. Not quite. But she is still the other half of me.

I don't know how to exist without her.

"All I'm saying is, some days, I wish we could sleep in," she grumbles.

I roll my eyes and straighten her scratchy blazer. Our brains are wired differently, she once told me. She can't read well, but I can. I don't talk, but she does. And I *like* routine. It's reassuring. Every morning, I know when I get to eat. Every night, I have a roof over my head and a bed to sleep in. We may not be comfortable here, but it's better than before.

Across the hallway, Nia Miller stifles a yawn. Underneath her bangs, she gives me a tired grin and waves. She's my age, Black, with her hair tied back in a curly ponytail, and ink stains on her sleeves. She has a few crumpled pages stuffed in the pockets of her pants. I gesture at her to push the paper deeper so the guards won't see it, and she does.

"Thanks," she mouths.

I smile. I like Nia. She's always drawing, though I don't think anyone's ever seen the work. That's okay. She shouldn't have to share if she doesn't want to.

Leah nudges me. "Eyes down."

Warden Davis and two of the guards show up at our wing. The warden stalks past, a clipboard in hand, staring at every single one of us like he's looking for something. I glance at him through my lashes. He wears a dark suit and an angry frown, and he towers over us.

Josie Watson, the white girl in the room next to ours, doesn't seem fazed by his presence. She meets his gaze. She has chestnut hair cropped past her ears, and her eyes are cold. When she sees me looking, she doesn't smile or wave, and I quickly look away. She scares me. She stabbed another girl, and I wouldn't put it past her to do it again.

"What is he doing?" I sign at Leah, when the warden reaches the other side of the hallway and marks something down.

Leah hushes me. "Not now."

She'll figure it out. And if not my sister, someone else will know. Or Warden Davis will tell us in one of his endless speeches about rules and good behavior. He believes everything is a teachable moment.

It's one of the reasons we all hold our breath until he's gone again, and the guards get us moving toward breakfast. That's what movement line is. Everything we do is controlled and supervised by the guards.

The rest of our wing falls in line around us.

Isabella Gonzales leads the way to breakfast. She's here because she got into a fight with her one of her teachers and got arrested for assault. She's one of the kindest people I've met. She's the only one aside from my sister who shares her dessert with me.

Chloe Hughes and Riley Jackson are next, following Isabella. The new kid, Emerson, brings up the rear. I don't know their last name. They got sent here three weeks ago, and the only thing I know is that they were allowed to bring a violin, but they aren't allowed to play it. They tried, once, after lights-out, and ended up in solitary for a full two days.

It's cruel, Leah said. But there is little here that isn't cruel.

I wish I could have a violin, even though I can't play. I wish I could have something that belongs to me.

When I said that to Leah, she replied, "I belong to you."

I shook my head. "That's not the same thing."

"It still matters."

She reaches out to squeeze my hand now and starts pulling me toward the cafeteria.

———

Mrs. Harris stands at the door, counting us in. She coughs when we approach her and raises an eyebrow at the two of us holding hands, but she doesn't say anything. I like her. She knows how much it matters to me.

"Thank you," Leah whispers.

Mrs. Harris shakes her head, and something like sadness flashes across her face. It's there and gone again, so maybe I didn't see right. Or maybe I imagined it.

Leah leans into me. "I saw it too." She may not always be able to concentrate well on what's happening around her, but she's always aware of me. "Do you think she's okay?"

I hope so.

I don't even have to say or sign it for Leah to know how I feel. "I hope so too. She's good people, like Granddad would say."

We grab our trays and line up to get our food. Today's breakfast menu is an apple, unidentifiable fruit juice, coffee, half a cup of cereal with milk, and two burned pancakes. The smell of sizzling-hot oil clogs my nostrils.

"At least we've finished up the leftover turkey," Leah mutters.

That's true. Three days of the same meal is more than enough for me.

A commotion near the door causes the breakfast line to grind to a halt, and I turn to figure out what's going on.

Two guards have pulled Emerson aside and have marched them up against the wall. One of the guards grabs the sleeve of Emerson's blazer, and it tears at the seams. "This is a disgrace."

Leah says they give us uniforms to wear here because they think it gives us a sense of pride. But the scratchy fabric makes my skin crawl. Some of the clothes are threadbare, and all of them are uncomfortable. And Emerson's uniform doesn't fit at all.

"Keep quiet," Leah hisses, when Emerson argues.

The sentiment is echoed by several people around us.

"If you act up, that dress code violation is going to be the least of your problems," the guard promises.

Every eye in the cafeteria is trained on Emerson and the guards now. Everyone wants to see what the new kid will do. Only the people at the table closest to the guards keep their head down and pretend to be focused on their food. In the farthest corner of the cafeteria, the boys from the west wing have huddled together. Their leader—Hunter—is standing on his seat to get a better look at what's happening.

He smiles thinly and mumbles something to his friend Reid, who laughs.

I nudge Leah, and when she sees what I'm looking at, she shakes her head. "New kid's going to get a reminder of who owns these hallways too."

I frown. Technically, the state does. Or Better Futures, the private company that controls Hope. It's where the none-too-subtle name comes from too. Hope for Better Futures. But if you ignore that, it's Hunter and his friends. And they have hungry smiles.

I hate it.

I take a step closer to Leah, and she reaches for my hand again, her fingers brushing mine. "Keep your head down," she whispers.

I do.

This is a part of the routine too. The guards flexing their

muscles. Hunter and his friends showing theirs. Leah told me the best thing anyone here can do is not draw attention to themselves.

Eventually, the guards release Emerson, and the tension in the cafeteria fades slightly. Everyone is ready to return to breakfast, until one of the guards throws a last comment in Emerson's direction, and Emerson flinches.

A girl a few places in line behind us sighs heavily. "*They* are nonbinary, and *their* pronouns are they and them." Her voice echoes in the quiet room.

When I turn, I see it's Grace Richardson, from the south wing. She rolls her eyes and picks up her tray again, though she must know what's coming. She is at Hope for aggravated assault. I believe she did it too. She's been here longer than Leah and me, longer than pretty much anyone, and she intimidates me.

Leah groans. "Come on, I want to eat."

A moment later, Grace's tray clatters on the floor when the guards grab her and pull her out of the line. Emerson stands forgotten, and they do the smartest thing they can—they fade into the background.

One of the guards who grabbed Grace shoves the line forward to get us all moving again, and I nearly get pushed off my feet. "Eyes forward!" he says. "You won't get any extra time to eat."

That's enough of a threat to get everyone focused on breakfast again, but I wish I could ignore the sounds of the struggle going on behind me. Grace's tray as it screeches across the floor. The guards' angry grunts when Grace struggles—and her muffled compliance once they've cuffed her. By the time Leah and I have gathered our breakfast, the guards have dragged Grace out of the cafeteria.

"She tried to help," I sign at Leah, once we've sat at our table. "She didn't do anything. She corrected them."

Leah stabs at her pancakes. "The guards don't like making mistakes. And they like it even less when someone points those mistakes out to them."

I take a bite of chewy cereal. I don't like the texture but being hungry is worse. "It makes no sense."

She shrugs. "I know."

"Are you like, psychic or something?" The voice comes from close behind me, and I swirl around.

Elias Thompson towers over me. He holds an empty tray, and he's munching on his apple core. He's pale, with hair so blond, it's almost white. He got arrested selling meth out of his high school's basement, and he's the type of person who walks around with mocking contempt for everything and everyone.

"Well?" He reaches over my shoulder and grabs my apple too.

Leah raises her eyebrows. Her hands are curled to fists. "I pay attention. Try it sometime."

"Cute." He smirks.

"I am," Leah says, without missing a beat. "You should put that back. It's my sister's."

Elias tilts his head. He stares my sister down and dares her to force him.

It only takes a beat. Reid and Maverick from Hunter's table notice that Elias is challenging us, and they get up and walk our way. Their soles squeak on the linoleum, and every conversation around us hushes. It always happens. A silent beat whenever Hunter or any of his friends are around. Elias realizes what's happening. He drops the apple on the table and turns on his heels. Reid follows him, and Maverick lingers near us.

"You okay?"

Leah told me I shouldn't scowl. Instead, I try to look grateful. I reach for the bruised apple and polish it on my sleeve.

"Yeah, thanks," Leah says. "He wasn't doing anything, just being his annoying self."

Maverick rolls his shoulders. "We'll make sure it doesn't happen again."

Leah's smile is tight-lipped. When Maverick reaches out to tousle my hair like I'm a kid or a pet, she very carefully shakes her head. *Don't anger them. Play along.*

I freeze and let him touch me.

Hunter took pity on us when we first arrived. He slung an arm around Leah's shoulders and told her: "I have a sister who's special too. I know how hard it is, but I'll make sure nothing happens to you while you're here."

She had to step on my foot to keep me from punching him, and we fought about it when we got to our room. I hate the word *special*. I hate his belief that I'm a burden—or anyone's precious possession. I hate the idea that I should be protected. I may not speak or think the same way Leah does, but that doesn't mean I'm less human than she is, and I can take care of myself.

It took Leah almost a week to convince me it wasn't about any of that—except the protection, maybe.

"Life is different here than it was back home," she said. "For better *and* for worse. Do you remember what Granddad used to tell us? There are good people who will help you, but there are also wolves in disguise. Hunter is a wolf."

"So?"

"We have to be careful with him and his crew, and I'd rather he eats others than that he tries to eat us."

"I'd rather he doesn't eat anyone at all." They all scared me.

"Also that, of course." She winced. "But...I can't protect you here. Not on my own. Not from everyone. He can."

So I learned to bite my lip when Hunter and his friends find ways to "help" us. I learned to accept it when they treat me like a porcelain doll that might break.

I like being human better, but when I spy Emerson huddled up in a corner and Grace's empty seat at her table, I know no one is quite human here.

two
EMERSON

"HEY, NEW KID." A VOICE cuts across the open area. I recognize that tone from the streets—mild curiosity with a threatening undercurrent. I push myself farther into the corner of the concrete yard. Bits of gravel crunch underneath my feet.

I've been waiting for this moment since the guards drew everyone's attention to me. I pluck at my ill-fitting blazer and swallow the nausea. The Hope Juvenile Treatment Center is no St. Agnes Academy, but some rules are universal. Every school has its predators.

Maybe I can pretend that I belong here—leaning against the wall, looking at the clouds, trying to figure out my place in the world. No threat to anyone.

A shrill whistle, from much closer. "Hey!"

I flinch and look up. A white boy with a fuzzy red buzz cut saunters in my direction. He holds his hands loosely behind his back. He's coming at me from an angle, cutting off my escape routes.

"New kid," he says again. "Why didn't you listen to me?"

I sigh. I want to keep my head down, sit here in the pale morning sun until I have to get to therapy, and make it through another day. I don't want any more trouble, not again. Still, I can't stop myself from muttering, "*Emerson*."

"New Emerson," he says.

"What?" I snap.

"What *what*?"

"What do you *want*?" I demand.

He laughs, but it sends shivers down my spine. "To warn you that your shirt is untucked. The rule is you have to look presentable, and you've got to follow the rules, right? I don't want you to get in trouble when you get to class."

He knows full well I learned that the hard way already. But, "Thanks."

I reach for my shirt, but a large hand clamps around my shoulder. "Hey! Wh—"

A fist connects with my stomach, and the air rushes out of me. "A reminder of these rules too."

I double over, and immediately his right fist cuts across my jaw. Pain blossoms across the left side of my face. I stumble and reach out to find my balance. The metallic taste of blood floods my mouth.

A hand grasps my hair, forcing me to look up. The boy has the long, slender fingers of a pianist. His mocking smile and blue eyes swim in and out of focus. "Hunter's in charge here. He gave you time to settle in."

I glance around to find help, but no one is close. The few teens on the far side of the yard steadfastly look the other way. The guard at the doorway is preoccupied with one of the other teens. That's probably on purpose.

I spit on the floor and try to shake free. "Tell him thanks."

Another punch to the stomach sets me straight. Or rather, folded over and dizzy. The world spins and twists around me, like I'm losing my connection to it. Maybe it's better that way. Maybe I can just get lost.

My assailant tightens his grip on me. "You're smart. That gets you nowhere. He wants to talk to you tonight, after lights-out. He'll be in the recreation room."

"Why?"

"Why *what*?"

I lick my lips and immediately wince. My bottom lip is swelling, and it's split open. "Why does he want to talk to me?"

The boy grins. I try to remember his name. Seth? Red? Reid? That's it. "Consider it the welcoming committee."

"Won't the recreation room be closed?" And more to the point, won't I get in trouble for walking the halls after bedtime?

Reid shakes my head none too gently. "Figure it out. So you'll be there?"

"Yeah." My bravado doesn't extend to challenging the only guy in the Hope Center with his own followers. Everyone warned me to expect a visit from one of them, one of these days. Like Reid said, those are the rules too. Unwritten, perhaps, but no less real.

"Good!" Reid lets go of my hair, and the sudden release causes me to stumble. I expect him to walk away, but before I can brace myself, another fist connects with my side, and then his leg sweeps my feet from under me. I crash to the ground, and the impact *hurts*. It reverberates through my arms and knees, and my skull feels like a tympan, the pain ringing in my ears.

I know I should get up. I shouldn't make a target of myself. But I lie with my face against the concrete until Reid's footsteps retreat. I have to find the courage to put myself back together again too.

If I could stay here, in this position, and not get up again, I would.

I don't belong here.

"Guess it's time for your initiation." Another voice rolls over me. A hand appears in my line of sight. When I turn my head, trying not to wince too hard, I can make out a face. Dark-brown hair, light-brown skin, laughing brown eyes. I see no threat in his gaze or in his posture.

"Khalil," he introduces himself.

I try to introduce myself too, but my throat is dry, and my head is spinning. Instead, I reach out to grasp his hand, and he gently guides me to a sitting position.

He crouches down beside me. "Wow, you're a mess."

"Thanks?" I touch the bruise on my cheek and wince. It feels warm underneath my hand, but I don't think Reid broke skin.

"Don't worry, no permanent damage."

Small mercies, I guess. I cough. "So what did you mean by initiation. Like…hazing?" The word feels out of place here, like an uncomfortable reminder of my old-old life, but it's the only thing I can think of.

"Nothing like that, unless you want to be part of Hunter's crew. Which, by the way, I would advise against. He's an asshole."

"I'm not—" I swallow the objection. "So what is it?"

"You know, asking you a few questions. Explaining the house rules. Making sure you have everything for a pleasant stay in this establishment."

I raise an eyebrow. "This place loves its rules, huh?"

Khalil smiles. "See, now you're getting it. Once you understand it, life in Hope really isn't that complicated."

"I don't think that's true," I say, before I can stop myself.

He doesn't even blink. "You're right. But look at it from the bright side: we have a roof over our head, steady food on the table, and people who are paid to tell us they believe in us. We should be grateful, or so I hear."

"So grateful, I'd be willing to commit a felony for it." I wince.

"That's the spirit." He hesitates for a moment, his eyes narrowing. "Did you?"

"What?"

Khalil raises an inquiring eyebrow. "Commit a felony?"

Same question. Different words. Everyone I talk to wants to know why I'm here.

I shrug. "Nah, I didn't do anything. I woke up here one morning."

Perhaps, one day, I'll wake up at home again.

He gets to his feet and brushes his hands on his navy-blue shirt. "Fine then, keep your secrets. I'll figure it out one way or another." He doesn't seem angry, just amused. He seems to be amused by everything here.

By the time I've scrambled to my feet and steadied myself against the wall, he's already walking away from me, back to the other side of the yard.

I lean back against the wall and breathe in the air. It's getting colder. Maybe the leaves are changing colors outside, though I can't see it from here. But if I close my eyes, I can pretend.

By the time we're counted back inside, I'm stiff and hurting all over. I place my hand on my side once and cringe. It feels like I've been tenderized.

The guard at the doorway frowns but doesn't say anything, which is a small mercy. Or negligence. Either/or. I could tell her what happened, of course. Part of me still wants to believe that authority figures have my best intentions at heart or that the guards only misgender me by accident. That if I tell her, she'll prevent it from happening again and make sure that Reid gets what he deserves.

But Hunter and his crew could never get away with what they do unless the guards *purposefully* looked the other way. Perhaps they think it builds character. Perhaps they simply don't care about us that much.

Like Father John, the old parish priest at our church, who thrived on telling people they were incorrigible sinners. No matter what we said or did. No matter how many Hail Marys we said. Incorrigible. I loved the church. I hated him. I thought things would be better when Father Michael took over.

What a fool I was.

Either way, saying something about Reid could be dangerous. So I keep my head down and my mouth shut and follow the bare, gray hallways straight to my therapist's office. My shoes squeak on the linoleum, and it makes me all too aware of myself. I have a right to be in the hall, but barely. Therapy and bathroom passes are the only acceptable reasons to be on our own during the day.

I pass another guard stationed outside the classroom area, where I would be if I didn't have therapy. He's staring at his phone. It must be exciting, because he barely looks up. Raised voices drift out from the inside.

One of the twins from my wing slips past him with a pencil and a bunch of empty paper. She winks and gives me a thumbs-up as she heads toward the bathroom.

I smile in return.

But when I knock on Jemma's door a few minutes later, the smile has faded, and tension has settled in my neck and shoulders. We didn't see each other last week—Jemma was home for Thanksgiving—and I'm still getting used to the idea of trusting her with my feelings. At least Confession has the theoretical option of anonymity.

Jemma doesn't look up from the report she's reading, and her long, auburn hair falls in strands across her face. She absently gestures for me to come inside. "Emerson, good to see you."

"Hi." I perch on the chair in front of her desk, legs folded underneath me. Jemma's office is as basic as can be. No endless bookcases or a couch to lie on, which is kind of what I'd expected when I heard we all had to go to therapy. But there are no visible cameras. The chairs are comfortable, even though they smell of fake leather. And one of the walls has a pretty cool mural of an ocean at sunrise. It makes the room feel cozy. Almost.

"We're here to talk about—" Jemma sets the report aside, and I brace myself. She sucks the air in through her teeth. "What happened?"

I shrug and lie. "I fell."

She narrows her brown eyes. "Sure. What *happened*?" She pushes her glasses higher up her nose and leans closer to me. "You can tell me, Emerson. Fights are not tolerated here, especially not hazing or gang activity." She says those last words like she stepped on a bug and felt it squish beneath her feet. "Everything you say in this room is confidential."

She looks at me expectantly.

Briefly, the opportunity is there.

Jemma is one of the reasons Hope is classified as a residential treatment center. We aren't just stuck here—we're provided with counseling and therapy. We have a communal garden where we can grow our own food, because it may teach us something about life, and there's the opportunity for other forms of work experience. Mrs. Vance, our teacher, worked in special education for nearly three decades before she came here.

Warden Davis calls it interdisciplinary treatment for emotionally troubled youth.

Fancy words that don't change the fact that the doors around us lock. Or that Jemma looks like she graduated college last year. Or that school is a small room with a secured desk for the teacher, sixteen of us, all at different levels, and fewer books than people.

When I arrived, once I was told what to expect, Jemma was the first person to sit down with me. She looked like she'd stepped right out of my former neighborhood, with her plaid pencil skirt and blue button-up, bow and all. She said it would be an intake conversation, but it took several hours and involved various multiple-choice questions, much like the psychological evaluation in detention. One of those "figure out what's wrong with you" assessments. Next, she and the guards observed me for three days to get insights into any problems I might have with adapting to my environment or with socializing.

Then Jemma created a personalized treatment plan. She wanted to work with me on what she calls my authority issues, my gender identity issues, and my commitment issues.

"To put it bluntly," she said one of those first days, "the board is aware that you are a status offender, and your assignment here is suboptimal. So we're willing to do what we can to help you with your needs."

I didn't think I had issues. Or needs beyond what we all have. Home. Purpose. Someone who listens. But if it means more time away from the others, I can't say I mind.

But I'm still locked up here. And I don't know Jemma well enough yet to know that she won't betray me too.

I push myself back in the chair. "I fell."

Right at the same moment, Jemma's computer *dings*. She glances at the screen and freezes. She clenches her hands to fists. Her glasses slide down her nose again. For the longest moment, she doesn't say anything at all. Then she sighs and leans back in her chair. "Okay, well, in that case, let's talk about your last couple of days."

And she doesn't push, and she doesn't try again.

I admittedly don't know her that well, and maybe I'm not used to this—to any of this—yet, but that seems odd.

Jemma folds her arms, listens, and doesn't take notes. Instead, she keeps glancing back at her computer. I don't know if she's angry at me for not trusting her or if she wants me to say anything else. But I *can't*. She must understand that.

When our allotted time is up, she passes me a chocolate from a small stash she keeps behind her desk. I wince when I put it in my mouth, and while my bruised cheek throbs, it tastes better than anything I've had here in the last couple of weeks. Perhaps it's a peace offering.

But she doesn't meet my eye when I get up and leave.

three
GRACE

EVERY TIME I THINK I'M better than this, I prove to myself that I'm not. I haven't learned a thing. I still let my anger take hold of me. The same thoughts keep running through my head over and over again.

Failure.

No one cares about you.

You'll be left here.

It's been hours since the guards dragged me out of the cafeteria. They took me to see Warden Davis, but he wasn't in his office, so they tossed me in solitary to wait. By now, I'm convinced that I've been forgotten entirely. The clock in the hallway is ticking so slowly that I barely believe time is passing.

We've been left here.

You'll be left here to die.

I wonder sometimes what it would look like if the people who run Hope gave up on us completely. They wouldn't actually kill us, I don't think. It would be an inconvenience to deal with all that paperwork. But some days, the worst days, when it feels like I'm only a hollow shell of anger, it's almost a comfort to think that they might be accidentally negligent. That they might forget about us.

On those days, it would be a relief.

Not today. Pacing around the solitary room, I remember all too well what it's like to spend a night in here. What it feels like to have my hands tied to the bed frame, unable to scratch and stretch and sleep. I don't want to be given another night like that for "acting up," but I don't know what I can do now to escape it. It'll be my ninth time in solitary this year, including two forty-eight-hour cooldown periods. Every time I come out, I feel a bit less like me, a bit less like a girl with dreams bigger than this place.

"Grace." A voice from near the door.

Fuck.

I freeze and glance around me. I've only been pacing here. I didn't leave a mark or destroy anything. They can only punish me for running my mouth.

"Grace." The voice grows more insistent. "Are you in here?"

The guards wouldn't ask me that, and though my heart still hammers out of control, I hesitate.

"Who's there?" I keep my voice as low as possible.

"It's me."

I roll my eyes at that, like I can see straight through the heavy door. But the answer tells me everything I need to know regardless, because there's only one person here who would pull a stunt like this.

I sit next to the door and pull my knees up to my chest. I imagine what he looks like on the other side of it. "What the fuck are you doing here, Casey? Are you trying to get us both in trouble?" I mentally go through the day's schedule. "Aren't you supposed to be in class?"

"Mrs. Vance left early. And I wanted to make sure you're okay."

I open my eyes wide, distracted despite myself. "Mrs. Punctuality-Is-the-Key-to-Happiness left early?"

"I think she got abducted by aliens," he says, somberly. "It's the only logical conclusion."

I snort. "Aliens?"

"Chest-bursters or face-huggers. Maybe we're all about to be eaten by giant squirrels." There's a smile in his voice, and I feel the corners of my mouth quirk up in response.

I imagine what he looks like, sitting there, his lanky body folded into a crouch. His dusty, dark hair framing a scarred, brown face, and his eyes sparkling. In the year and a half since I got here, he's become my best friend. The only one who makes this place remotely habitable, his wild ideas an escape I never knew I needed.

I shake my head. "You're—without question—the weirdest person I know," I say. "But I'm okay. Thanks for checking."

"I'll be waiting for you when you get out," he promises. "I saved you some food from lunch."

I breathe a little easier at that, at the idea of an after. "Get out before anyone catches you, please."

"See you, Star Kid."

It's late afternoon when Rock and Scissors come to free me from solitary and bring me to Warden Davis. Neither one of them acknowledges the time or the fact that my stomach is rumbling and my head is pounding. They're both pale and distracted. Usually they're two of the good ones. The guards we can count on to joke around, who don't treat us as criminals but as humans— not like the two who took me out of the cafeteria this morning.

But Rock lets me out of the room without a jab or a smart comment. Scissors flanks me quietly as we walk. The cell used for solitary confinement isn't part of the four residential wings of Hope or close to the communal areas. Instead, it's near the various offices. While these hallways look cleaner than ours, they're all but abandoned today. They're quieter than I've ever seen them before.

I can't stand the unnecessary silence for a moment longer.

I clear my throat. "What has you both so distracted?" I nearly laugh. "*Did* the aliens land?"

Scissors opens his mouth to respond, but Rock—who has fallen in on my other side—grunts. "Shut up, Grace. You don't want to get into any more trouble than you're already in. Not now."

"I don't want to get into trouble. I wanted to eat breakfast and lunch. I want to eat dinner, I guess, by now." I fight to keep the accusation—and the hunger—from my voice.

"If you'd followed the rules, you wouldn't have been in there waiting for the warden in the first place."

"Right, so I should let you all misgender the new kid and not say anything?" I mean to *think* it and not *say* it, but that's kind of always been my problem. Tone down one comment and the other slips out.

Rock grabs me by the arm and pushes me to the wall, forcefully, face first. For a brief moment, I'm convinced he'll zip-tie me up and march me back to solitary, and pure terror courses through me. *Good* in here doesn't mean the same as it does in the outside world. It simply means it takes longer for the guards to snap.

He leans in close. His breath is hot on my cheek, and it smells of stale coffee and gum. It reminds me of too much. I force myself not to flinch. Not to think. Not to struggle.

"I'm complying, okay? I'm complying," I mutter, almost out of habit.

"You better be." He leans in until it hurts, and I cringe. "You are responsible for the choices you make, Grace, and for the consequences of those choices. You could've followed the rules, and none of this would've happened. None of this *would* happen."

It sounds like he's talking about something other than my throwaway comment, but I can't for the life of me figure out what. His words run through my mind and turn and twist.

If Ian would've kept his hands to himself, none of this would've happened either. If our school had listened to the girl he was assaulting or to me instead of their golden boy. The star of the swimming team. The kid without a history of lying. If the police had listened to us. If justice were justice.

But I learned early on how rare that is.

So I let my shoulders go slack and release the tension from my body. After a while, when my neck starts to ache and I'm certain my hips will be bruised from the collision with the rough stone, Rock registers that I'm not putting up a fight, and he lets me go.

I expect him to push me forward to Warden Davis's office, make another angry comment about how, if I don't learn, I'll be stuck here all the way until my twenty-first birthday, despite the fact that no one's ever been here that long.

Instead, he takes a step back and brushes his hands. He jerks his head in Scissors's direction. "You take her to Davis. I'm done with this mess."

Scissors steps in to hold me, his movements automatic and trained into him, even though I have no escape. His voice holds a warning when he turns to Rock, and his hands tighten around my arms. "Henry…"

Right. I keep forgetting they have normal names too.

Rock must shake his head or something, because Scissors's grip slackens. "Yeah, okay. Stay safe."

And before I can react or ask what the fuck is going on, Rock turns and walks back through the hallway, leaving Scissors and me staring at each other in awkward silence.

Then he pushes me in the right direction, and his voice is softer. Tired. "Not a word, Grace. For once. Not a word."

I know. I need to find a way to not say everything that pops into my brain. But here's the thing I've learned about Hope: we're not taught to moderate ourselves; we're taught to be silent. Don't speak up. Don't talk back. Don't question too much, too loudly, too often.

At some point, we'll stop using our voice altogether. Because what's the point if no one listens? What's the point if we're only punished?

Maybe that's when they'll call me *rehabilitated*. Maybe then they'll care. Not when I'm better, but when I'm the Grace they want me to be and I've lost myself completely.

The worst thing is: it's effective. I'm a coward. Maybe I am a bad person. Once we get to Warden Davis's office, I simply stand there, arms to my sides, and prepare to let his words wash over me.

Normally, Warden Davis sits behind his desk to lecture us.

He'll stare at me with his cold, blue eyes until I'm uncomfortable, and he'll tap his fancy pen against the wooden desktop. *Tap-tap-tap.* Today, he is in the midst of packing files into a briefcase, and he doesn't so much as look at me. One of the filing cabinets along the wall is open, and several folders are sticking out.

I stare at his short-cropped, gray hair and try not to fidget.

"Miss Richardson, we've had this conversation too many times now. You are here at Hope because you were given a second chance in life, in spite of your flagrant disregard of both law and your fellow student's personhood. You are here because Arkansas and Better Futures believed we could rehabilitate you and turn you into a productive member of society. But this has always required work from your side, and I'm afraid to say I do not see the progress we hoped for. Despite our help and continuous efforts, you let your emotions get the better of you on an all-too-regular basis. Sometimes, I wonder if you want to make life worse for yourself."

His words are like ice through my veins. My throat is so dry, I wouldn't know how to speak if I wanted to. Worse? Worse how?

Solitary is only meant to be for a couple of hours, according to the guidelines—a day or two at most. But Hope has other ways to punish us. We've all heard the stories of teens being taken from here to be sent back to a closed facility. Sometimes for a couple of weeks or so, as a time-out, to scare them. Sometimes they don't come back at all.

The mere thought of it makes me want to vomit. I hate it

here, but everywhere else is hell. And I *didn't do anything*. I only told the guards to stop misgendering the new kid. I only struggled when they cuffed me. I can be *good*. I know I keep messing up, but—

"Of course, Better Futures was built on the belief that even delinquent teens deserve understanding and care. We would never simply wash our hands of you. But everything that happens from this point on will be on your own head. These are the consequences of your own actions."

His words eerily mirror Rock's outburst. Warden Davis looks up from sorting the documents, expecting some kind of acknowledgment—even if I don't know exactly what I'm acknowledging.

I swallow hard and manage a barely audible, "Yes, sir."

He softens a bit at that. "You're a good girl, Grace. I truly wish we could've done better by you."

I don't know how to respond to that. I don't know what he's saying. And it isn't until the broad hand of Scissors rests on my shoulder that I realize this is it. I've been dismissed.

The guard steers me toward the door and gives me a gentle nudge. "Go on, clean yourself up."

I'm trembling all over, but my hand is surprisingly steady when I push open the door. I walk out and part of me expects to find Rock there, to escort me back to solitary, but the hallway is empty.

I'm alone.

So I keep on walking. One foot in front of the other. And Warden Davis's words bounce through my head. Teasing me. Haunting me.

Why wasn't I punished for what happened in the cafeteria? And why did Warden Davis's dismissal sound like a goodbye?

It's all I can do to make it to my room. Where the walls are empty but for mold stains and a hint of faded graffiti. Where the bed is uncomfortable, but at least it has no restraints. And where I make it to my tiny bathroom to throw up.

After I've rinsed my mouth and cleaned my teeth, I sit down on my bed with its itchy woolen blanket and think.

Something strange is going on here, and I want to know what it is. Because if this place doesn't make sense anymore either, I don't know what will. I hate it here, but at least I know what's expected of me.

I *don't* want to make life worse for myself.

It takes me all too long to realize that this trembling inside me is fear, pure and breathtaking. I haven't felt this afraid in a long time. Not since that first night after I got arrested. And the last night before my court hearing. I'm far more comfortable with anger than I am with fear.

I kick my shoes off and send them flying across the room.

I don't go see Casey. I sleepwalk through dinner. I don't reply when people talk to me, only in single syllables when the guards say something. I can't even taste what I'm eating. All I can do is observe and consider.

One of the guards shouts at Sofia when she accidentally drops a spoon—and he kicks it out of her reach. Another guard purposefully looks the other way when Joshua steals an extra cup of pudding. Halfway through dinner, Warden Davis passes by the cafeteria on his way out. He has a long coat over his suit and a briefcase in his hand. He shakes hands with the guards on duty. In the doorway, he turns back to look at all of us.

When our eyes meet, his mouth thins, and he shakes his head. Then he leaves.

During recreation, several guards do the same thing: they come in, shake hands with those on duty, and leave. With every one of them who passes by, the discomfort inside of me grows— and so does the annoyance at being kept in the dark.

Once I'm back in my room after lights-out, the solitude is too oppressing and the questions in my mind are too many. I want to know what's going on here. I *need* to know what's going on here. We have a right to it, don't we?

Without any care for consequences anymore, I get dressed. I pull my hair into a messy braid. And I walk out of my room.

four
EMERSON

THE IRONY IS, FOR MOST of my life, I was a good Catholic girl. I never broke rules. I loved going to Mass every Sunday. I would dutifully go to Confession too. Sometimes I miss it. I miss the Emerson I thought I was. Maybe things would be easier if I could have gone on pretending to be that girl. In another life, maybe. A parallel universe.

But in this universe, I'm sneaking through the darkened hallways of a juvenile jail to meet the residential bully, because apparently, I have no sense of self-preservation whatsoever, and I don't have anyone to pray to.

But I guess this is a rule too, isn't it? And if this is the only way to fit in, if this is the only way to find a glimmer of belonging here, I'll do it. Hunter is waiting for me. So I go.

Since my room is at the very end of the east wing, it's terrifying to sneak toward the common areas. My footsteps on the stained linoleum floor are never entirely silent and neither is the hallway around me. In one of the rooms to my right, someone is talking in their sleep. A little ways farther down, I can hear someone crying.

The only thing missing is the pounding of the guards' boots and the loud middle-of-the-night conversations.

My steps echo, almost like someone is following me. If I'm caught outside of my room at this time of night, I'll be in so much trouble.

I follow the hallway until it gets to the cross section with the three other wings. The light is brighter here, the shadows darker. I duck down—like that makes me less visible—and am crossing the large open space toward the common areas and the administrative wing when it happens.

"Weird."

I nearly jump out of my skin. The soft voice comes from close by, but it rings like a bell. I can't figure out who spoke. I *can* jump back and push myself against the wall. My heart hammers up a storm, and my knees shake.

Someone laughs coldly. "Chill, new kid. I'm not here to turn you in."

A girl steps out of the shadows on the other side of the room. It's the same girl who corrected the guards when they misgendered me. She's wearing a faded shirt and pajama bottoms and somehow still looks more at ease than I do in my dark shirt and uniform pants. She has her mousy hair pulled back in a braid, but despite her confident words, her eyes look haunted.

"Who are you?" *What do you want?* almost slips out too. My voice only shakes a little.

"Grace. South wing." She takes a step toward me, offering me a wry smile. "Nice to officially meet you, I guess."

We probably shouldn't be having this conversation here, in the middle of an open area, but I'm not sure what'll happen if I walk away.

"Are you part of the welcome committee?"

She raises her hands, as if I'm some kind of skittish animal. "Not my thing. I happened to pass by." A totally normal thing to do in the middle of the night.

"So what's weird?" I ask.

Grace turns away from me and points toward the blinking red light from a security cam. "You passed at least two different cameras, but no one has come to check on you. Last time I was that naive, I was in solitary before I even made it out of the hallway."

Oh.

Fear squeezes my throat. Someone could have—*should* have noticed me. I didn't even take the cameras into consideration. "I'm not really used to this yet," I squeak.

She snorts. "I can tell." There's an edge to her voice, like she's tired or has been crying. "But this is not normal."

"What do you mean?" Maybe the guards are preoccupied. Maybe we should turn around and go back to our rooms before they notice us.

"Long day. Long story." Grace throws a glance in the direction of the north wing, but then she shakes her head. "Come on, I'll show you the best way to get to the recreation room unseen. Unless you want to turn around?"

The absurdity of what I'm doing has crept up on me, but I can't simply turn away. "I think I should get this over with."

"If it makes you feel any better," Grace says, "you'll live."

"Good?" I probably don't sound very convinced, but Grace doesn't say anything, and the best option I have is to follow her. She moves with purpose and abandon.

It takes me roughly five minutes to realize that we're not going straight for the recreation room but taking a long way around. A *very* long way around. We're not walking toward the common areas but toward the main guard station.

Unease and fear settle heavy in my stomach.

"Wait. What are you doing?" I hiss.

She gestures for me to be quiet. "Checking on something."

"*Grace...*"

"Trust me."

Before I can do anything else, like stop her, or run away, or tell her I don't trust her, or try to let the floor swallow me, she pounds on the heavy-duty door.

The loud bangs vibrate through the air around us. I grab

Grace by the shoulders, and I yank her back from the door. "What is *wrong* with you? Are you completely out of your mind? Do you know the trouble we're in—"

Anger sparks in her eyes, and she slaps my hands away. "Shut up. Listen!"

I close my mouth.

Nothing.

Absolute silence settles around us again, and no one responds to Grace's racket. Grace's hands tremble, and her breath is shallow. Her mouth works, but no sound comes out. The door doesn't open. No response.

I love silence. Silence is what makes music. But this silence is uncomfortable and threatening. "We shouldn't be—"

"Hush." Grace does the next unthinkable thing and reaches forward to open the door to the guard station. Usually, it's one of the doors inside of the Hope Center that is permanently locked. Medium security only goes so far. Not tonight. It creaks when it opens, and the darkness inside practically spills out.

No guards. No lights. None of the surveillance monitors are on.

Grace's shoulders drop, and she clenches her fists. "I knew it."

"What?"

"I knew something was up."

I shake my head. "So what—"

"We're alone."

I blink. "What do you mean? We're not supposed to be alone." The words spill out of me uncontrollably.

Grace narrows her eyes, and I can feel the distance and the ignorance between us. "Something happened outside, I think. The whole staff has been acting all weird. Distracted or something. I don't know."

I nearly laugh, because what else can I do? "I didn't even notice."

Come to think of it, didn't I? I remember Jemma staring at the computer screen, like she didn't hear a word of what I was telling her. The guard who didn't see the twin sneaking around in the hallway.

"Told you this wasn't normal," Grace says.

"What isn't? Tattling to the guards? That won't get you anywhere."

Another voice from the shadows. Again, I jump. I'm not meant for this sneaking around, even when, apparently, there are no guards here to stop me. When Reid saunters into our line of sight, his movements casually predatorial, my unease doesn't falter. Especially not when I see the other boys behind him, down the hallway. All of Hunter's crew, with their leader in the middle. They're far enough away that I can't make out their expressions, but they seem to be purposefully blocking our exit.

Reid grins at me. "We were waiting for you."

I can still feel his hands on me. I can still feel the ghosts of his punches. I force myself to remain upright so I don't crumble.

Grace turns around, and the set line of her mouth betrays her annoyance. She's not the type of person to be intimidated easily. "What is this, a midnight picnic? Go away."

Reid shrugs. He jerks his head backward in the direction of the others. "Hunter wants to see the new kid, and when they didn't show, well... You know how it is."

With those few words, the tension of the night grabs me. I was going to this initiation willingly, but I foolishly forgot about it for a moment, and now I'm trapped.

One of the other boys walks up to me.

"It's bullshit, is how it is," Grace mutters. She takes a deep breath and steps into the guard station.

Reid gasps—and the sound echoes throughout the hallway. "Whoa, Grace, what are you doing?"

She doesn't answer, and he turns to me. "What is *happening* here?"

"The guards are gone," I say, once I've finally found my voice. "They're not patrolling either. They're...gone."

His shock is palpable—and it's mirrored on the faces of the people behind him. Some of them have been here for years. Guards are part of daily life. Being observed constantly is part of being here. And with no reasonable explanation, we're left with an emptiness that has the gravitational pull of a black hole.

The camera lights still blink, but if we're only being observed from a distance, that hardly matters now, does it? Unless... "Grace, do you think this is a test of some sort? A psychological experiment to see what we'll do?"

I read about prison experiments in school. Why else would they leave?

Reid scrunches up his face. "There's no way that's legal."

"Oh, like that's ever stopped them," Grace comments from inside. She pokes her head out. "Nothing's here. No sign of why they're gone or where. No letters or notes. No hot coffee either. Doesn't look like anyone's been here all night."

She tosses a candy bar my way, and I barely manage to grab it.

"Eat up," she says. "You look peaky."

I stare at it, not hungry in the slightest.

"There's no one on patrol either?" Reid asks. One of the boys who followed Reid has turned and is spreading the word. At a small gesture from Hunter, two others run into opposite directions.

"Not in our wings," Grace says. "Presumably not in yours either, and I can't imagine everyone's hiding up north."

"I have a few people checking the premises," Hunter says, walking up to all of us—but especially me. He's a lanky white boy with dirty-blond hair and sharp cheekbones. He stops next to me and places an arm around my shoulders. When he leans in, I can feel the hilt of a knife press into my side. No doubt he feels me tense up immediately.

He smiles at me. His voice is musical and smooth as honey. "We were planning to have fun tonight, but I did not expect the night to be *this* good."

I must've squirmed, because Grace steps forward. "Lay off, Hunter. You're a creep."

Hunter lets go of me, and I stumble backward. It happens

so fast, it takes my brain a second or two to catch up. He grabs Grace by the arm and twists her with such force, she goes crashing into the wall. Before she can pull back or defend herself, he is on her, and I see the flicker of a blade near her chin. While she inches away from the knife, he licks his lips. With the same charismatic voice, he says, "I'm happy to remind you of the rules here. But for tonight, it seems, we have more important issues at hand."

She swallows.

"Understood?"

"Yes."

He flicks his knife up in the air and catches it deftly as he gives Grace some breathing room again. She doesn't immediately move. She clings to the wall like it's the only thing that keeps her standing, and I'm fairly sure I'm the only one who sees a whole roller coaster of emotions play out across her face. Fear. Anger. Heartbreak.

She pushes herself up and brushes her hands on her pajama pants, and whatever mask she wears slips back into place. Only the shadows in her eyes remain. "What is your plan then, oh wise and magnanimous leader of all of us lowly folk?"

Hope buzzes with stories about Hunter. Stories that even I've heard. Stories that he killed another boy without reason or provocation. That he's unpredictable and dangerous.

I believe everyone always has a reason for their actions. But when I see the glint in his eyes, I also believe the dangerous part.

"Well, it seems to me, with no one here to stop us, tonight might be an excellent time for a midnight stroll. We may not even want to come back."

Even Reid blinks at that.

"You want to break out?" Grace's voice rises two incredulous octaves.

"Those are such strong words. Let's call it an excursion. We'll see where it leads."

I clear my throat. "Have fun."

"Oh, no." Hunter sounds obnoxiously pleased with himself. "Can't leave witnesses behind. You're coming with, of course." He turns to Reid. "Go wake the twins too. I don't want to think about what happens to them without our protection here."

Reid flicks him a salute of sorts. "Sure thing."

"No." For the first time tonight, fear is apparent in Grace's voice, and it echoes exactly how I feel. "Do you know will happen to us if we're caught breaking out? I want a *life* after this, Hunter. I want a future."

"And I'm providing you with one," Hunter says, like it's entirely reasonable to suggest escaping prison. "If our wonderful zookeepers at Better Futures wanted us to remain here, they would've guarded us better. Haven't we been taught to reach for opportunities? This is one."

Grace's nostrils flare. "I won't stand in your way."

"You won't, because you're coming with."

"Then let me at least get—"

"No."

"Hunter…" Grace is tense all over. Her eyes are frantic.

"Yes?" There's a challenge in Hunter's voice. He glances at his two remaining bodyguards, who haven't said a word at all but who are both taller and stronger than Grace and I.

Grace's resistance drops. "Fuck you."

"I knew you'd see reason." He smiles, and all I can think about is the good Catholic girl who would never have been in this situation. Who would have prayed for protection and deliverance from this boy and his dangerous plans.

But I am here. And I can't pray. Not anymore.

five
LOGAN

BEING WOKEN UP IN THE middle of the night isn't part of our routine. I hate it. Having someone else in our room in the middle of the night is even worse. I see the shadow hanging over me, feel the hand on my shoulder, and I want to scream and scramble, but my brain overloads and the only option I have is to tremble.

Don't touch me.

On the other side of the room, Leah leaps out of bed. The long-sleeved shirt she's using as a pajama top billows around her. She scowls. "Get out." She pushes the shadow away and comes to my rescue like she always does. She crouches next to me and holds out a hand.

I stare at it, and my hands twitch and flap. She doesn't make a move. She doesn't react to the voice in the background. She waits. And when I reach out and grab her hand, she squeezes. I cling to her. I cling to what is left of me.

Don't ever let me go.

My breathing eases, and the familiar sights and sounds soothe me. The uncomfortable bed with its ratty mattress. The near constant dripping of the faucet in the corner. The tears in the walls. The torn-up school library book I signed out loud to Leah before we went to sleep.

Reid.

Oh.

I pull back from Leah and glance at the boy in our room. "Why is he here?" I sign.

She narrows her eyes but doesn't turn around. "Good question. Reid, why are you here?"

"Hunter wants to see you."

"In the middle of the night?"

"The guards are gone. He wants to get out."

And with that, Leah stills. It's not the same kind of freezing that I experience, but I recognize it all the same. Too many possibilities, too many feelings, too many thoughts all mashed up against each other. She breathes out deeply and closes her eyes, and for once, I can't tell what she's thinking.

"Out out?" she asks, quietly.

"Hunter doesn't want to leave you on your own here."

He doesn't think we'll make it, most likely. He doesn't think I'll make it.

But we can't.

I push myself up in sitting position, my knees up to my chest and the blanket up to my chin, and nudge Leah. She glances up at me, and I can see a spark in her eyes. A dangerous glint I've seen before. "We can't," I sign. "We'll get in trouble."

It was the very first thing they told us. The doors inside remain open. The doors to the outside remain closed. That doesn't change because the guards aren't here.

"Don't you want to see the world again?" Leah asks softly.

"I don't want to get in trouble."

"If there's no one here, no one can find out," she says. It reminds me a little too much of the conversation we had right before we torched the warehouse. *Don't you want revenge?* she'd asked me.

Someone was there. Someone did find out. Someone nearly died.

But I went along with it then. I'll go along with it now. She knows that. She always does.

"I don't like it."

"I'll take care of you."

She always does too.

"Where will we go?"

She turns to Reid, who doesn't—can't—understand my question. Only Leah knows the language we speak.

"Where will we go?" she repeats. Her voice cracks, and she coughs.

He shrugs. "Wherever Hunter wants to go, I guess. Are you getting dressed?"

"Get out then," she says. "Yes."

He places himself outside the door, and I start my morning routine at night. Get dressed. Brush my teeth. Brush my hair. I can't help but wonder about his answer. We'll go wherever Hunter does. Because I recognize that feeling.

I'll go wherever Leah does.

Reid takes us to the center's entrance hall and the heavy-duty doors that separate us from the outside world. We've only ever used them once. Only to enter, never to leave. Hunter is there with his crew. Six of them in total, including Maverick and Reid. Emerson is there, crouched down and staring at the floor, alongside Grace.

Hunter lights up when he sees us. He always does. Leah says it's because I make him think of his sister, and we should encourage that side of him.

I think it only makes him more dangerous.

"If it isn't my favorite sisters in this building." He steps toward us, and I take a step back. It's habit. It's instinct when faced with a predator. His mask slips for a second, before he throws an arm over Leah's shoulder, and I'm the only one who sees that she cringes.

"Are you ready for the wide, open outside?" he asks.

I'm not, but thankfully it's not like he expects me to answer him.

"Always!" Leah plasters on a smile, while Emerson frowns. I'm glad I'm not the only one who's uncertain about this.

"Fine, whatever, let's do this," Grace says. "Since it's not like we have a choice or whatever." Before anyone can stop her, she pushes open the door, and we all suck in a deep breath.

The door gives.

It creaks and it's heavy and the only thing I can think about is how definitive it sounded when it closed behind us—but now it's opening. Slowly. Until Hunter snaps his fingers and three of the boys on his crew jump forward to push, and the door swings open wide.

It isn't quite as simple as one door. Behind it is a small registration desk, for visitors and lawyers to announce themselves before they're guided to the reception area, where tall windows let in more sky than we ever see inside. But this door is the one that locks us in. Or did, at least.

Now it's open. No one on the other side can stop us.

"So now what?" Emerson asks, eyes wide open, fists clenched.

"Do you have a home to go to, new kid?" Hunter asks, not unkindly.

Emerson shakes their head.

"In that case, the first step is out of this godforsaken place, and you can figure out the rest from there." With that, Hunter steps through, dragging Leah with him. I follow without hesitation, because I always have, and so does everyone else. All ten of us.

Hunter quickens his pace. Reid follows. Before long, we're all running, like we're in a movie. Even me, though I'm not sure what we'll find outside. Past the metal detectors. Out of the other set of doors.

Outside.

Outside.

Outside.

There's a world outside. We all stop and breathe because we haven't seen it in weeks or months or even years.

Hope Juvenile Treatment Center lies amid a small clearing. A piece of elevated grasslands between the wild oak and hickory trees and mountain ranges of the Ozarks. It could be a wilderness camp too, cut off from all kinds of civilization, surrounded by endless *world.*

We run out. Into the cold night. Off the dirt road that leads to Hope. Onto the grass that's soft underneath our feet. I stumble. I let myself fall, hands first, to feel it. I'm not the only one either. Meanwhile, Emerson has dropped to their knees and is clutching their stomach like they're about to throw up. Grace stands outside the door, and she's staring up at the stars—*the stars.* An owl hoots in one of the trees, and Maverick whoops loudly in response.

"Freedom!"

Hunter cuffs him across the head, but he's grinning too. "Quiet. We're still too close to that hellhole. Let's keep going."

None of us want to move. We want to sit here and breathe in the crisp, free air. I want to stick close to what I know. Maverick and Colton—boys in Hunter's crew—are laughing about a raunchy joke. Grace is still staring up at the sky like she wants to memorize every star and every cloud and every inch of darkness. I don't look up. The endless sky and the thousands of lights overwhelm me.

Leah crouches down next to me, and the way she smiles at me aches. "We can go anywhere from here, if we stick together," she says. "If we keep going, we never have to worry about social services or being separated."

"We'd still have to eat and find a place to sleep."

She shakes her head. "I thought about it. All we have to do is cross the state lines. Find another city to live in. Be more careful than we were before, and never lose sight of each other."

"Live on the streets again?"

"Not for long. I'll find a job. I'll provide for us."

I have no clue what that would look like. After our granddad died and we had nowhere to go, we'd hole up in empty buildings and dream together. Of a small apartment with a dozen cats. I could do administrative work and Leah could find a waitressing job, and at the end of the day, it would be the two of us together, and we'd be happy.

I don't think anyone will hire two girls who set fire to a building with people in it.

I don't know what the world holds.

But I reach for Leah's hand, and we cling to each other, and I don't tell her how afraid I am. Hope is structured. We have a roof over our head and food to eat every day. Our teacher doesn't shout at Leah when she can't keep up with reading, doesn't shout at me when I don't speak up in class. It may be cruel, but the world is cruel too.

We sit until Hunter comes to fetch us. He sees us holding hands and smiles at Leah. "You're good to her," he says.

She frowns a little. "We're good to each other."

He smirks. "Of course. We'll have to keep moving."

Once he turns his back, I make a disgusted sound, deep in my throat, and sign viciously, "I hate him."

"Hush, you." Leah smacks at my hands, but she smiles.

Even in the little while since we sat down here, the sky's grown darker. It's well past midnight. Well past any sort of witching hour. All is quiet when we follow the dirt road out of here. Or at least quiet compared to Hope. Another owl hoots in the distance, and I hear rustling off the path, like a rat or a possum.

I kick at some fallen leaves. "Do you think the others will leave Hope too?" Tonight, tomorrow, whenever. If for some reason the guards don't come back.

Leah glances at the buildings slowly disappearing behind us and shrugs. "Dunno. I imagine they will once they realize the guards are gone."

"The other teens?" Emerson says from my other side. They still have their arms wrapped around their chest. "I can't imagine anyone choosing to stay at Hope. That is, unless the guards show up again in the morning. I don't know what'll happen if they do. I don't know what'll happen to us."

I raise my eyebrows, and Emerson colors. They glance back between the two of us. "I figured you were talking about everyone who's left," they say.

I nod, but I can feel Leah tense next to me.

"We were having a *private* conversation," she snaps.

Emerson colors deeper. It makes them look almost purple in the little light we have, and I elbow Leah.

"It's okay. Do you think that'll happen? Do you think the guards will come back?"

Emerson watches my signs carefully and then turns to Leah. I have to elbow her again before she begrudgingly translates.

"I don't know," Emerson says. "They seemed distracted all day, so maybe something is wrong? If we're lucky, we'll never find out." They furrow their brow. "I saw one of you sneak out with paper, right? That's not something you can usually do."

I nod. They're right about that, but the guards *were* distracted.

Leah's eyes widen. "Did you?"

"Nia was running out," I explain. It only makes me wonder if she'll escape too. And if it's easier for us to try than it would be for her.

"You can't get caught with those." Leah sighs. "And she can't either. It will only make life harder for her."

"But I was trying to help."

Leah closes her eyes and sighs. "I know, but it doesn't work like that. We're not treated equally."

Nia is at Hope for larceny and resisting arrest, because

someone thought she tried to shoplift—even though she never really stole anything. Meanwhile, Leah and I have been caught with stolen food or pads more than once, but we never got anything more than *a stern talking to*, as Leah put it. Even at Hope, the guards pay more attention to Nia than they do to us. It doesn't sound like justice to me.

Something of my outrage must have been visible on my face, because Emerson nods. "It isn't fair."

"It isn't." Leah turns to the road ahead. "It'll be better out there."

"Will it?"

"It has to be."

If nothing else, under the countless stars, it's certainly brighter. We make it a mile or so away from Hope when the dirt road takes a sharp turn toward the mountains.

From here, a narrow mountain road leads toward the nearest town. Sam's Throne, a small town right at the edge of the Ozarks. It was where Leah and I were transferred from the court's jurisdiction to the care of a local guard. We waited for nearly two hours, and the court clerk refused to let us go to the bathroom. It made the drive uncomfortable, but at least there were no roadblocks.

Not like the one that currently protects the pass. With barricades and floodlights that seem to come out of nowhere.

And soldiers, heavily armed. With guns pointed in our direction.

six
GRACE

"TURN BACK TO WHERE YOU came from!"

I knew this was a bad idea. I can't put into words how good it feels to be under an open night sky, to see stars and clouds go on forever, unobscured, endless. I don't know how to wrap my mind around the overwhelming joy of walking without having to stop.

But leaving Hope goes against every fiber of my being. Not because I want to be there, but because I want to make it out. Properly. I want to prove to everyone—but most of all myself— that I can find a way to be good. To be better than this.

Instead I find myself once more with a gun pointed at me, and a familiar, bone-numbing terror spreads through me.

Hunter clears his throat and raises his hands. He takes a careful step forward. "What is going on?"

"Stay back!"

Hunter freezes.

"Farther, all of you!"

Something heavy settles in my stomach. We all take a few steps back.

The roadblock is set up with barred traffic barricades and a truck parked sideways across the road. It's manned by at least four soldiers, and none of them look particularly excited about ten teens showing up in the middle of the night. Two soldiers are wearing neck gaiters pulled up over their mouth and nose, and they whisper among themselves. One runs to a truck a little ways farther down the road.

"We're just trying to get to Sam's Throne," Hunter says, when he gets no answer to his initial question.

I push my fists into my pockets to keep from reaching for him and pulling him back.

"Stay there, and show us your permit!" The same voice has an edge of fear to it now, and that only ever makes things worse.

"What is happening?" Emerson whispers behind me. I can't make out the hushed answer, but it's probably a variation of *nothing good*.

The soldier who ran back returns with an officer. The officer motions at the guards to keep their post, then steps in front of the barricades. He hooks his thumbs around his belt. The absence of the weapon doesn't make him look any less menacing, especially when the soldiers behind him still have their guns trained on us.

"Go back to where you came from, and you won't get into trouble, kids," he says, presumably trying to sound older than he looks, trying to de-escalate whatever this is.

"Do they know who we are?" A soft voice. Leah, probably.

"We live in Sam's Throne!" Hunter says boldly. "We're *trying* to go back to where we came from."

I bite my tongue. I want to *hit* him. They've already recognized us. Emerson isn't the only one in part uniform, for goodness's sake. Reid wears a navy-blue sweater with HJTC in bright-yellow letters on its back. What is Hunter going to do? Convince them that we're harmless fugitives, so don't mind us?

The officer—lieutenant something-or-other, judging by his insignias but lack of name tag—scoffs. He shakes his head. "Nice try. You're Hope kids. Keep your distance, go back to where you came from, and we will all pretend this never happened."

I raise my eyebrows, because that's wildly, ridiculously generous. But if it's good enough for them, it's good enough for me. They know who we are. We have to get out of here.

I reach for Hunter's arm. "C'mon, let's go."

Hunter frowns, and he silently stares past the soldiers at the mountain pass. The barricade effectively blocks it from all sides, with barriers on the other side of the soldiers too. No one will get in or out of town from here.

Maverick elbows his way forward, past Hunter and me, and immediately the soldiers tense again. "Why?"

His question is backed up by several others from Hunter's crew. "Yeah. What's going on?"

"What are you doing here?"

"Why can't we pass?"

It's curiosity mixed with bravado. It's like they've forgotten that we're technically prisoners on the run.

I wait for Hunter to tell them that it doesn't matter, that we have to go back. Because he must see what I see, feel what I feel: that cold certainty, crawling its way up from my feet to my legs to my spine. Lieutenant What's-His-Face glances back at one of the other soldiers, and she immediately tightens her grip around her gun. Despite his forced relaxed appearance, this situation is a powder keg.

"We want to know what's happening," Reid demands.

I glance around. Reid stands close to us, his arms crossed, and his face pale. At the far edge, Emerson has begun to back away, while Leah and Logan cling to each other. They understand as well as I do that curiosity comes at a price.

Except Hunter still doesn't do anything.

"That's fair, sir," one of the soldiers says. She's a young woman, with kind, hazel eyes and her hair in a ponytail. She's not much older than we are. "They have a right to know as much as anyone else does."

We all turn around to look at them. At the officer. He squares his shoulders and tilts his chin up. I'm sure he intends to look imposing, but under the light of the barricade, with shadowed mountains flanking us, he merely looks small.

The lieutenant rubs his face, adjusts his gaiter, and after a few seconds, he comes to a decision. "Several days ago, right before Thanksgiving, there was an outbreak of a respiratory disease in several cities across the state and the country. The disease appears to be highly contagious and deadly, and since the outbreak happened as everyone was traveling, it's been able to spread rapidly across the country. The government placed the state in total lockdown. No one can leave their houses or travel outside of the town borders without a permit."

Oh.

"An outbreak?" Reid asks. "Like...a plague?"

The lieutenant swallows, then nods. "Exactly like that, yes."

So not chest-bursters then. That's my first, ridiculous thought. No aliens. But I'm not sure this is any better. A plague? A respiratory disease? What does that even mean?

Behind me, someone coughs, and the effect is almost immediate. Two of the guards turn and train their weapons in our direction. The lieutenant steps back. A wave of fear washes over us.

I raise my hands and try to find my voice. I try to ignore the refrain in my head and the rapid beating of my heart. *We're complying. We're complying. We're complying.* "We'll go back. Right, Hunter?" I address him, more than the soldiers. I need him to see reason, because once he does, the others will follow.

Maverick shakes his head. "No, we need to know more. So people got sick? Why does that mean we need to stay inside? Who will take care of us?"

"Who will provide us with food and medical care?" Reid chimes in. "What if we get infected?"

"What kind of disease?"

"What are the symptoms?"

"What will happen to us?"

They're solid questions, and we deserve answers, especially if this lockdown means our guards won't come back to us. But now is clearly not the time. The soldiers in front of us tighten their ranks, and the boys from Hunter's crew shift uncomfortably.

"We'll figure it out," I try. "We'll go back to the center, get everyone together, and regroup. Call for help. Figure out what's going on." I lower my voice. "But we won't be able to get through here. Look at them. We—"

Reid raises his chin. "No. I want to know. I want answers. What will happen to us if we go back?" He's balled his hands into fists. He won't back down.

The lieutenant shakes his head. "I don't know. I *do* know nothing good will happen to you if you stay here or try to push through."

It's a very thinly veiled threat—so much for de-escalation. His words are followed by angry mutters from Hunter's crew around me. Emerson is whispering something under their breath, and the twins hold on to each other. My stomach flips. I don't want to be here, stuck between boys and their terrible decisions once more. I want to turn around and go back.

"So we have to sit tight and wait for a deadly disease to

pass—or for the government to forget about us?" Maverick laughs bitterly. He is walking around the group like he's looking for another way out, but there's only thick patches of hickory trees around us and rough slopes that are impossible to climb at night. Perhaps there are other ways out of here—shallow streams or trails—but not with armed guards observing our every move.

One of the soldiers keeps Maverick in his sights.

"They won't forget about us." I try to keep my voice down. They *won't*. Right? No matter how much it feels like that sometimes, they won't. They *can't*. The authorities will find a solution—or we will. But we have to get out of here.

"You're naive if you believe that, Grace," Maverick says. "Do you really think they care about us?"

"No, but..." Maybe part of me *does*. Deep breaths. The cold November air chills me from the inside out. "C'mon, let's go. Let's go back. Find one of the computers. Figure out what's going on and—I don't know—*appeal* to someone."

I place my hand on Hunter's arm, pull him aside, and repeat the words. Hunter frowns. He seems torn between Maverick and me. I've never seen him this uncertain before. But if he moves, the rest of the crew will fall in line. He's the key to getting us all safely out of here.

Reid growls. "No. I hate it. I'm not going to sit around and see what happens." He slaps my hand away and places himself in front of Hunter. "We're in this together, right? You always said you'd take care of us, and now we need each other. I can't go back.

Fuck, I *can't*. I hate those walls, I hate the smell, I hate the food. I don't want to sit there and wait for some kind of plague to find us, and I don't want to sit there until someone decides that it's safe enough to *feed us*. What will we even do without guards around?"

"Exactly!"

"I don't want to go back either!"

"Let's go!"

Once Maverick picks up Reid's declaration—with a snarled "I won't be locked up again"—Hunter shakes himself and nods. "I agree. We can't let them send us back."

The words rattle me to the bone. "So what would you do?" I place myself between Hunter and the guards and try to keep my voice down.

"There's…what, five of them? We outnumber them." Reid glances over my shoulder and smirks. His eyes are cold and dangerous.

"They have *guns*," I hiss.

"We have the element of surprise," he says. "They won't expect us to do anything. Not really."

"Of course they don't! Because rushing a group of armed soldiers is *ridiculous*." I want to grab him and punch him until he sees sense. "Are you really that ignorant? Are you completely unaware of the situation around you? I want to get out of Hope too. Don't you think I'm tired of living between the same walls and doing what other people tell me to do? But I want to *survive,* Reid." More than that, I want to live, but I won't admit to that.

"We all do," Reid says, his voice low and threatening when he turns to his best friend. "Don't we, Hunter?"

Hunter's jawline flexes. He knows a challenge when he hears it. "Reid's right, we have to do something. We can't go back. Maybe we can't get through here, but we'll find another way around."

"Through the woods?" I ask incredulously. "Over the mountains? Good luck. Try that when it's light out if you want. I'll take my chances back home." The words leave my mouth before I can truly consider them. *Home*. Fuck. What does that even mean? How could I *say* that?

Because you have no other home, a little voice in the back of my mind tells me. *You don't belong anywhere else*.

Shut up, I tell it.

But if I had any chance of convincing Reid or Hunter or any of the others, I've lost it with that single word. A slip of the tongue and I'm no longer worth listening to. I see it in the way the boys turn from me, I feel it in the scornful gaze from Hunter. Reid spits on the floor in front of me.

"We'll retreat and try to find our way around them," Hunter continues, his voice rising in strength, as if I'd never spoken. "Find another route toward Sam's Throne. We won't go back to Hope."

He locks eyes with Reid, a quiet demand for him to fall in line. But Reid doesn't look down. I'm witnessing some kind of shift in power, because Hunter takes a step closer, and Reid straightens to meet him.

Reid slowly shakes his head. "No. We're here now. We keep going."

"It's too dangerous, man," Hunter says. He indicates the soldiers, who are still keeping a watchful guard.

Reid folds his arms. "It's worth a try."

"They'll shoot you," Hunter insists.

But it doesn't seem to be a threat to Reid. "Then they'll shoot me. I can't go back."

Hunter reaches out to him. "We won't. I promise you, we won't."

Reid smiles bitterly, like he regrets what he has to say. It's the same stunt I saw from Warden Davis on the regular. That "I'm not sad, I'm disappointed" frown. "You hesitated for so long. What's to say you won't change your mind when we turn back? What's to say Miss Let's Go Home won't change it for you?"

I keep my mouth shut, because it's the sensible thing to do. Our crowd is filled with whispers. Crew members who drift from Hunter to Reid and back. Everyone feels it now, and briefly, the soldiers don't matter, because this is our world. This is our normal.

Hunter grabs Reid by the neck and pulls him close. "I *won't*." His voice is low and menacing, and it would be enough to pull me in line.

Reid reaches out and pats Hunter's cheek. "I don't trust you, friend." He disentangles himself from Hunter's grasp and checks him, casually pushing him aside. "We're here. We keep going."

His declaration is met with murmured agreements. People who hesitate between him and Hunter. Reid winces and turns to Hunter one last time. "We're too close now," he says. "Don't you see? I can't go back. I can't. *I can't.* I have to try."

So he does.

Time slows down.

Reid rushes past us, because he hasn't yet learned that the world isn't made for people like us. He runs toward the soldiers. And with no hesitation whatsoever, one of them lifts his weapon.

Takes aim.

And fires.

seven

EMERSON

THE SOUND OF THE SHOT echoes around us. It's followed by shouting—and screams. The shouting comes from the soldiers. Two others have pointed their guns at us, and they'll shoot. I know they'll shoot. They're scared and we're scared, and I don't know who's screaming, but my throat feels raw.

"Reid!"

Reid stumbles closer to the small gap between two barricades before he reaches for his chest and topples over.

This can't be happening. It can't be. *Oh God. Protect us.* I try to fumble my way around a prayer, but my mind refuses to catch up. *Let no evil befall us.* I left that side of me behind a long time ago.

It can't be happening.

It is.

It's too much. Sneaking out and finding out about—what? A plague? A pandemic? They're *shooting* at us.

This isn't real.

Hunter tries to run forward, but Grace clings to him. So do some of the others. He's strong enough—or desperate enough—to push forward regardless. Trying to get to where Reid has fallen, in spite of the soldiers on high alert.

Reid lies splayed on the ground, one arm spread out, the other underneath him. One leg at a weird angle. It twitches until it stops twitching.

Are the bruises on his knuckles from where he beat me, or is it something else? Why was he at Hope? What was his story? I can't ask him now.

A pool of blood spreads under him, like tar under the night sky. He doesn't cough. He doesn't give any indication that he's hurt. He doesn't breathe.

"Reid! Come on, man!" Hunter manages to reach him, and he all but drags Grace with him.

Immediately, two soldiers step forward, guns trained on them. Another shout. The officer, again. They reverse their weapons and use the butts of the guns to slam Hunter and Grace aside and away from the barricades. Grace goes sprawling across the road, and Hunter stumbles. He raises his hand to his head, to feel for blood perhaps, and shakes himself.

"Reid!" His voice cracks.

I want to run forward to see if everyone's all right and stumble backward all at the same time, but I stand frozen. A year ago, I had everything. I had a family and a place to call home. Now I'm in the middle of nowhere, watching other kids get shot. Is this what my parents wanted for me when they kicked me out? Perhaps this is what purgatory feels like.

God...

One of the soldiers shoves Hunter away again. It's the spark, and we're all ready to explode. The rest of the crew surges forward. Leah zooms past me, on her way to Grace or Hunter or Reid, I don't even know. It happens so fast.

When the other boys move forward, the rest of the soldiers step toward them and form a buffer between us and Reid. All of them use their guns to bludgeon and push and create distance. Leah somehow slips through. Perhaps because she flanks them. Perhaps because she doesn't register as a threat.

She makes it all the way to Reid's body.

Next to me, Logan is keening, a soft, penetrating sound. She's gone entirely pale.

I reach for her hand, but she doesn't reach back.

Leah shakes Reid by the shoulders and tries to wake him up. He doesn't stir. He only twitches as she moves him. It's impossible to tell if it's him or if it's Leah.

The only time I can remember seeing death up close was when my grandfather died. I was seven, and I didn't really understand what happened. I didn't know what to expect from the service or the wake, but I vividly remember expecting him to get up at the end of it. Resurrection, maybe. Rousing from a slumber, really.

One of the soldiers makes for Leah. She puts her gun away and tries to pry Leah off Reid. She's gentle in a determined sort of way. It's obvious they aren't as intimidated by a slender girl, and I hate that for so many different reasons.

Leah fights. She struggles. She pushes at the soldier without any coordination whatsoever. "Let me go, let me go, let me get to him."

The soldier grabs her by a wrist and uses the momentum to pivot Leah away from Reid and back toward us. Leah lets herself be turned, and once she faces the woman, she makes a claw with her hand and *scratches*.

The soldier releases her with a yelp and a thrust, and it sends Leah stumbling backward. Another soldier uses his gun to push her away. Leah trips over her own feet and collides with Grace, who is scrambling to find purchase.

Next to me, Logan straightens, poised to fight or protect her sister. I reach out to grab her, knowing that she'll hate me for it—

When another loud gunshot shatters the night sky.

I scream.

Was I screaming before too?

Following the second gunshot, everything and everyone freezes. The soldiers, in front of the barricades and Reid. Hunter and his crew, trying to get to their friend. Leah and

Grace and their tangled collection of limbs. The soldier who got scratched—and who keeps a few steps distance between herself and the others.

"Stop this." The lieutenant's voice is loud and clear. He's holding a gun pointed at the sky, like he's willing to shoot the stars themselves. "Do not attempt to come closer again, or we'll be forced to use any means necessary to defend ourselves."

Defend? The word barely registers. From whom? A bunch of unarmed teens in the face of fully armed soldiers. That's ludicrous.

"We have to get to him," one of the boys says. I don't know his name. I don't care. He points at Reid, who is still lying amid the barricades on the road, but he has no force behind his declaration. His cheeks are streaked with tears. Several crew members have raised their hands and are walking back. It's been drilled into them to follow orders.

"You have to turn around," the lieutenant counters. "Go back to where you came from. Everyone is under orders to remain in their homes, and that includes you. We'll dispose of the body."

The words are a gut punch. My hands twitch to cross myself. I should say a prayer for him. Anything.

Grace pushes herself up to her feet, and unlike Hunter, she is bleeding from a head wound. She pulls Leah with her. Leah rests her hands on her knees and coughs. She's struggling to catch her breath. Grace places an arm around her shoulders and gently guides her to an upright position.

The soldiers hold their line around the barricades, though one of them glances at the soldier with the scratch wound. He shudders. It's like he's never seen blood before—or anyone in distress.

I don't stop Logan when she runs toward her sister and takes her from Grace's grasp. Hunter offers Grace a shoulder to lean on, and I find myself on her other side. She sways and straightens herself. None of us has consciously decided to fall back, but we do. Faced with the fear and anger of the soldiers. The inevitability of Reid's...body.

And the impenetrable gaze of the lieutenant, who now stands alone, between us and his men. He stands at ease, his hands folded behind his back, and his eyes find mine.

We look at each other.

What are you sending us back to? I wish I could ask him.

He narrows his eyes, and his shoulders drop, imperceptibly. While we help Grace and Leah away from here, while we leave Reid's body behind, the lieutenant shakes his head.

He doesn't turn around. He keeps staring while we retreat. Maybe he's just following orders. Maybe he would've done something different if he had the choice. Maybe he's sorry for sending us back to a correctional facility that's been abandoned because our lives aren't a priority in the face of a plague.

But inaction in the face of injustice is injustice all the same. And it's the same refrain that's stuck in my head, over and over and over again.

Why didn't you do something to stop them? Why didn't you do something to stop them? Why didn't you do—

I don't know if I'm trying to reach the lieutenant or my priest or God. It all bleeds together at some point. Authority figures you're supposed to trust but who'll let you down.

My court-appointed lawyer, who couldn't—or didn't want to—find ways to help me after I was arrested for "running away from home," though I had actually been kicked out.

Father Michael, who I came out to in the pews of our church. When my skin felt too tight and my heart couldn't stop racing, I needed him to tell me that we were all made perfect, created after the likeness and image of God. I wanted him to tell me it would all be okay and someone would be there for me. And instead, he told my parents.

My parents, who forced me to choose between conversion therapy, exorcism, and leaving. As long as I "chose" to be non-binary, they said, there wasn't a place for me under their roof. My mother prayed for me. My father turned away.

Why didn't you do something to stop them?

Grace leans heavily on me when we make our way back to the Hope Juvenile Treatment Center. The head wound has stopped bleeding, but a bright-red bruise is spreading along the side of her face and her jaw, and she moans when we jostle her too much.

"How did we all get here?" she asks softly. I don't know if anyone but me hears.

But I don't have an answer.

eight
GRACE

THE HOPE JUVENILE TREATMENT CENTER looks no different when it appears before us again. It's the same ugly building we left some three hours ago. A concrete box with a concrete yard. A slate-gray outcropping on a moonlit night, surrounded by darkness and a barbed wire fence encircling the grounds. The lackluster communal garden. The ramshackle shed. A sports field and a gym that we all avoid as much as we can.

It hasn't changed, but we have.

"God, what a desolate place," Emerson mutters at my side. Hunter has drifted back to help one of the other boys, and Emerson tries their best to support me alone, but the closer we get to the building, the more they stumble. Exhaustion. Fear. I don't know. I disentangle myself and bite my lip while trying to stay upright.

"I believe the word you're looking for is *hell*," Maverick snaps.

I wince. *Hell*, what a place to call home.

And my head *pounds*. I press a hand against my eye, and the world tilts around me as pain flares through me. I refuse to fall, but it takes everything I have to stay upright. I lean with my hands on my knees and breathe in hard.

Fuck.

"Are you okay?" Emerson asks.

I don't dignify that with a response. No, I'm not.

At least I don't have to worry anymore about what it would look like if they give up on us completely. It looks like this. The ten—no, the nine of us. Beat up and terrified. The others have ground to a halt too. Leah sways on her feet. Hunter has ripped off part of his shirt and used it to patch up someone's arm. He has a smear of blood across his face, but I don't think it's his.

I knew we were wrong to leave here, but I didn't expect the world around us to be on fire. Why wouldn't they tell us? We have a right to know. We have a right to try to survive.

No one cares about us.

You'd think I would have grown used to that, but I haven't. Despite the armor of anger I've drawn up around myself, there's still a small part of me that looks at Hope like I looked at all the homes I've stayed at. As a chance. An opportunity. A "this time it will be better." This time I'll find a way to be the person I was meant to be.

These are the consequences of our actions, Warden Davis said. The bastard. He knew, and he didn't do anything.

That spark of anger that's always lurking beneath my skin burns brighter. It's hot and hungry, all the more so against the chilly night sky, and it helps me straighten despite the pain. It helps me take the next step. And the next. "Come on, let's keep going."

"Yes, please." Surprisingly, Leah is the first to catch up with me, Logan immediately in her wake.

With a foul look at Hope, Maverick snaps, "Why? Do you think the plague will catch up with us if we wait?"

"Mav…" Hunter comes up behind the twins. His voice holds a warning. He uses his sleeve to wipe at the blood on his face.

"What are we going back for, anyway?" Maverick demands.

Hunter stares him down. "Supplies. If we're taking the long way around, I want to be prepared. We'll take whoever wants to come with."

"Like anyone will want to stay in that hellhole." Maverick snorts, but he falls in line, stomping through the dried leaves as he follows Hunter.

His words nag at me, as I'm sure they're intended to.

I don't want to stay. But I definitely don't want to leave and try to survive the middle of nowhere.

Next to me, Leah plucks at her hand. "I don't think the plague will catch up with us," she says softly, "but I'd like to clean this." Her fingers are bloody from where she scratched the guard, and she has a few scratches herself too. They're bright red and angry against her pale skin.

Oh. I shudder. "Yeah, good plan. There must be first aid kits somewhere inside." And painkillers too, hopefully.

Leah shivers, and on her other side, Logan narrows her eyes. She signs something, and Leah shakes her head. "Don't worry, I'm fine. It's a—a scratch. And it's cold out."

Logan scrunches up her face. She signs again, and Leah shrugs. "Yeah, well, we didn't know that when we got out, did we?"

I have an inkling what they're talking about, but I don't want to get mixed up in it. Everyone at Hope knows that the twins exist in their own little world, and they're protected by Hunter and his friends. I'm sure they'll leave with them too.

While the two of them argue, I glance at Leah. I wonder about the soldiers who shied away from her—from all of us. Should we be more worried? Does this disease spread through scratches? Could any of our guards have infected us before they left?

I'm not sure I want to know.

We stick closely together, all the way back into the building. The lights at the entrance are dark, and so is the registration desk. We pass through the first set of doors, breathing in the same stale air we left behind. If we'd never left, the world could have ceased to exist around us, and we would never have known.

"Home, sweet home," Hunter drawls. He holds the second door open for me, and I swing at him.

He sidesteps my weak attempt with ease, and pain laces through me. I hate him. I hate all of them. I hate the unconscious relief I feel when I slip through these doors, like something inside me recognizes this as the place where I belong.

"Nice try," Hunter says. He reaches out and taps my bruised cheek. "Let's wake the others. We need an action plan. I won't stay here a minute more than is necessary."

He sounds like he expects all of us to follow his lead, and by the looks of it, he might be right. Logan and Leah are already walking toward their wing, and at Hunter's command, the others begin to spread out too.

Emerson clears their throat. "We should wash our hands first." We all turn to them, and they swallow hard. "You know, just in case."

Maverick narrows his eyes and takes a step in their direction. "You think we might be sick?" A whole, complicated range of emotions passes over his face. From confusion to fear to disgust. It makes the lines of his face look harder.

"I don't know," they say. "But I don't want to risk it."

My shoulders drop.

"Do you think it'll *help*?" one of the other boys asks.

"I don't know that either."

Emerson's words fall heavy in the silence around us. Three boys of Hunter's crew exchange glances. Logan steps closer to Leah and reaches for her unharmed hand.

"But we should try," Emerson adds, as an afterthought.

Hunter unexpectedly graces them with a smile. "New kid has the right idea. Wash up. Wake the rest of those rejects. We'll meet in the recreation room in fifteen."

I lean a hand against the wall and use that to keep myself upright as I walk back to my room.

The last time I stumbled through the hallways of Hope with my head pounding and bruises all over was an initiation night too. Mine. I wasn't saved by the end of the world. I let Hunter and his friends beat me, and it was vicious and measured and purposeful. I answered their curious questions and their invasive questions, and no one put a stop to any of it. It was part of life at Hope as much as the unannounced room inspections, the schoolbooks that were held together with tape, and the days in solitary.

That night, when I stumbled back out of the recreation room and began to learn how to avoid the guards, Casey waited for me in my room. He wasn't a threat. Not quite a friend yet either. Simply Casey, who, on my first day, set his lunch plate at my table and claimed the seat next to mine, like it was the first day of high school instead. Casey, who wanted to make sure I was okay.

When I get back to my room now, I'm not okay, and there's no one waiting for me. I'm shivering. It's almost as chilly here as it was outside, and when I wash my hands and the cut across my eyebrow, the water is near freezing. At least the cold numbs the pain.

I press a wet washcloth against my face. Does Casey feel safer here? Do any of the others? Or am I the weird one out?

I set my jaw. I pull on an extra shirt and walk to the recreation room, where I'm surrounded by yawns and confusion, and Hunter's crew acts like they're the traffic wardens of Hope, rushing everyone until we're all gathered. Counting us in.

The recreation room is the only place that feels remotely like it's ours. The walls are covered in murals and graffiti tags. One of the cabinets holds a collection of board games (though most of the dice and the pawns are long since missing). In one of the corners stands a pathetic fake Christmas tree, left over from last year's festivities. Give it a couple of weeks and it'll be timely again. One shelf holds a collection of five books. Well, four and a half.

Hunter's at the front of the room, near the game cabinet. The unofficial boss of Hope. He has his arms crossed, and he taps his foot. His hair is wild and unruly, but it doesn't make him look less intimidating.

When I walk up to him, the corner of his mouth quirks up. "Good to be home again?"

I grasp the edge of a table. "Fuck you."

He raises an eyebrow, and he shifts his weight so he towers over me. "You know the rules that apply in here will apply outside too, right?"

I tilt back my head so I can look him in the eye, and I speak slowly, enunciating every word. "Good, because I'm not going."

I want to see Paris. I want to see Vinnytsia, where my first foster family was from. I want to try out as many towns and cities across the world and find the one where I belong. I have no idea who I can be yet, but I know I'm meant to be more than a number in a system. So many of us are. I want to figure out who I am when you peel the anger away.

I don't want to be shot like a dog by soldiers who don't care for us.

I do not want to die outside.

Satisfaction straightens my shoulders when Hunter frowns and leans back. "You're not." It's a statement, not a question.

"I'm not," I repeat. "You can take your friends on a wild goose chase through the mountains, but I'll stay here where I'll have a roof over my head, food to eat, and oh, what was the other thing again? A future."

He scoffs. "You're adorable when you're upset."

"And you're an asshole who couldn't even protect his friend from getting shot," I snap.

It happens before I can stop him. He grabs me by the front of my shirt and pulls me close, angling his own body so the rest of the room doesn't see what's happening between us. Not that anyone would step in regardless.

"Don't you *dare*," he hisses quietly.

I tense all over. I refuse to flinch away from him and instead lean in closer. "I'll take my chances in Hope. Let. Me. Go."

He doesn't. Not immediately. He holds me close, and it's as

if he stares right through me. Then he shakes his head. "If you think you'll have a future here, you're a fool, Grace." He drops my shirt, and I nearly lose my balance. "But I don't need you slowing me down. For that matter, anyone else who wants to stay here with you and die is welcome to do so. Just know that everything that happens to them will be your responsibility."

I flatten my shirt and try to keep my head from spinning. My stomach twists. Being responsible for everyone certainly wasn't my plan, but if that what it takes to stay safe, so be it. I'll figure it out.

The room fills up fast around us. We count thirty-something, and it wasn't built for quite that many, but we're used to that. Though I can't help but wonder now if we should all be together in such a small space. What does a plague look like, anyway?

At the back of the room, Casey frowns and pushes through to try to get to us, but I quietly shake my head. Not now. Please.

He settles down on one of the tables and folds his arms.

When the last group of people enters the room, Maverick climbs on a table and counts heads. He nods in Hunter's direction. "We're all here."

"Good," Hunter says. "Let's start. Grace?"

"What?"

"You go first," he says, his voice calm and reasonable.

A headache takes up residence behind my eyes, and all I want to do is punch him. Just once. But everyone is looking at us, so I tighten my fists, and with a painful smile, I nod. "Fine."

I clear my throat and wait for silence to settle around us, and then I start. "A couple of days ago, there was an outbreak of the plague. We're all here together because the guards have left us."

nine
LOGAN

NOTHING GOES ACCORDING TO OUR routine anymore. I don't understand how Grace and Hunter find words for what happened tonight, but they do. When Grace sways, Hunter steps in to provide details, and together they tell the whole story. One word at a time. I couldn't do it. I don't have the signs. It's all balled up in a restlessness inside of me, and not even stimming will make me feel better.

Next to me, Leah coughs. She slumped in one of the chairs, her wounded hand cradled against her chest. We cleaned it as well as possible with our foul-smelling soap, and then we tied a clean shirt around it. We should find bandages in the infirmary after this.

I nudge her with my toe, make her look at me. "Are you sure you're all right?"

Leah blinks and doesn't focus. She isn't. I understand her as well as I do myself and maybe even better. She's the other half of me.

She shakes her head and keeps her voice down. "I'm fine. I promise."

"You don't look fine."

"Wow, thanks."

"That's not what I mean."

"I know." She tries to smile, but it looks crooked.

"I'm worried," I tell her.

Every time I blink, every time I close my eyes, every time I let my thoughts wander, I see the same scene over and over and over again.

The soldier, raising his gun. Reid, falling to the ground. And Leah, rushing past me to get to him, to fight with the soldiers, to leave me behind. We promised to never leave each other. No matter what happened, no matter where we were. We promised to never leave each other.

"I propose to stay here," Grace says at the front of the room. She licks her lips, like she's nervous. "None of us came to Hope out of our own volition, but like it or not, it's the safest place we have. We have a roof over our heads. We have food to keep us going. We can sit it out until help comes, instead of becoming fugitives on the run."

"What about our families?" someone asks.

"I'd imagine your families would want you to be safe too," Grace says. "You can call home if you want to, but they'll understand we're protected here. Besides, there is no easy way to leave now. Not unless you want to risk getting shot."

Leah coughs again, but the sudden rumble of voices around me drowns out the sound.

I shuffle closer to my sister and squeeze her hand.

At the front of the room, Hunter physically turns away from Grace and addresses the crowd. "You've heard her. Those who want to stay here and die can do so. But the truth is, no one will come for you. No one will help you. The world outside might be dangerous, but we know what to look out for now, and at least we'll be free. We're leaving as soon as we've gathered enough supplies."

"Where will you go?" someone else from the crowd asks. Josie, probably, but I'm not entirely sure. Too many people stand between us.

Hunter shrugs. "Anywhere but here. If you have parents, you can call them, and we'll help you find your way back home. It doesn't have to be simple; we'll figure it out."

Past the roadblocks? How?

"Anywhere but here sounds good to me." Josie pushes past several others toward the rest of the west wing crew. Two of the boys elbow each other and laugh and leer.

"I'll take my chances here, thanks," another person calls.

"Can you promise us we won't get shot on sight?"

"Can *you* promise us we won't die of that disease anyway?"

The questions go back and forth.

Anywhere but here sounds *terrible* to me, but I look at Leah all the same. She wanted to see the world again earlier tonight. "If you still want to leave, I'll follow you."

She doesn't immediately answer. She needs time to add up all the pros and cons. Figure out what's best.

Meanwhile, all the boys from the west wing band together. Another girl joins them and comes to stand next to Josie. Saoirse Sullivan. The only girl in Hope with flaming-red hair and more freckles than I could possibly count.

Hesitatingly, Joshua Taylor walks over to the group as well. Joshua's latest tall tale was that he got caught running messages for a mafia boss. Two weeks ago, he told the new kid that he got caught in a sting operation. Leah says she also heard him confess to building a bomb once. Probably none of those are true.

He and Saoirse are kind. Hunter's crew will protect us. I can easily imagine the pros that Leah is gathering now. I pull at a bit of rough skin around my cuticles until it bleeds.

Leah covers my hand with hers. The shirt we used as bandages has shifted and opened. The scratches are wider now, like she pulled at them the way I do. Her hand is red and warmer. Her eyes are still distant, but she pulls me close enough, our foreheads touch. "You want to stay here, right?"

I nod.

She sighs deeply. "Yeah. I think—I don't know what'll happen to us outside. I don't know how to protect you. I don't know..." Her voice trails off, and I wait until I'm sure she doesn't want to say anything else.

"I don't need you to protect me." I pull back enough to make room for my signs. "We can stay here for now. Until it gets better outside. It can't stay like this forever."

"If it gets better, the guards might come back."

I frown. "We'll have to be careful to find the right moment then."

"Yeah, we will."

"We're in this together." My signs hold somewhere between a statement and a question. Our only option is for us to be in this together. Right?

Leah nods. "Always."

"And always."

My shoulders drop a little. My jaw unclenches. In the end, this is really all that matters. The two of us, together. Even in here. Even if the world is ending.

Hunter's new crew counts seven when he stomps out of the room. Four boys from the west wing—excluding Hunter himself—plus Joshua, Josie, and Saoirse. Everything I know about all of them bounces through my head. Josie and her knives. Saoirse and her fourth nonviolent offense. Hunter, who killed someone.

It means Andrew Riker will be the only one left in the west wing. He's quiet. The only boy in the west wing who didn't join Hunter's group. Leah thinks he's intimidating. He has a history of violence.

I like him because he barely speaks more than I do.

It means there'll be twenty-two of us left. Seven in the south wing. Seven in the east wing. Seven in the north wing. Andrew on his own.

"We'll figure out how to go from here in the morning," Grace says. She appears to ignore the fact that the sky outside is a little brighter than it was. I like it. I want to go back to normal too. "None of you are obligated to stay, but I hope you do. We can be safe here, together, until help comes. We'll hack into the computers to find more information."

At the front of the crowd, someone raises their hand. "I can help with the computers." I almost smile. Isaiah Wood. He's a soft-spoken Black boy everyone knows as the Professor because he knows everything about everything. Of course he can hack into the computers.

Grace nods. "We'll make it through, I promise. They'll find a way to stop the spread, and this will all be over soon."

She makes it sound like she knows what she's doing, but she can't possibly. No one can.

"Diseases don't just go away." Emerson's voice is so soft, I doubt Grace hears. I doubt anyone hears, except for maybe Leah and me. "You can't promise we'll survive."

"We can only try," Leah whispers.

And even when you think you'll make it through, sometimes you don't.

I dream about the fire, that night. We'd stayed in the warehouse often enough that we both knew how to get around without being seen. I'd never been the best at stealth or any sort of coordination, but here I only had to follow Leah.

She carried the gasoline.

I carried the matches.

We snuck inside through the same busted door we always used, past the aisles full of mostly empty storage racks. This building had fallen into disuse years ago. The owner obviously didn't care for it. But with an open door and a roof that protected against rain and walls to hide from prying eyes, there was always someone who could make good use of the place.

Leah first heard of the warehouse through gossip on the streets of Hot Springs. A girl who was passing through told her about the location. She said it was a safe house when she stayed there a year or two ago.

It wasn't a safe house when we were there. Just another location you had to pay to enter. But it was winter, and we had nowhere else to go, so we did. We paid with stolen food and stolen goods, with kisses and with touches, until the touches became something else and I couldn't say anything.

Leah spread the gasoline across the floor and the racks. The smell of it cloyed at my nose and choked me. I stuffed part of my sleeve into my mouth to keep from coughing and betraying our presence. Some nights I choke on the sleeve and wake with tears in my eyes.

Other nights, I simply skip ahead to the next image seared into my mind.

Leah emptied the jerrican and quietly placed it in a corner. In my dream, it's always the same thing. I want to scream at her and shout at her not to do that, because it won't burn, and it can be traced back to us. But I never try.

Instead I feel the sensation of the matches between my fingers. It was one of those small matchboxes, crumbled and used. It held exactly three matches, and I fumbled the first when I took it out, letting it slip between my fingers.

Leah growled, low in her throat, and I winced.

"Are you sure we should do this?"

Her signs were never quite as supple and smooth as mine. I once told her she signed with an accent, and she'd laughed at that. She told me she couldn't have an accent, because we were the ones who invented the language.

"We have to. For everyone who comes here and thinks it's a safe place."

I sucked my cheeks in. "Maybe it won't be so bad for others."

"I'm not willing to find out." She took the matches from my hands and lit both with one strike, like Granddad used to light his cigars. She handed me one, kept the other to herself, and smiled.

"Together, okay?"

"Always."

"And always."

We stood hand in hand as the fire spread along the gasoline, deeper into the warehouse. The flames looked like sprinters stuck in a race together, rushing down the lines, and it was fascinating.

We stood there until the fire roared so loudly, I could cough without anyone noticing—

And then I heard someone else cough too.

The smoke swirled around us, making shapes and nightmarish visions, but the coughing became louder and louder. It clawed at me, like I could feel it in my own throat, like I was suffocating on the hot air too.

I open my eyes and find the room is bathed in light. It's dawn. It's well past dawn. The lights in our room are on, because no one thought to flip the timer switch when they left us.

And the coughing hasn't stopped.

I reach for my throat. Breathe in deeply and savor the cool air. Sit up.

In the bed next to mine, Leah is coughing continuously. She's thrashing around, and I don't understand how she can still be asleep.

I *move*. Out of my own bed and two steps to hers. I crouch down next to her and reach for her hand. She always wakes when I touch her.

Today she doesn't.

I squeeze her hand. Rub circles with my thumb and feel her fingers claw around mine. I reach up and touch her cheek because she keeps coughing and shaking.

She's as hot as the warehouse was. She's radiating heat. And when I pull my hand away from her cheek, my fingers come back wet.

Red.

Bloody.

Her eyes spin rapidly beneath her lids, and she's twisting and turning away from me. She coughs again, and a bit of spittle lands on my face. A thin line of bright-red blood trickles from the corner of her mouth toward the pillow.

I grab her shoulders and shake hard to wake her up. Desperation grasps me and tumbles out of me, and I'm whimpering. I don't know how to make the sound make sense. I don't know how to stop.

She. Still. Won't. Wake.

Leah. Leah. Leah.

She stops thrashing. The trickle of blood stems. Her eyes still. Her hands fall limp to her side. Briefly, I'm convinced she's stopped breathing too. In my head, I *scream.*

She gasps like her lungs have forgotten how to take oxygen from the air, like she's drowning on dry land.

And she stills again.

I want to pound her chest. I want to shake her. I want her to wake up, because she promised me always and always, and I'm so terrified, I can hardly remember how to breathe myself. I want to scream.

I do the only thing that makes sense to me. I reach down and hug her, as close as I can, and hold her because I refuse to let her slip away. She doesn't struggle, but when she coughs, her entire body racks, and the bed around her is stained with red.

I gently place her back on the bed, turn around, and run.

ten
GRACE

THIS IS THE WAY THE world ends. Not with a bang but with a knock on my door.

Casey lies on my bed, hands behind his head, and I lie curled up across his chest. Casey snores a little, and his arm twitches. His heart beats steadily underneath my cheek. I hear it. I feel it.

We never do anything but sleep in the same bed, and it's the safest place in the world for both of us. We soak up each other's presence. Find comfort and courage in each other. This is the only place where Casey can relax at night, ever since the guards found out that he can only sleep when it's quiet.

I've always wondered if this is what it's like to have a brother.

When someone pounds on the door, Casey's heart skips a beat. He tenses, from sleep to fight-or-flight in a second.

I sit upright before I'm fully aware of what I'm doing. "Who is it?" My voice croaks. It's morning. I must have slept some, though it seemed an impossibility. I rub at my eyes.

"What's going on?" Casey's voice isn't any less ragged. I reach for his hand and squeeze it.

Heavy pounding. It reverberates through the room.

"Calm down, I'm coming."

I stumble across the room, trying to catch up. Last night feels like a cruel nightmare. Maybe I dreamed it all. Except if I did, we've been left in our rooms way past movement line. My head still feels sore. I push open the door, and Logan stumbles in.

That's when everything falls to pieces.

The twins are Hunter's pets. We share our school hours, but we're in different wings. I'm okay with that. I can't wrap my mind around the fact that they apparently tried to kill someone.

But I also can't wrap my mind around the fact that one of them is here, now. Still in pajamas. Her hair a wild bird's nest. "What do you want?"

Logan signs at me frantically, panic in her pale-green eyes. Her hands are stained with blood, and they tremble when she isn't signing.

All the warnings from the soldiers flood my brain. A plague. So contagious that everyone's confined to their houses.

"No. Go away." I shake my head. We were supposed to be safe here. I want to *stay* because it's safe here. *Fuck, no.*

"What's happening?" The bed creaks, and Casey gets up too. He walks toward the two of us and pauses. "Oh."

Logan signs again. Palms up, her fingers curled toward her. She pulls the hands toward her heart. Then another sign. One hand balls into a fist, and she wraps it with the other. Her right hand is the bloodiest of the two, with red stains crawling up to her sleeves.

I have no idea what she's saying. I never learned sign language, and I can only pay attention to the blood.

I take a step back. "Are you ill? You're bleeding."

She blows out a breath and shakes her head. She reaches for me.

I take another step back. I would slam the door in her face if I could. Does it matter if we keep our distance? Have we all been infected already?

"She needs help." Casey takes a step closer to me, and his comforting presence does nothing to waylay the anxiety creeping up on me. It presents like it always does: in the desperate need to destroy before I'm destroyed.

"If you're not sick, is someone else?" he asks.

Logan's shoulders drop, and she nods.

"Your sister?"

Another nod. Logan swallows. She reaches out a hand again and gestures.

Casey walks past me, and I grab his shirt. I suddenly understand the soldiers so well right now, and I hate it. I *hate* it. "If this is it...if this is that disease, we can't help. We'll have to stay away." I refuse to look at Logan when I say that, but it's true.

"It's not like we have medical care. The kindest thing we can do is keep our distance and make sure no one else gets infected." The words taste sour in my mouth.

It's here already, my treacherous brain says. *It doesn't matter.*

"Grace." Casey takes my hand and slowly pries open my fingers. He looks at me with mind-numbing sadness in his eyes. "If that plague is as terrifying as you said it was, then the kindest thing we can do is take care of each other."

He nods in Logan's direction and follows her out the door, leaving me standing there, staring at the hallway. And it's all I can do not to shout after them.

That first night, when he waited for me after my initiation, he held me when I cried, and he told me all of us here only have one job. "We survive. Whatever we do, we survive."

I wanted to tell him I didn't know how, but something of the truth slipped out. "I don't know if I can."

"You have to believe it." His intense desperation took my breath away. He held on to my arms so hard, I thought they'd bruise. Bruise upon bruise. "You have to," he said. "Repeat what I told you."

"We survive. Whatever we do, we survive."

I'm only trying to survive now, Case, like I promised you.

I take a step back and swipe at the plastic cup with my toothbrush that stands on the edge of the metal sink. It goes clattering across the floor. It doesn't make me feel better at all.

With the lights on and the doors open, it's clear I'm not the only one awake. Several girls are mulling about, walking through the hallway aimlessly. We have no movement line. No set hour for breakfast. No one to prepare us breakfast either.

I hate the lot of them—Warden Davis, the guards, the soldiers. Hunter, for telling me I'm responsible for everyone. That's what gets me going. I want to be better than them.

I wouldn't be, if I didn't help Leah and Logan.

Saoirse stops me before I make it three steps out of my room. I shake her hand off me immediately.

"She's sick, isn't she?" She's as intense as she's ever been. "One of the twins? I saw her."

And I can't lie, not about this. "The other twin. Her sister."

She pales, making her freckles stand out even more on her already-light skin. She pulls at an imaginary thread on her sleeve, like she doesn't want to look at me when she asks the question. "Is it that disease you talked about? The plague?"

I shrug. "I don't know."

"We have to get out of here." Her head snaps up, and she has steel in her eyes. "Hunter was right. We have to go as soon as possible."

"Then go," I growl, angrier at myself than I am at her. "If any one of us has been infected already, it doesn't matter. I'm going over there to help."

She backs away. "You're out of your mind!"

"I guess I am." I turn. "Good luck, Saoirse. I hope you and the rest of the crew get out of here safely. I really do."

Getting to the east wing is no easy task. Every few steps or so, someone stops me, like I have all the answers to their questions. I sigh and run my hand through my hair. It's all tangled because I haven't had a chance to brush it yet. I have morning breath because I haven't brushed my teeth either. The day has only just begun, and I'm already tired.

Mei Fujita and Serenity Jones are in the midst of some kind of fight when I pass them, and Serenity snatches my arm and pulls me in. She's a head taller than I am, and she *glares* at me, her light skin flushed red with anger. She doesn't live up to her name at all.

"Is it true they're leaving us here to die?"

After taking the lead with Hunter, everyone looks to me, but I barely know what I'm doing beyond finding a way to survive. "I don't know."

"You were there, you heard what those soldiers said."

I wince. "They didn't know either. They're here to enforce lockdown."

"But we'll need food and—" She waves her hand, encompassing the whole building, and I don't know exactly what she means, but I also don't want to stick around to find out.

I pull my arm from her grasp. "We told them."

"They'll figure something out," Mei says, and I think she *wants* it to be true more than she actually believes it, but that counts for something. "Right, Grace?"

"Right. I hope so. I have to go. Get some breakfast, if you can."

The Professor stops me when I cross the open space between wings. Isaiah is eating an apple and pacing back and forth. He looks up but not at me when I walk through. I've never seen him make eye contact with anyone, no matter how much the guards tried to force him.

"I can help with the computers," he says, an exact repetition of his words last night. "Where would you like me to start?"

Why is that my call? I bite my lip and force myself not to snap at him. Instead, I try to decide what makes sense. "The warden's computer, if you can."

"Of course." He nods, takes another bite.

"Find everything you can about the disease. It should be all over the news. Find out what it looks like. How it spreads. What we can do." It's disconcerting that he doesn't look at me, but he hears me. And this is more comfortable for him, so whatever. "Find out how we can keep each other safe."

"Yes. Anything else?"

So much more, but nothing that's pressing right now. "Find out if we can expect help? But keep that quiet for now." I hate asking that, but if it spreads... "Let me know. No one else."

Isaiah doesn't seem fazed. If there's one person here who sees all the possible options, all the possible complications, it's him. He spends way too much time in his own head, but he seems to like it there, so who are we to tell him otherwise? It's not like the real world is necessarily a better place to be.

By the time I make it halfway into the east wing, Logan and

Casey are already carrying Leah out. My heart squeezes when I see them, when I see how pale and unresponsive Leah is. When I see Casey touch her. When I see the stains of her blood on her pajama shirt.

She's barely conscious. Occasionally, her head lolls back and she coughs. Her breath sounds rasping and...*wrong*. I have no other word for it. It sounds like she's trying to breathe but isn't.

The few people who wander this hallway stay far away from the three of them, but their whispered worries echo against the concrete walls. Some of them physically back away.

A respiratory disease. Highly contagious.

Is this it? Is it starting?

I rub my eyes and try to get my thoughts in order. "You should bring her to the infirmary. I don't know what medical equipment we have, but Isaiah is looking into what we can do." *If anything.* "And we can quarantine her there."

Logan snarls at those words, but Casey nods. "Stay back, Grace."

I do. I push myself against the wall as they pass me, like those few feet will make a difference when we all spent time together last night.

Leah coughs again. I flinch.

I follow Casey and Leah to the commons and try to ignore the whispering behind us, around us, in front of us. The shocked looks. The panicked retreats. *What is happening?*

I'm not entirely sure either.

Casey notices the reactions and gently steers the long way around. Past the cafeteria, instead of through. Past the classroom and tiny little library with beat-up books and pages bound together without covers. He throws me a look over his shoulder. "Word will spread soon. You should talk to the others."

I shake my head. "Why me? I have no idea what to say."

He's honest enough not to deny that. "You did last night, and you made people listen to you. We need someone to keep the calm, and you can do it."

"I…" I'm not calm. I don't know how. I don't know where to start.

"Please, Grace. Trust me."

I do. I always do.

But there's a difference between pulling a ridiculous stunt because your best friend asks you—like that time in middle school when Amy, my best friend at the time, and I cut each other's hair and dyed parts of it black with her aunt's leftover hair color—and navigating the end of the world because you didn't know when to keep your mouth shut.

Once Casey and the twins reach the infirmary, I don't stick around to see if they need my help; I turn around and make my way to the cafeteria. It feels wrong, to be able to *wander*.

But the cafeteria looks like it did yesterday and the day before and every day since I came here. Bright fluorescent lights. Tables with attached seats in drab gray. Late-autumn skies filtering in through the windows. Not everyone is here, but people have drifted in to eat. They stuck to their assigned places, mostly. We have food on the tables.

Raided rations of cereals, like we've never had cereal before. Fruit enough for all of us. The smell of scrambled—and slightly burned—eggs wafts in from the kitchen.

The biggest difference between today and any other day is that people are talking to each other. They're worried and anxious but talking. Some of them are laughing. Word hasn't spread here yet.

I don't want to be the one to tell them.

I clear my throat. No one looks at me.

I clap my hands. At the first table, two people turn around, glance at me, and go back to their food.

"Can I get everyone's—"

The door on the other side of the room slams open, and Hunter stalks in. He's dressed in his work uniform, and he has a bag slung over his shoulder. The rest of his crew lingers near the door. "We're going," he announces. "One last chance for those who want to come!"

He spots me, and a cruel smile spreads across his face. "Or you can remain here, with her, and your very own plague victims."

He does what I couldn't. The entire room is silent. Someone places their cup on their tray, and several people at once hush them.

"What do you mean?"

"Did someone get sick?"

One of the other boys stands up, but the girl next to him drags him down. She looks to me. "Grace? Is it true?"

"Everyone, *listen up*." I grab a tray and slam it against the metal counter. "Leah—one of the twins—fell ill. We don't know if what she has is the new disease. Her sister and Casey helped her to the infirmary. We're trying to figure out what we can do."

I wait for crude and fearful suggestions, but the deep silence is somehow worse. The worry and fear when they all look to me. It drains me and leaves me scrambling for the right words.

"She didn't look good. We'll try to take care of her," I say. "I don't know what will come of us. I honestly don't. But we're trying to figure out when help will come, and until then we have a roof over our head, food on our plates." I gesture at the tables.

Hunter scoffs, and something like ice and rage and failure settles in my stomach. Maybe he's right. I said last night we'd stay here, but maybe it's better to leave and find our fortune somewhere else. Maybe all of this is my fear speaking. Maybe I'm not just scared of the plague but of losing the little bit of world I understand.

But fuck it, is that so bad?

"We have resources, we have beds, we have an infirmary in case others are infected too. We have each other. We can *take care* of each other. We don't know how to protect ourselves from the disease yet, but we can protect ourselves from hunger and cold and needless violence." I feel as cruel as Hunter right then, and when he laughs and rolls his eyes, the cruelty slips away from me. "I won't promise you you're safe here. But Hunter can't promise you that either. Because if we were exposed to the disease last night, so was he. So were all of them."

Hunter's eyes flash, and the fear around me is suffocating. The murmurs. The terrified expressions.

Hunter spits on the ground and pushes past me, into the kitchen. "We take what we can carry," he calls out over his shoulders to the rest of the crew. "And then we leave. The rest of them can rot, for all I care."

Phone call between Xavier and his brother

FRANCISCO: Xavi? You okay? I didn't expect to hear from you until the weekend.

XAVIER: Is it true?

FRANCISCO: What?

XAVIER: The plague. Those outbreaks, right? Is it as bad as they say it is?

FRANCISCO: Ah, shit. I hoped you'd be spared from that over there, what with that whole wilderness location and such.

XAVIER: We're in the Ozarks. We're not on Mars.

FRANCISCO: I don't know what they're saying, but the answer is probably yes. It's as bad as they say it is.

XAVIER: Oh.

FRANCISCO: Our hospital is filling up. It's only a matter of time before we need to turn people away. It's everywhere. It spreads so rapidly, it's like a tidal wave, and no one is prepared.

XAVIER: What about you? Are you prepared? Will you be safe?

FRANCISCO: I don't know.

FRANCISCO: We have good protective gear, so we're fine for now. But I worry there won't be enough. Not for us. Not for the nurses. And the board isn't offering anything beyond gloves to the cleaners.

XAVIER: I hate that.

FRANCISCO: You and me both, bro.

XAVIER: Can't you do something about it?

FRANCISCO: I'm trying. But it's not like hospital boards frequently listen to interns. They say it's not currently a priority.

FRANCISCO: I can't imagine what it'll be like here when the staff gets infected. When we have to start turning people away. I swore an oath when I started med school.

XAVIER: Are you at work now?

FRANCISCO: I'm on break, but yes. It's resident hours for the interns too, so we can have as many beds available as possible.

XAVIER: Well, we'll have beds available here soon enough.

[silence]

FRANCISCO: Xavi? What do you mean?

XAVIER: The guards left when everything locked down. So some of the others are planning on leaving too.

FRANCISCO: Left you? As in, they left you unattended? That's wildly irresponsible.

XAVIER: Looks like we're not currently a priority either.

FRANCISCO: [muffled] ...*be right there. Give me a minute.*

FRANCISCO: Fuck, one of the attendings needs me. I've got to go, but I'll look into it during my next break, I promise. Be safe out there, please? I need to know that you're safe. I love you.

This phone call has been disconnected.

Phone call between Elias and his uncle

MR. THOMPSON: What do you want?

ELIAS: We...um, we heard about that plague thing here. It's—I wanted to know how you are—how are you all doing? You and Aunt Vera and Hazel.

MR. THOMPSON: Hmph. Buying into that nonsense that we're all doomed, are you? I thought they taught you there better than to believe in ghost stories. If it isn't big pharma wanting to profit off us, it's the government trying to keep us fearful and docile. It won't work on me.

ELIAS: The news we're getting—

MR. THOMPSON: Overblown, all of it. It's a bad flu season, nothing more. Everyone gets sick in winter, right?

ELIAS: But—

MR. THOMPSON: What a time for you to start caring about family anyway. Couldn't have thought about that before you got yourself in this mess? Could've taken care of your mother when she was ill. Could've gotten a real job. Could've been at the funeral like a caring son.

ELIAS: Uncle—

This phone call has been disconnected.

ELIAS: I just wanted to know you're all right.

eleven
EMERSON

THIS IS WHAT THE PLAGUE looks like.

It's not illness, at first. It's fear. The type of fear that nags at the back of your thoughts, that crawls like a parasite under your skin. It's like every bruise that brushes against my clothes.

This is the fear I felt after my parents kicked me out. The difference between living in a well-lit home with food on the table, pictures to remind you of where you belong, and caring words—and the coldness of night, where every shadowed corner may be dangerous. The fear of not knowing how to survive.

It's the type of fear that claws at your chest and makes it hard to breathe.

Is this how it starts? Or is it simply anxiety? Are my hands trembling because I'm infected, or am I tired? Does my head hurt, my stomach hurt, my throat hurt because I'm scared, or is this how I'll die? How can I die when I don't know what it means to live?

Maybe I should leave with Hunter and his friends. The very thought of it terrifies me. I don't trust them not to hurt me. I don't trust them to protect me. But how can I trust the people in here?

Maybe I should go home. I bite my lip. Like my parents would accept a fugitive from the Hope Juvenile Treatment Center. The very thought of it. I don't want to imagine what would happen if I showed up at their doorstep now.

Except.

My chest aches at the thought of home. I miss it. I miss my room with its soft bed covered with cushions, the shelf full of sheet music, and the musty, sea-green curtains. I miss the songs from the record player drifting from the living room to every corner in the house. I miss the smell of the lasagna my mom cooks.

I miss the home I thought I knew back when I was who my parents thought I was. It was the only place where I've ever felt completely protected from the evils of the world. And I want to feel safe again. I want to curl up against my father on our faded leather sofa and hear his voice rumble in his chest when he tells me it'll all be okay, that God has a grand plan for me.

"Even in the darkest times," he told me, "if you follow God's light, He will be with you. If you're overwhelmed and scared, pray, and He will give you purpose and peace."

I still believed that. I want to believe it now.

But I tried to pray, when they kicked me out. When my so-called friends turned me away and I spent nights out in the open. When I wandered into churches in search of warmth or food or recognition. I never felt any lighter.

In that half year between my parents shutting the door on me and the police arresting me, the only real peace I ever felt was in a drop-in house in Little Rock, where I met a trans girl with kind eyes and a penchant for chaos. Mica. We only spent two days together before she disappeared to another shelter, but she accepted me. She called me Emerson. She stole clothes for me that clung to my body in all the *right* places. She danced around my mistrust like it didn't exist. She helped me cut my hair. After everyone who made me feel broken, she was the first to see me whole.

That was peace. Whatever God's light was supposed to be, it had only given me pain.

I try to pray now—in the privacy of my own room—but I might as well be talking at a wall. At the broken wardrobe. At my violin case.

If I leave now, could I bring it with me again?

My violin is the single personal possession I was allowed to keep here, against normal regulations. Presumably because the warden thought I wouldn't be able to harm anyone—or myself—with a graceful instrument.

Jemma's voice in my mind. *The board is aware that you are a status offender, and your assignment here is suboptimal. So*

we're willing to do what we can to help you with your needs.
She was supposed to help me. Why didn't *she* do anything to
stop this?

I take the tarnished bronze saint medal attached to one of
the straps and turn it over between my fingers. On the saint side,
it shows a man with heavy eyebrows holding a holy book. He's
smiling. A flame is etched above his head. I trace the raised edges
with my thumb.

Saint Jude, pray for us.

My dad gave me the medal the night before my audition
for the St. Agnes school orchestra. Between stage fright and
repeatedly messing up the piece I wanted to play and increas-
ing dysphoria, I'd felt out of sorts for days. My parents simply
thought I was worried, so the night before, my dad sat with me.

"This was my older brother's," he said. "Patrick gave it to
me before he left for seminary. It's time for you to have it. To
remind you that you always have someone willing to listen when
you worry and who won't judge you when you do."

I guess he was talking about Saint Jude, because it certainly
wasn't true for him.

Is this God's plan for me? Is this my grand purpose in life?

I looked up the devotions to Saint Jude a few days later
and found a prayer for hopeless cases. The lost cases. He must
have known that. Maybe he thought it inspirational, but for me
it was a reminder that something was wrong. That I didn't—
wouldn't—fit, no matter how hard I tried.

And still I kept it.

I turn the medallion over and over. It's not shiny enough to reflect the light, but the differences in color and texture are still clear.

I could leave now, but where would I go? I don't think anywhere out there would be better than here. I don't ever want to be denied again. I'd rather take care of myself, and this is the safest place to do so.

I stay on my knees for a heartbeat longer. My fingers on the medal. My thoughts far away. *Saint Jude, pray for us.*

All of us hopeless and desperate cases.

Hunter's crew leaves Hope with bombast, like they're staging a Hollywood jailbreak instead of walking out of the front door. At the very last moment, a ninth person joins the group. A brown boy with sad eyes. I don't know his name, but he's the only boy in the west wing who wasn't part of Hunter's crew initially. He wears his work clothes and carries a duffel bag, though it looks relatively light and empty compared to the others. Underneath his short-cropped hair, he is tense.

When he walks up to Hunter and the rest of the group, several of us stand and watch. A girl from the other wing rushes up to him and grabs his arm. "*Andrew.* What are you *doing*?" She chokes on the sentence and coughs.

"Serenity." Andrew shakes his head. "I can't stay here on my own. I don't know how dangerous it is, and I—I can't."

"You wouldn't *be* on your own, you fool." She punches his arm. It's all too clear her anger comes from worry too. "I'd stay with you."

"You could come with," he suggests, but his words hold no force, no conviction. I'm not sure even he knows exactly what he's doing, and certainly Hunter doesn't care, because he's already marched through the door.

Serenity glances back at the rest of us, standing at a distance like a silent and awkward farewell committee. Her hesitation is all he needs. He slips from her grasp and walks out, shoulders slumped, without looking back.

She stands there. On her own, torn between him and here.

Until the doors swing shut.

Another girl breaks the ranks of our silent vigil and runs toward Serenity. She wraps her arms around her, and Serenity clings to her and sobs. Others begin to scatter and go back to their rooms or the recreation yard. Despite the absence of guards, all the conversations are soft and careful.

I understand why they stay. They have something here the outside won't offer. Community. Certainty. A way to call their families. A roof over our heads. A place we've known for weeks or months or years. A sense of belonging. Something to desperately cling to.

Where there's love and community, there is God. Father Michael was always fond of saying that.

But when the hallway is nearly empty and the girls break

apart, Serenity gasps. Like she's drowning on dry land and there's no oxygen around her. She reaches for her throat and starts to cough. It sounds like she did when she choked on the words before, but when she brings her hand up to her lips, her fingers come back bloody. "Mei..." she croaks.

And then she topples over.

"Serenity? Serenity!" Mei catches the girl before she collapses and hoists an arm over her shoulders, fighting to keep her upright. Her eyes dart across the hallway and land on the two of us left here. Me and a third girl from their wing. "Faith! Help!"

Faith has covered her hand with her mouth.

"We need to get Serenity to the infirmary," Mei says, her voice strained. "Help carry her."

Serenity continues to cough, and her rasping breath makes my bones ache. It makes me feel like I'm not getting enough oxygen either. Is this how it starts?

Next to me, Faith shakes herself. She swallows hard. "I can do that. I can *do* that. I won't get sick, will I?"

Mei cringes. "I don't know."

I do. *Saint Jude, pray for us.*

Because this is what the plague sounds like. Inevitability. Serenity wasn't there last night. She wasn't with us. Was deciding to stay here a death sentence? If two of us are sick already, it'll only be a matter of time before we all are.

Faith steps up on Serenity's other side and hoists another

arm over her shoulders. Mei pushes a stand of hair out of her face and leaves a smear of blood on her forehead. Her hands are trembling. Serenity's coughs leave droplets of blood across her clothes and the floor.

Mei glances my way. "Go find Grace. Tell her what's going on."

The words push through the terror, and I nod. "I will."

When they start half walking, half carrying Serenity in the direction of the infirmary, I clear my throat and add, "I'll clean up the blood too." It seems like a sensible thing to do. Like washing our hands. Like staying where there's food and cover.

I don't know if it makes a difference. I don't know what the right choices are. I don't know if we've already made far too many mistakes.

But I can't go back. This is all I am now, and if I'm staying here amid this whole forsaken mess, I need a purpose. No one can promise us we'll survive. The best we can hope for is to go out fighting.

Or cleaning, as the case may be.

Can we get sick from touching other people's clothes? Can we get sick from running our hands over the same door handles? Are we doomed for breathing in the same air?

This is what plague smells like. Chlorine and sweat.

I can bleach the blood stains, but I can't scrub away the fear.

twelve

LOGAN

NO ONE TELLS ME WHAT to do. I wash up in the bathroom, and then I stay outside the infirmary. Inside is too dangerous, but I cannot be without Leah. I do not know how to be. I do not want to be either.

I pace, first. Then I find a place to stand. My hands flap against my legs, and I rock back and forth on my heels. Every time I do, the soles of my shoes squeak on the floor. I stare at the dark-blue door to the infirmary.

Casey showed up at the door once before, when the girls carried Serenity Jones to the infirmary. She was quieter than I've ever seen her. If it hadn't been for the trembling rise and fall of her chest, she might've been gone already. Mei carried her to the doorstep and pounded on the door until Casey opened up. She immediately took a step back when he helped Serenity in.

It nagged at me that she assumed Casey would stay in the infirmary. Like he made that choice once he carried Leah in, and now he wouldn't be able to go back. He didn't challenge it though. He simply helped Serenity cross the threshold and closed the door behind him.

When he opens the door again, he's paler. He pulls down the cloth he's bound in front of his mouth and stands on the threshold for a small eternity, staring at me, and at the hallway, as if to muster the courage to walk out.

I sign at him. "I can help, if you need me." He frowns but doesn't respond, so I continue. "You shouldn't do this alone. I want to be with my sister."

After a beat, he shakes his head. "You shouldn't be here. You can't do anything for her now."

"Do you know what you're doing?" I sign.

He doesn't respond to my question. "Your sister is resting. You need to rest too. You can't stay here all day long."

"What does that mean, she's resting? She looked like she was—" I abruptly stop, ball my hands to fists.

Casey rubs his eyes. "I took some of the antibiotics and gave them to her. Tylenol too. I don't know if it'll help, but she isn't coughing up blood anymore. She's...sleeping, best I can tell. Her fever hasn't broken yet."

"I have nowhere else to go, and I want to know if she'll be

okay," I sign, but I don't know if he understands me. He probably doesn't.

"You need to stay back when I come out. And don't—don't go in. We need to quarantine them—us."

"Are you sick too?" I ask.

Am I? Will I be?

"I'll try to let you know how she's doing, I promise. I need you to stay back." Casey tilts his head like he's waiting for me to acknowledge his words, even though he never acknowledged any of mine. Still, I nod.

"I'm glad you understand what I'm saying, at least." He sucks in a deep breath then slips out to the bathroom.

I stay exactly where I am. I keep an eye on the door but don't move. I won't go in. My sister wouldn't want me to—even if I do.

What would happen though? If I got sick, I would have to stay with her too. I've already spent so much time with her. Would it be such a bad thing? Wouldn't it be better if we stuck together?

The minutes slip by, the opportunity opens. I could pretend I didn't understand him after all. Everyone always assumes I don't.

My hands clench by my side. I don't have any other place in the world than beside my sister. But I don't move. I wouldn't just put myself at risk, but Casey and the others. Leah would hate me for it.

And I think I would too.

When Casey returns, droplets of water cling to his face and his hair is wet too. "You should go, back to the others or to your room or wherever you're comfortable. I'll stay here with your sister and Serenity."

"Do you need to eat or drink something?" I ask.

I'm not feeling particularly hungry or thirsty, but we've been here for the better part of the day, late into the afternoon, and he might be. Meals are part of our routine.

He shakes his head. "I wish I could understand what you were trying to say. I'm sorry."

Yeah. Me too. I eye the back of my hands because I don't know what else to say. It's not like he'll suddenly understand it now. Leah is the only one who ever does. Even Granddad didn't—he didn't care to try. He told us once, "If one of you's too stupid to talk, you find another way to tell me what you need. I ain't got no time to guess." So we did. First out of anger at his cruel words, then because it meant safety between us. Leah and I built our own language. She always understood that there are so many different ways to speak.

Casey speaks up again. "I'll take care of your sister, Logan," he says quietly. "I'm here. There's nowhere else for me to go. But you can't stay." He glances past me, and his face softens. Some kind of intense emotion sparks in his eyes. "She can't stay, Grace. And you shouldn't be here either."

I swirl around and find Grace walking up. She halts at a

distance and folds her arms. She has a handful of paper crunched up in one hand. Her lips tremble, before she swallows and juts out her jaw. "Neither should you. I told you to bring her to the infirmary, not *stay inside*."

"So, what would you like me to do then? Leave the two of them in a bed and abandon them?"

"Of course not, but I thought—"

"We have no medical care, in case you've forgotten."

"I also know that, but—"

Casey folds his arms. "I can't leave them here. I won't."

"I don't want you to get sick, dammit! It's the fucking plague, and I don't want you to get sick." Grace raises her voice, and I flinch. I push my back harder against the wall, like it might swallow me.

Casey rakes his fingers through his hair, and all the worry and anger seeps out of him. "I don't want to either. I really would have preferred first contact to this. But I meant what I said. If this is it, the kindest thing we can do is take care of each other."

Grace's jaw ticks. She clenches her hands. "You remember what you said to me on my first day here? No one here truly cares about each other."

"Well, I also said you couldn't trust me."

"Oh, fuck you." Grace shakes her head, but she doesn't seem angry anymore. Leah told me once, there are a thousand ways to say *I hate you* and some of them mean *I love you* instead.

Casey's expressions go through a complicated journey. He

crumples like he might cry, but he swallows hard and narrows his eyes. He breathes out through his mouth, and somehow, in spite of everything, he manages to smile. "I was wrong. When I told you to survive. Surviving isn't enough."

Grace swipes at her eyes. "*Fine*. But surviving is where we start. You're not allowed to get sick, do you hear me? I don't know how I got to be the one in charge here, but if I am, then I forbid it. I forbid you from getting sick." She uses the papers she's holding like a pointer, to underline her words.

"Yessir." Casey tips an imaginary hat.

Neither of them says what I think: if only it were as simple as that. But maybe that's not what they mean. Maybe they know that as well as I do.

Casey nods his head in my direction again. "Please take her away from here, Grace. Let me take care of them, but protect yourselves too. Please." He directs the last word at me, and I can feel my shoulders drop, because that's what Leah would want me to do too. Protect myself. Be careful. Even if I want to find a way to protect her instead.

Grace sighs deeply and walks past me. She pauses at a respectable distance from Casey and places the papers on the floor. "Isaiah found more information on the disease. It's not good, but it may be helpful. I'll be back soon, okay?"

"I'd rather you didn't."

"Well, tough. I want to hear how the two inside are doing, and we have to plan for how to handle this until help comes."

She steps back, toward me. "I can't do this alone. I don't want to do this alone."

None of us *should* do this alone. But I can't tell them that, not in any way that they would understand. So, instead, I push my hands into my pockets and wait for Grace to lead the way. Out of here, away from my sister. To be torn in half. To be useful.

Somehow, Grace understands.

When she walks back to the main area, she speaks to me in a low voice that is probably exhaustion, but it reminds me of Leah. "I wanted to stay here because it's familiar. It's the closest thing to home I have, and I don't think I'm the only one. We're all outcasts and rejects."

I can't deny that, no matter how much I want to.

"But I didn't think—" She shakes her head. "If we stay here, we need to make this place habitable long-term. We need to take care of ourselves until someone comes for us, right? And that means we all need to pull our weight, like Case is doing..." She hesitates at that. "We need to take inventory of the food we have. And cook food. Do you know how to cook?"

I nod. Leah and I used to do the cooking and the cleaning and the laundry at Granddad's. He took care of himself before we came, but once we were there, he simply decided those tasks were ours now. Leah hated cooking, but I didn't mind it. I always liked creating stuff. And that way, at least, I knew what I was eating.

"Would you be willing to do kitchen duty?" Grace asks.

I nod again. I might as well. I just—

I look down at my hands and back at Grace. Shrug.

She follows my line of sight. "Yeah, we'll have to figure out the best way for you to communicate with others and for all of us to understand you."

I push my mouth into a forced smile.

Grace notices it, because she winces. "I'm sorry it's not easier. I don't think anyone here knows sign language."

It wouldn't have made a difference, since my signs are mine and Leah's. No one taught me how to sign properly in school. No one took the time to listen.

"Do you read and write?" Grace asks. We turn the corner, and she guides me toward the kitchen. I follow because that's what she expects, but now that we have left the infirmary behind, the weight of the day settles on my shoulders, and I would just as easily find my room and lie down.

Especially because it was quiet near the infirmary, but it's loud here. People are shouting and arguing. Isabella sobs into the shoulders of a brown boy with long, dark hair. "My father is sick. They don't think he'll make it through the night. So many people are dying, Xavier."

When we walk past them, it's clear Xavier's eyes are red too. His hands around her are trembling. "My brother said it's overwhelming the hospitals. I don't know how this could happen."

Elias leans against the wall, fists balled. "My uncle says it's all a hoax. He told me I shouldn't buy into it."

"Yeah, my mom said the same this morning. But she's sick now." Chloe Hughes stands across the hall from him, staring harshly into the distance. She's always been tall and lanky, but it looks like she might fold over.

Grace tenses when she hears the conversations back and forth. "Fuck."

I frown.

She's better at reading me than Casey. "I'd forgotten about the phone calls." She laughs at that and shakes her head, but her laugh is cold and full of pain. "I don't know how I forgot. I'm trying to keep track of everything, but—"

I reach out and skim her sleeve. Not enough to touch her. Enough to let her know... I don't know. That I understand? That I'm there? That I haven't answered her question yet?

I make a scribbling motion with my hand.

She nods. "Thanks, Logan. And good."

When we get to the kitchen, another person is there already. Nia Miller, with her ever-present pen and ink stains on her hands. She has some of the paper we stole from the classroom folded up in her pockets. A piece lies on the counter in front of her, scrawls all over it. The kitchen still smells faintly of toast and coffee.

She startles when we walk in. Her whole body tenses before she realizes it's the two of us and not a guard.

"Logan will help take inventory," Grace says, by way of introduction. "Please be careful to keep your distance from each other."

"We will." Nia is already moving again, between the counter and the large pantry. With the doors open, endless cans and cartons peek out, but there's plenty of empty space too. If the plague doesn't kill us, we'll have to keep each other alive.

Grace frowns. "Hunter didn't leave us much."

Nia turns to her, a carton in hand. "I think we may be at the end of a delivery cycle, actually. Do you think we can expect anything else?"

Grace's nostrils flare, and she grimaces. "I'll ask Isaiah to check."

"Good." Nia points me toward a second door across from the pantry. "I started with the dry food," she says. "You can make a list of what's in the freezer. We probably need to get through the cooked meals first. We can figure out food for tonight later. Grab a piece of fruit if you haven't eaten yet. It won't last anyway."

I turn around in time to see the doors close behind Grace, and that's it. It's Nia and me now. I scour the kitchen for more paper and a pen, nibble on a pear, and start my new job counting cooked meals, leftover turkey, and endless jars of peanut butter.

It's good to know what we have. It's good to have a purpose. If I can't be with my sister, I'll focus on doing the best job I can—and I think it would make Leah proud.

WHAT IS YERSINIA PESTIS? AN INTRODUCTION

- Y. pestis is a gram-negative bacterium, widely known by the disease it causes: the plague. The plague is known to take three forms: bubonic, septicemic, and pneumonic.

- Pneumonic plague arises from infection in the lungs. It can develop from inhaling infectious droplets or from other untreated forms of plague that spread to the lungs.

- Y. pestis has been on the CDC's National Notifiable Diseases Surveillance System since the system's inception. With outbreaks in at least a dozen cities, Y. pestis is a nightmare scenario come true for scientists.

- Some scientists believe the current and multidrug-resistant P21 variant is not naturally occurring but has been genetically weaponized, but as of yet, no evidence exists to back up that claim.

Historically speaking, the plague may be best known as having caused the 14th century Black Death, a pandemic that killed an estimated 30 to 60 percent of the population of Europe, North Africa, and Asia. But there have been multiple plague pandemics throughout history, as well as many localized outbreaks.

In modern times too, plague cases continue to occur, and the plague is said to be endemic in at least two dozen countries across the world. It has always been considered a threat to human health, but up until recently, it was a controlled threat and one with an effective treatment.

Following an outbreak of the plague in several cities across the country, doctors, hospitals, and scientists are discovering that this current strain of Y. pestis—*Yersinia pestis modernis,* with its current variant P21, which presents predominantly as pneumonic plague—has developed a multidrug resistance. It cannot be treated with the antibiotics normally used to treat victims.

Multidrug resistance in Y. pestis is not new. It was first discovered last century, and it's been a source for concern for scientists. But while there have been multiple cases since, they have never occurred on this scale.

Additionally, the way infections are spreading suggests that this variant may be more virulent than what we were used to. While it was previously understood that transmission of infected droplets is the only way that plague can spread between people, and that people therefore had to have been in close contact with each other, initial case spread also suggests infections following fleeting contacts.

Without early treatment, the pneumonic plague has a near 100 percent fatality rate. Even with early treatment, the IFR remains high. But compared to fatality rates of other recent outbreaks, it appears that this plague variant—at least—is not as immediately deadly as the original strain.

thirteen
GRACE

WE'VE BEEN LEFT HERE TO DIE. It's the same refrain, in the back of my mind, over and over again, along with all the things we don't have. Generous supplies. Medication. Help. Perhaps I shouldn't have said anything to Hunter. I could have let everyone leave and simply let myself stay behind with Case.

But I didn't. I told others they could stay too.

We've been left here to die. And so we have to figure out ways to live.

"It's the pneumonic plague," I tell everyone at dinner. I've climbed up and sat down on the food serving station, so I can see the eighteen people in front of me. Everyone but Leah and Serenity.

Everyone keeps a little distance from each other, but none

so much as Casey. I told him to come here for food, but he's pale and uncomfortable. Everyone gives him a wide berth while we're eating our precooked meals.

I fight to keep my voice even when I give them the details, confirming what some already heard when they called home. Isaiah was able to get into Warden Davis's computer, but the information he's found has only made things worse. *The* plague instead of *a* plague. The actual, medieval plague, but with a modern, virulent strain. *Yersinia pestis modernis.*

"Others will get sick. It's inevitable. This plague is contagious, and it's deadly, but that doesn't mean we can't do anything. We can be careful. We'll keep our distance from each other. Wash our hands. Fashion ourselves masks. Clean everything we touch. Quarantine if you don't feel well. Stick to your rooms."

"And put up a sign like a plague cross?" someone calls out.

It takes me a moment to identify the speaker. Khalil Nassif. He leans his chair back on the hind legs. He's crossed his arms, and his dark eyebrows draw together in a frown.

He meant the words like a challenge, I'm sure, but... "If that's what it takes. If you get sick, the rest of us will make sure you have food and water. I don't know when help will come—" I glance in Isaiah's direction and swallow hard. "I don't know *if* help will come."

According to Isaiah, Better Futures knew about the plague outbreak a few days before the guards left. The instructions from upper management were for the warden and the staff to leave and go home to quarantine. The company wanted them to be safe and not risk their lives guarding us.

"Their exact words were 'It's not worth it,'" Isaiah told me. "Nothing more than that. There was nothing ensuring we're safe or healthy or fed. There was nothing about anyone coming for us."

I asked him to reach out to Better Futures regardless. Email, call if necessary. "Maybe the authorities need time to decide what to do. They can still come for us," I said. Something cracked in my voice at those words, but what else was I supposed to say?

How do we move forward from here? What happens next? Should we figure out kitchen duties for all of us and take inventory of the medical supplies? What happens if our food runs out before winter comes? Why on earth should we stay here?

"But we'll take care of each other," I tell everyone, "because that's what we have to do. Casey will stay in the infirmary, and he'll look after the sick for as long as he can. We don't have many beds. We don't have much in the way of medication. But we'll make do." If the plague is resistant to everything anyway, medication doesn't matter. "If anyone wants to help him, they would be more than welcome."

Dead silence. Of course.

"We have plenty of other work to do too. We're here together. We'll make it through together." I can't keep the annoyance out of my voice, so I check my hastily scribbled list. "Nia and Logan are on kitchen duty. They're in the process of taking inventory. They could use more volunteers."

After another long pause, Elias raises his hand in the very back of the room. His light hair flops around his face. "I can cook."

"Yeah, you can," someone mutters.

"Like actual food too, thanks," he shoots back. "I used to cook for my mother," he adds sheepishly—quietly.

In the six months he's been here, I've never seen him do anything useful. I had a whole list of assumptions about the guy, but those perceptions all shift uncomfortably. "Cool, thanks."

I make a note, pretending for all the world like I know what I'm doing, and continue. "Isaiah will use the warden's computer to keep up with information about the plague and life outside for as long as we can. We'll try to have updates for you every day. If you have specific questions or locations you want to hear about, let him know, and he'll take care of it."

In my periphery, Isaiah nods. When I asked him about this, he immediately started making lists of everything to check up on. And if anyone wants to know about their homes or their families, they have a way to ask and figure it out.

"In addition, the phones should work for the foreseeable future, so you can call home any time you want."

The words are followed by a wave of murmurs. A sense of relief—and pain, for the people like me, who have nowhere to call. Worry about their loved ones. And about us.

"We're going to need people on cleaning duty as well and people to tend the garden." I have a whole list of tasks to divvy up between all of us. The garden was actually Emerson's idea.

"If no one comes for us," Emerson reasoned, "we'll need the food."

"To grow ourselves?" I didn't want to ask how long they anticipated us being here, on our own. They seemed like someone prepared for the worst.

They shrugged. "If necessary."

"It would take months."

"Yes." The finality to their voice sucked the air out of me.

At least the garden and the chores are a good way to keep everyone busy. That is, perhaps, the only real lesson I've learned here. Can't get into trouble when you're kept busy.

Well, it's *harder* to get into trouble anyhow.

Emerson is the first to offer taking up garden duty, as expected. Riley Jackson joins them. So do Mei Fujita and Faith Lang. After another moment or two, Khalil raises a hand too.

Unexpectedly, Walker Green is the first to sign up for the cleaning squad. When he first arrived, everyone pegged him for a rich white boy who would only be kept here a month, to be scared straight. It's been almost a year. He shrugs when I raise my eyebrows. "Might as well make myself useful, and I'm better with my hands than with my brain anyway."

Sofia Rodriguez follows. She doesn't say anything, and she

has her arms wrapped around her chest. The scar across her eye has grown pale against her brown skin.

From there, everyone claims something to do. Mackenzi offers to be our handyman, though we don't really have anything she can fix yet. Others sign up for laundry duty and still others for guard duty, though I don't know what they want to guard us against. A tentative trade begins too. Swapping out positions so no one has to do the same thing every day.

I have no idea yet if any of this will work, but when I look at the group of them—of us—I think we might stand a chance. Case still keeps to himself, and Nia and Logan are behind me, on the other side of the kitchen counter, but there is more vibrancy and life to the group than I've seen in ages.

The world is crumbling all around us, but we have the chance to build something that is ours. A small outpost against the coming storm, where we're safe and protected, because we're the ones who secure and protect ourselves.

And then someone coughs.

Immediately, our tentative house of cards collapses. The voices disappear and silence settles. Energy makes way for deep, abiding fear once more. Everyone turns around to try to figure out where the sound came from.

Another cough.

Quiet.

Maybe that's it. Maybe it's someone eating too quickly or choking on a sip of water.

Then, at the farthest edge of the room, comes the sound of something hitting the floor. Everyone sitting around the table pushes themselves from their seats and backs away.

I stand up on the serving station to see what's happening, but I hear it first.

The intense, racking cough that sends shivers down my spine. Mei described it like drowning on dry land, and that's what it sounds like.

I jump down and carefully move closer. Someone is lying on the floor.

"Help me." The voice sounds cracked and ragged.

Aleesha Mantis is trying to push herself to her feet, but her arms don't have the strength. She coughs again and again and again, and it sounds like it's coming from deep inside her, like she's trying to eject something lodged inside her lungs.

She trembles and shakes.

I take another step closer.

Tears are rolling down her cheeks, and while she manages to sit up, she's gasping for breath. "It—it hurts."

"Bring her to the infirmary." Case's voice, behind me. He's picked up his tray and brought it back to the serving counter. His eyes find mine but for a heartbeat.

I nod. I find my own voice. Because this is what we do now too. "Come on, she needs medical attention. We need to get her to infirmary."

Unexpectedly, it took longer for people to volunteer for

cooking. The girls who shared a table with Aleesha walk around it to help her up, but Walker and Khalil get there first. As if in tandem, they reach down and pull her gently to her feet, offer her support on either side.

At one of the other tables, Sofia leaps up and—once Aleesha and the boys have made their way past her—beelines for the kitchen. "I'll clean up. Everyone keep their distance," she states.

Her actions are brisk and brook no discussion. Nia immediately steps back and lets her enter to grab water and detergent and sponges.

I was afraid of desperation, but tonight, here at the end of the world, we find determination instead.

Aleesha manages to stumble to the door, supported by Walker and Khalil. She sways back and forth between them. Her head lolls. Her lithe dancer's frame strains under the weight of her racking coughs. No blood yet, but judging by the sound of her gasping breaths, that's only a matter of time.

Casey is already running toward the infirmary to prepare a bed for her.

Phone call between Walker and his mother

MRS. GREEN: Walker?

WALKER: Hi, Mom.

MRS. GREEN: I...I didn't think you'd call home.

WALKER: I didn't mean to, but with everything... How are you?
How's Dad? How's Tibby?

MRS. GREEN: Tibby's okay. The school's closed, so she spends
her days up in her room on her computer and chatting with
her friends. They're playing this type of game together...
I don't know what it is, but it's distracting her. At least this
way, she isn't scared mindless like the rest of us.

WALKER: That's good, isn't it?

MRS. GREEN: Yeah. I hope so.

WALKER: Is it as bad out there as they say it is?

MRS. GREEN: I don't know what they're saying, Walker.

WALKER: Just that...it's everywhere. People are dying.

MRS. GREEN: Ah.

MRS. GREEN: I imagine it will blow over in time. People talk so much.

WALKER: I guess. How are you and Dad?

MRS. GREEN: I'm doing okay. I've been meeting up with Mrs. Davis from across the road and Mrs. McCoy. We are under lockdown orders, of course, but they can't expect us all to stay home indefinitely. We need company to find solace with each other.

WALKER: Solace? Why—

MRS. GREEN: You know your dad regretted turning you in, don't you? He spoke about it often. He believed he did the right thing, but maybe we've been too harsh. Once he recovers, the two of you should talk.

WALKER: Once he what? What is going on, Mom?

WALKER: Mom?

MRS. GREEN: I'm sorry, Walker. I'll give Tibby your love. Stay safe out there, okay? I think you might be safest of all of us now.

This phone call has been disconnected.

PLAGUE OUTBREAK AND PANIC SPREADS ACROSS THE NATION

- Following outbreaks of a virulent strain of Y. pestis in cities and counties across the nation, the president calls for a calm and measured response.
- The rapid spread of the disease has caused governors in at least half the affected states to declare a state of emergency and institute harsh lockdown measures.
- Government agencies are investigating the possibility of bioterrorism or other forms of chemical warfare, though without any proof so far.

What started with a few seemingly unrelated cases of pneumonia shortly before Thanksgiving has devolved into a rapidly spreading new disease. In the past week alone, more than 275,000 cases have been counted, with nearly 80,000 deaths.

While the first death was confirmed ten days ago, scientists theorize that this new strain of Y. pestis has been in the country for at least fourteen days, with initial cases either undiagnosed or unrecognized altogether. It's possible that initial outbreaks stem from the near invisibility of those cases or the expansiveness and virulence of initial vectors.

Unnamed sources within the CDC say they are instead working under the assumption that the index case—who is as of yet unidentified—traveled knowingly or unknowingly while infectious, with airports and other forms of transport creating a viable environment for endemic spread of the disease during the holiday rush.

What appeared to be localized outbreaks at first is now turning into uncontrollable spread in three states, with the rates of infection and death climbing exponentially in at least half a dozen others.

A presidential task force of scientists has been instated to create rapid-response alternatives for treatment, containment, and vaccination. Existing plague vaccines are available in other countries but not currently in the United States, and none have proved effective against inhalation and airborne variants of Y. pestis.

Kitchen Inventory List

- 60 cooked meals (That's enough to keep us going for three days. I know it sounds like a lot, but there are 21 of us, and I don't think there'll be another food delivery anytime soon. We were supposed to get one this week, I think. I don't expect we'll see it now.)
- Frozen packages of meat (chicken and beef)
- 3 frozen tubs of butter
- 15 loaves of bread
- 75 eggs
- 3 bags of rice (50 lb each)
- 2 bags of potatoes (50 lb each)
- 4 bags of beans (50 lb each)
- 5 bags of flour (25 lb each)
- 1 tray with 6 cans of tuna
- 2 trays with 8 cans of green beans
- 1 tray with 8 cans of chickpeas
- 2 trays with 8 cans of carrots (Ew.)
- 1 bag of lentils
- 10 boxes of cereal
- 12 boxes of mac and cheese
- Vegetable stock powder
- Five packets of ramen
- 25 fruit cups
- 2 cups of past-its-shelf-date chocolate pudding

- 3 oversize boxes of granola bars (peanut butter and protein)
- 2 trays with 12 jars of peanut butter
- Half a bag of raisins
- 3 gallons of milk
- 5 gallons of some kind of juice ←—It says orange. It doesn't look like orange juice.
- 2 containers of instant coffee
- Leftover instant soup
- An absolutely ridiculous amount of tea
- Salt
- Pepper
- Sugar
- Honey
- Ketchup
- Mustard ←—It probably shouldn't have a white layer on top.
- Vinegar

fourteen
EMERSON

THE WORLD CAN CHANGE AND change again in a few days' time. I'm not sure I'll ever catch up enough to grow used to it.

It's been seven days since we were abandoned. Out of the twenty-two of us, one third of us are sick. The infirmary is overflowing.

And the garden won't grow. Rationally, I know it wouldn't in a few days, but I hoped to see some improvement. I don't know why I even offered to do this. I don't know anything about gardening. I'd only been to the communal garden twice before, and it's a mess.

When our little squad showed up with shears and shovels, most of the plant beds were covered with fallen leaves, while some of the plants were pruned to be nothing more than stick figures, and—according to Khalil—no one had planted any fall crops. I nearly laughed at that. To everything there is a season, and a time for every matter under heaven. Even here. We did what we could. Under a drizzle of rain, with the drops tapping out a rhythm on the shed's wooden roof, we set about to cleaning the leaves and the dead twigs, and covering the roots of the trees and plants with straw from the shed.

But a week later, the leaves are still changing colors and falling. Faith started coughing two days ago, and she's in the west wing now, alongside Chloe Hughes. The infirmary only had space for five beds.

The four of us have gathered in the small shed. An intimidating collection of garden tools lean in the corner. Dust motes float in the air, and the smell of fertilizer permeates the beams. And all I can think about is how this garden is a metaphor for all of us: far more dead than alive.

"It's meant to be educational," Khalil says with a sigh. He was here when the garden was first planted. He's standing in front of a worktable, and he's sifting through packets of seeds we found in the drawers. "Learn to care for a peach tree and reap what you sow? Something like that. They said it would be great for 'people like me.'" He makes air quotes with his hands.

"What does that even *mean*?"

He shrugs. "Occupational therapy for all of us with ADHD and other weird brains? Not that they'd ever acknowledge those labels, mind you. They just call what we have behavioral problems and criminal tendencies."

Riley rolls her eyes. "Right, those." She clears out some cobwebs around her head.

"So how do we make any of this nutritional?" I ask, gesturing at the seed packets.

"Well, we can eat persimmons in a couple of weeks." Khalil looks at the orange trees in the corner of the garden with a wistfulness that aches. They're flanked by other trees, but they're the only ones that look like they're bearing fruit.

"Besides, it's not like we'll actually need to be able to sustain ourselves," Mei says, with more determination than I'd ever felt about anything in my life. She's holding a hand rake and uses it to pick at her nails. "Isaiah said as much last night. The state senate promised to look into the situation in prisons and residential facilities. They'll come for us."

Riley scoffs. "They'll think about us. And then decide they have other priorities. They left us here in the first place, remember?"

"Grace said there were no plans. That doesn't mean they can't still *make* plans," Mei objects. "It's only been a week."

"It's only been a week here. It's been longer on the outside," Khalil says.

Silence.

"It's a mess out there. They *will* come."

Riley picks up a packet of cucumber seeds and frowns at it

over her makeshift mask. The bright yellow fabric pops against her dark skin. "Of course. And who knows, maybe they'll decide to let us all go and live free and happily ever after. And the plague will magically disappear, and we'll find unicorns in the wild."

I can't help but agree with her. Isaiah *did* mention the state senate adopting a resolution to look at incarcerated populations, but he also spoke about outbreaks in the juvenile detention center, and it didn't sound like they were doing anything about that. It didn't sound like they *could* do anything about anything. Death rates continue to rise, and from Isaiah's news reports, daily life has almost ground to a halt.

If a third of us are sick and it's the same outside, it must be chaos. There've been pandemics throughout history, and everyone knew there would be another one sooner or later. The literal plague must have been on scientists' watch list. But I don't think anyone could have anticipated this—not anything like this. The news stories call it a nightmare scenario, and not for nothing. We have no better antibiotics or other treatment.

It nags at me. The question of what it's like back home. Are my parents sick or safe? Can they still go to church? Does their faith make them less afraid?

Maybe I should try to call. Be the better person. Father Michael would tell me to honor my parents.

"Maybe you can simply give up," Mei snaps. "But I won't."

Riley shakes her head and mutters something under her breath.

Mei narrows her eyes. "What was that?"

"We should ask Isaiah to find us information on fall and winter crops," I say, before the situation escalates further and we lose more precious time to fighting between ourselves. If I'm honest, that's the main reason why we've only cleaned the garden and done nothing else yet. Everyone is scared and touchy. I nearly punched Khalil yesterday when he reached out and poked my shoulder, and two days before that, Faith snapped a rake in two with the sheer force of her frustration.

"We have some," Khalil says, putting seeds aside. "Beets and carrots and kale. Some of them should've been planted already, but we can try."

"Ew, kale." I say it to make him smile, before I can stop myself.

Thankfully, he simply glowers. "It's food."

"Yeah, fair enough." I hold out my hands to take some of the seed packets. "We should try."

"We can plant the seeds and take care of them. We can make something grow."

"Reap what you sow?" I wince.

"Something like that." At this, the corners of his eyes crinkle, but it's nothing more than a ghost of a smile. How do you smile when the world is breaking?

We carry our shovels into the garden and dig row upon row. One seed at a time. An hour in, my back hurts and so do a variety of muscles I didn't know I had. My hands ache from holding the shovel. I might grow calluses, but I don't have them yet. This is work. It's hard, but it's comfortable. The garden has a gentle peace to it, to the four of us working in tandem, without words to spare but in the knowledge that we're together. And on the other side of the fence, we have more ground to plow, if we need to.

Seeds in good earth.

One of Father Michael's sermons about the Parable of the Sower floods back to me. He insisted that we should strive to be good and fruitful soil for the word of God and not let ourselves be distracted by the cares of the world or swayed by any hardship. Only those seeds planted in the good soil will bear fruit and truth and justice.

What am I now? What would he think of me, if he saw me here? A seed among thorns? Or maybe I've grown into those very thorns myself. Let me get taken away and eaten by the birds; I won't grow on good soil anymore.

I ram my shovel into the ground with fierce abandon, until wood splinters dig into my hands and the work replaces my thoughts. Until someone at the entrance to the garden calls out.

All four of us immediately pause our work. I glance sideways to Riley, and all of us feel the same immediate, overwhelming fear crawl up our spine.

Near the gate stands Grace. She's pale. She's lost so much weight in only a week, and I don't think she's slept at all. She's developing a permanent frown. Her hands clench and unclench at her side, and she scans the garden until she sees Mei.

"I thought you'd want to know—" Her voice trips, and she clears her throat. "I'm sorry, Mei. I thought you'd want to know. Serenity died today."

The world can change and change again over the course of a single day too. Serenity dies. She may be the first, but she certainly won't be the last. All of us know that, but there's a difference between knowing and seeing it happen. It's fear that goes from realistic to real in the blink of an eye, especially when, midway through dinner, Isabella collapses.

Casey—already sitting on his own—gets up and helps her. He leaves the remainder of his food to grow cold, and we finish our meal in silence.

It only makes it worse.

Father Michael's words about seeds in good soil echo in my mind. The dead plants. The fallen leaves. The harsh scraping of shovels through dirt. All of it combined forms a constant buzz like a violin with a misshapen fingerboard. I cannot still it and I cannot ignore it, and I don't know how to stop myself from breaking, one piece at a time.

Serenity should not have died here today, alone, away from any family she might have. None of us should be here. Not like this.

If we're seeds among thorns, that isn't our fault.

The thoughts keep nagging at me, overwhelming enough to

tremble my bones and try to break me from the inside. It doesn't stop until I find myself back in my room, my violin case in hand.

The air here is cold and humid, and it's no good for a fragile instrument like this. But all that matters is the familiar movement of my hands as I unclasp the case and take out the instrument. Take out the bow.

I *can't* think. Thinking hurts, and I need something, anything to stem the pain.

I let my muscle memory guide me through tuning, let my audible memory guide me to the right tones. They all sound colder and shriller, struggling as much with being here as I am.

My hands hurt. Holding a violin bow is nothing at all like holding a shovel.

But it doesn't matter.

It should hurt.

I don't know how else to pull the ache from my bones.

I close my eyes and *play*. One of my favorite pieces: an arrangement of Albinoni's "Adagio in G Minor" for solo violin. I've never managed to play it slow enough, but tonight I do. It yearns and it aches, and it tears through the air. It teases more hopeful themes combined with baroque drama, and underneath it all is a sadness that leaves me empty and alone.

All I can do is let the music speak. I make mistakes. I miss notes. I put all my pain into it. And by the end of the piece, I breathe. My sorrow and my restlessness click into place.

I'm no great violinist by any means, but making music makes

me feel alive. It makes me feel like I have a purpose. To soothe, to rejoice, to celebrate. Father Michael's words still linger in the back of my mind, but they're quieter now.

I *will* let myself be distracted by the cares of the world.

Outside my door, I've amassed a silent audience. Logan sways back and forth. She has her hands folded—one hand over a fist—and holds them near her heart. Nia is clinging to Riley and has tears in her eyes. Xavier is deadly pale but smiling.

"That was beautiful."

I nod in acknowledgment but don't look up to see who spoke. Gently, carefully, I place my violin back in her case. When I put the case back in its corner, my fingers brush the bronze medal, and I take a deep breath—

I walk out. Past the onlookers. Through the east wing and toward the communal areas. It's the same route I took the night Hunter demanded to see me, the night when everything changed.

What I'm about to do now will change everything again. At least for me.

I brush my fingers along the rough spots on my hands.

Past the open space between wings. Past the cafeteria.

I don't stop until I get to the infirmary, and when I do, my heart is racing. My hands are shaking. I don't even notice it until I knock.

When Casey opens the door, the first thing I hear is coughing on the other side. It sounds like someone is choking.

"Emerson." Casey tilts his head. He has a torn shirt bound

over his mouth and nose. Blood spatters stain his clothes, and his skin is gray. "What are you doing here? Are you sick? We've cleaned out rooms in—"

I shake my head to interrupt him. "No, it's not that. It's about Serenity."

He doesn't say anything.

"Where is she?" I immediately correct myself: "I mean, where is her body?"

His face falls. "She's here, still. I've talked to Grace about a way to—" He breathes in sharply. "We need to find a good way to deal with—with the victims, but we haven't yet. I can't carry her out on my own."

"I'll help," I say.

Something in his expression crumbles. "I appreciate the thought, but you shouldn't be here."

"I want to." I swallow and try to make him understand. "She shouldn't have been here either. She deserves to have someone take care of her, at the end. You were there. And now I will be. She shouldn't be alone."

He frowns. "What are you saying?"

"There's good earth outside of the fence. I know because I spent most of my day outside. I've been digging holes all day. I can dig a grave too."

The words hang in the air between us.

"Emerson..." Casey hesitates.

"She deserves to have someone give her a proper goodbye."

I do the only thing that makes sense. I reach out to take his hand. "You've made this choice. Trust me to make mine."

It's been a long time since I've asked for anyone's trust.

Casey nods. "Are you certain?"

"I'll eat with you tomorrow."

And in the end, it's as simple as that. A choice. A decision. A seed in good earth. I follow Casey into the infirmary, and I try not to flinch at the sight of the sick teens. Leah is in the farthest bed, and she's pale and quiet. Aleesha is coughing near constantly.

I try not to think about the air I breathe—the air we share that smells stale and sick—even though I'm wearing a mask. I simply help Casey carry Serenity out. He's wrapped her in the linen sheets from her bed, as stained with blood as his clothes are.

She's heavy. Heavier than I thought she would be—but at the same time, maybe lighter too. When we carry her out of the building and off the grounds, as the night falls around us, I don't feel afraid for the first time since I can remember. When Casey leaves me and I go to grab the shovel from the shed, the same peace and purpose I felt when I was planting overwhelms me.

This might kill me, but the dead won't judge me.

And Serenity doesn't have to be alone.

"I'm not a priest," I tell her when I dig. "Or any sort of holy person. I would be offended if you called me that. I don't know how to commit your body to the earth or if you'd even want that. I don't know if such a thing like life after death exists. I don't know if there's a God either. But I want you to know, you'll be remembered. *I'll* remember you. And I hope you find your way home."

GOVERNORS MOBILIZE NATIONAL GUARD AS CASES CONTINUE TO RISE

- National Guard to provide lockdown support as well as mortuary affairs support across five different states.
- Mass graves and freezer trucks to provide a temporary solution in dealing with rising death toll.
- White nationalist groups have been protesting the use of lockdown measures, claiming their right to freedom supersedes others' right to live.

With cases continuing to rise, the federal and state governments are reaching for drastic measures to restrict the community spread of the new plague as much as possible. From local stay-at-home or shelter-in-place orders to mask mandates and curfews, everything is being done to keep the healthcare system from collapsing.

Governor Brooks (AR, D) stated, "The best way to keep ourselves and our fellow citizens safe in this time of uncertainty is to follow local and state guidelines as strictly as possible. I was proud to be one of the first governors to mobilize the National Guard to assist in maintaining our lockdown and curfew measures. As of today, they will also assist in recovering bodies of plague victims across the state. This is not an easy measure, but it is a necessary one." She continued to say, "I am grateful to all of our brave soldiers who are assisting in this."

In cities across the nation, the announcement of stricter

measures led to protests by local militias, originalists, and, in some cases, churches. The vast majority of these protests have been disbanded by National Guard soldiers and local law enforcement, citing the various shelter-in-place orders.

Scientists across the nation—and, in fact, across the world—have come together virtually to discuss the possibilities of treating a multidrug-resistant illness. An insider, who wishes to remain unnamed, says that there is frustration among scientists at the lack of urgency among governments in recent years. At the same time, this insider expresses a careful optimism at the research that has been done and is sure to be continued given the current state of affairs. "Antimicrobial resistance is one of the biggest public health threats of our time. When it comes to multidrug-resistant cases of Y. pestis, we have seen hopeful results in experiments with phage therapy. With time, funds, and global collaboration, breakthroughs might finally be possible."

An official communiqué from the presidential task force cautioned against expecting too much from these exploratory meetings. "While treatment is a crucial focus, our main concern is to find the quickest and best solution for this crisis. As such, we will keep investing heavily in developing better vaccines and researching all other avenues of containment."

Until such time as a solution can be found, the presidential task force advises everyone to abide by the rules. Quarantine when possible. Socially distance when not. Wear a mask at all times.

Phone call between Sofia and her brother

SOFIA: Hey, it's me.

LUCA: Wow.

SOFIA: Yeah. Look, I'm sorry, I didn't want to call you out of the blue, but—

LUCA: I like hearing from you. Are you okay? Is the plague there too?

LUCA: Lie to me if it is. I'd like to believe you'll be safe.

SOFIA: You're ridiculous.

SOFIA: Okay, no plague here. Everything is totally and completely fine, and we're living like kings.

LUCA: Cool. That's what I like to hear. No need to come bust you out then?

SOFIA: Nah, never. I'm good. We've got this.

LUCA: You don't sound convincing.

SOFIA: You told me to lie.

LUCA: Fair enough.

SOFIA: So how are things on your side?

LUCA: Same old. There may be a lockdown, but that doesn't mean everyone sits safely at home. I still take the bus every morning and every evening, and I'm hardly the only one. Still gotta produce food. Still gotta feed people. Still gotta care for them. They haven't figured out how to handle that part without all of us yet. Lockdown might be great if we all lived in a future with replicators and emergency medical holograms and shit, but we're not there yet.

SOFIA: Nerd.

LUCA: Watch it.

SOFIA: You'll be careful though right? Can't lose you too.

LUCA: You won't be rid of me anytime soon.

LUCA: Your room is here waiting for you.

SOFIA: Good. I...I'd really like to come home. Soon. When I can.

LUCA: When the world goes back to normal again, right?

SOFIA: Right. That. When it does, beam me over or whatever you call it.

LUCA: Wow, ouch.

LUCA: I've missed you.

LUCA: It's good to hear your voice. Promise me you'll check in with me as much as you can?

SOFIA: I've missed you too, bro.

LUCA: Promise?

SOFIA: Yeah, of course. Always.

This phone call has been disconnected.

Burial rites for Chloe Hughes

You'd think I'd get better at this, but death doesn't become any easier. Loss doesn't become any easier. We never truly had a chance to meet, outside of recreation time and dinners. You scared me. I'm sorry for that.

You didn't deserve this, Chloe. None of us did, and none of us do. But yours won't be the last grave. Too many of us are sick. Too many of us are showing signs of sickness. So here we are. You won't be alone. I don't know if that's a comfort.

I wish I had anything more hopeful or beautiful to say, but maybe this. The music I played before you fell ill was a part of Britten's War Requiem. It's not meant to be played by a single violin. No requiem is. It's meant to be sung. It's meant to be orchestrated. It's meant to be beautiful and ethereal and guide the dead to a place of rest. This one is meant to be angry too, and that's why I love it.

I hope it resonated with you. I hope it guides you.

I hope you find a place to rest. I promise I'll remember you.

fifteen
GRACE

I CARRY TWO LISTS OF names with me, everywhere I go. On the first: Serenity, Aleesha, Walker, Chloe. On the second: Leah, Isabella, Jeremy, Faith…

Mei.

She came down with it this morning. She made it to the garden, where she collapsed.

Walker Green went to sleep and never woke up. Emerson and Casey carried him out. I don't know what we would do without the two of them. And at least I can talk to Casey from a distance. Emerson speaks, but they don't let anyone get close.

It's been only two weeks since Reid was shot. It feels like a lifetime. In more ways than one, it has been lifetimes.

I grab the kitchen knife from under my mattress and strap it to my belt. With my toe, I nudge the shards from a broken cup to the corner of the room. I had coffee in my room to figure out the work lists when Emerson came to tell me about Walker. It was the only thing at hand I could break.

We do what we must to survive. Especially since there's still no word from anyone at Better Futures, despite Isaiah emailing and calling them. Several others have asked family members to reach out too, but it's the same voicemail every time. And no one can come get us here.

As for other options, they've all proved fruitless too. No one trusts the Department of Human Services enough to reach out to them. The outside world could not care less about what happens here. They consider us difficult at best and worthless at worst. So we have to take care of ourselves.

When I edge out of my room, Sofia is leaning against the door of Aleesha's now-empty room. She's dressed in her work uniform, her hair cut short, a scarf tied over her nose and mouth. We've shared the same wing for years and never really talked. Not beyond forced, perfunctory words in group therapy.

She was convicted for assault. Like me, I think she did it. We've all got stories, haven't we?

We're the only ones left here now.

"Took you long enough," she says, by way of greeting.

"Couldn't sleep."

"All the more reason to get up earlier."

I don't dignify that with a response. Truth is, I spent most of the night awake, staring up at the ceiling. The same two lists of names running through my head, while the narrow bed felt lonely and too big.

It's not like I can get close to Case now, and I'd never admit it, but I miss his touch. I miss human touch, period. I'm starving for it. We've cut down on rations, to be on the safe side, but it means my stomach is constantly growling, and my skin is yearning too.

"Are you certain you want to do this?" I ask. Sofia is pale and has dark circles under her eyes.

Sofia shrugs. "We need food, don't we? Don't get to be picky about the methods when you're hungry."

Yeah, we need food. No one comes for us, and it means we have no food deliveries either. We have bags of rice and beans to keep us going for a few weeks at best. Potatoes. Peanut butter. Vegetable stock powder and instant coffee. Ramen from the guard station, some chocolates from the therapist's office, and a tin of glazed pecans from the warden's desk. But we're rapidly running out of meat and vegetable supplies. I didn't think all of us together would eat this much.

I don't want to gamble on a few weeks.

We might all be dead in a few weeks.

If we aren't, I don't want to try to live through the winter cold with beets and persimmons and what little else Khalil and Riley manage to grow. I can see a future past that—with a spring garden and vegetables in summer, but between now and then extends a deep, hungry chasm. We don't have enough to stock up, so we need to be able to feed ourselves.

So I snuck out last night and set traps in the woods around Hope. Or at least, I tried.

"Are you sure it'll work?" Sofia asks. She brandishes her own knife. We both need something to use if I caught an animal and it isn't dead yet.

"No."

It's been years since I lived with the Podolskys. They were my first foster family when I entered the system. To my three-year-old brain, they were already ancient when I got there, and I had to leave the week before my tenth birthday, because Baba Podolsky broke her hip, and they couldn't take care of me any longer. But it was a good place to be. It's the only place I remember fondly. The place whose phone number I whispered to myself over and over again.

Mr. Podolsky taught me to build snare traps to catch the rats and vermin that ran around their basement and backyard. He taught me to forage wild garlic and mushrooms. He showed me the constellations.

Baba Podolsky told me about Paris and how she traveled there when she was in her twenties, to find a handsome gentleman to fall in love with. Apparently, that was what my birth mother had done too. Or at least, I still had the photo of the man I'd been told was my father—broad-shouldered with mousy hair like mine and glasses perched on the tip of his nose. He laughed at something only he could see, ruining his posing in front of the Eiffel Tower.

I kept the picture safe all through staying with my first three foster families. At least one of those families told me college wasn't for people like me, but the closer I came to high school, the more I entertained the idea of studying abroad and trying to find him. I only remembered my mother vaguely—and not fondly—but he became a larger-than-life figure to me. Someone who would see me and accept me.

He might have been a tourist for all I knew, but the mere thought of finding him and finding a home to belong to kept me going. It gave me reason to try my best.

In my fourth home, Doctor Coleman tore the picture to shreds in front of me. He called it discipline. The consequences of my own choices. If only I'd listened better. If only I'd given him the respect he deserved.

If only.

I wonder how the Podolskys are doing now. I hope they're safe.

"I want to know, if we don't…" Sofia hesitates briefly when we walk out the door to the outside. It's still a strange feeling to not have anybody stop us, shout at us, send us to solitary. I'm not sure when it'll become easier. "If we don't find food now, how bad is it? I know what Isaiah told us. I know things are bad on the outside. I know what my sister tells me too. But how bad will it be here?"

A hesitation underlies her words. Like she didn't want to ask this question, but she couldn't *not*.

Tension races up my jaw and neck. I glance around to make sure no one else is within earshot and measure my words. "It's not terrible, yet."

She grunts. "Sounds comforting, thanks."

"Would you rather I lied to you?" I demand. "We need to stock up."

"For how long?"

"I don't know," I snap. "For as long as we can. For as long as we must."

Sofia's voice remains calm and collected when she asks, "Do you think they'll find a cure?"

I breathe out hard. Isaiah tries to find information about that on a daily basis. So far, nothing, but it's only been a couple of weeks. At least, that's what I'm telling myself. I can't imagine being here for months or years. I don't want to imagine either. I'll grow old before I grow older. "I hope so."

"Yeah, me too." Sofia is silent all through our walk into the woods, but it's a silence of unspoken words, and I wait for her to continue. "I want to travel before I die. Do you think we'll ever travel again? I want to flirt with girls and kiss them. I want to learn Spanish, so I can talk to my niblings. I want to work with kids like us when I grow up, but I don't want to grow up yet."

We leave the path toward my first snare trap. I mull over her words. "Are you afraid to get sick?"

"Aren't you?" she shoots back.

"I don't know." The weird thing is, I don't think so. Of all the things that keep me up at night, that's not one of them. "I'm afraid others will get sick."

"Like your boyfriend?"

"He's not—" I stop when I see her wiggle her eyebrows.

"Chill, I'm joking. You remember we share a wing, right? I would've heard if you had your boy over for better times." She wiggles her eyebrows.

I roll my eyes. "You know relationships aren't just about sex, right?" Sofia is right that the walls of Hope are thin enough that we can hear others make out, but I don't care about sex. Or romance.

"Sure. Not my thing, but totally valid. Anyway, yeah, I'm afraid to get sick. I'm afraid to die." She tilts her head. Her brown eyes sparkle. "I'm afraid to spend all my time with the rest of you rejects."

I snort. "Join the club."

I let the woods distract me. The wind still rustles through the trees like the world is the same as it ever was. The water from a nearby stream rushes over sloping rocks, and all around us, birds chatter. I try to remember where exactly I placed the trap. I guide Sofia around a clearing, too far to the east, back toward the narrow stream that's downhill from here.

When we find the trap, it's sprung, the bait is gone, but there's no catch in sight.

"Fuck."

I kneel down and reset the trap. I made bait ahead of time. Some of the carrots that were left in the garden. Peanut butter and crackers. The same things Mr. Podolsky used. Bits and pieces we can stand to lose, but not if I don't catch anything.

I triple-check the trap for the third time, when Sofia places a hand on my shoulder. "C'mon, let's go. Show me the next trap."

So I do.

The next one is empty too. Something cold and hard settles in my stomach.

I breathe in deeply and try to focus. The air smells of wildflowers and decaying leaves, and it cloys my nose through the thin layer of fabric.

Sofia, to her credit, doesn't ask me again if I know what I'm doing. Perhaps because the answer is spectacularly obvious. She follows me farther into the woods, and she talks about the last girl she fell in love with before she got sent here. She tries to keep her voice down, but she probably spooks any wildlife in the vicinity.

It's not a bad thing. It's not like we're hunting with our kitchen knives—though we may have to figure out how to do that before long, if I can't figure this out.

When we get closer to the third trap, I hear rustling and snarling and screeching. I raise my hand, and Sofia stops midway through her sentence.

I point.

On my cue, we both approach the trap from different directions, Sofia going the long way around and me inching closer from here.

Another few steps, and it's clear what's making the sound.

The third trap sprung, and it snared a raccoon. But the snare didn't strangle it the way it did with Mr. Podolsky's rats. Instead, the raccoon is struggling and hissing, even though he's clearly wounded.

My stomach drops. The annoyance makes way for nausea—and regret. I shouldn't have done this. We're good, still. We have food enough to make it through another week or so. We can cut our rations further. I could've waited. I could've gone out then. I should've asked Isaiah to find me the latest information on snare traps instead of relying on my memory. I *did* have him look up wild garlic bulbs to remind me how to forage those, but—

I don't realize that I've growled until Sofia comes closer to me and takes my hand. I don't realize how hungry I am for contact until her fingers touch mine and I don't want to do anything but cling to her—and not let go.

I pull back as though she's burned me. "We should be careful. We should keep our distance."

"Do you want me to do it?" The worry in her eyes only makes my hesitation worse.

The raccoon is still struggling, fighting for its life, and bile rises in my throat. I can be violent when I'm angry, but this is different. The raccoon is defenseless. I want to take the easy way out and say *Yes, please. Please kill this animal that I captured. Let me pretend I have nothing to do with this.*

Instead I kneel down next to it, and I take my knife. If I can break bones, I can do this too.

The raccoon screeches. It frantically tries to get away from me. Maybe it knows what's coming. Maybe it's simply the instinct to survive.

This is survival too. It has to be.

I reverse my grip on the knife so I can use it as a blunt weapon. I want to close my eyes, but I understand what a terrible idea that would be. Instead, I breathe in, hold my breath and my hands steady, and the moment I spy an opening between the raccoon's flailing claws, I let the knife come down. The impact resonates through my hand, and the raccoon goes limp.

Before I can stop to think, before I can stop to breathe even, I bludgeon it again, then I flip the knife over and stab it.

Behind me, Sofia gags.

I can't. I have to make sure it's dead. I have to make sure it's not in any pain.

But once I have, once I've made sure it doesn't breathe anymore, I drop the knife right next to the trap, stumble a few paces away, and vomit.

Necessity makes monsters of us all.

Another Kitchen Inventory List

Or: learning to appreciate what nature gives us

- 2 bags of rice (50 lb each)
- 1 1/2 bags of potatoes (50 lb each)
- 3 bags of beans (50 lb each)
- 4 bags of flour (25 lb each)
- 2 loaves of bread that look fairly edible
- 5 boxes of cereal *(Which is definitely still edible even without milk)*
- 2 cans of tuna
- 5 cans of green beans
- 8 cans of chickpeas
- 2 cans of carrots
- 1 bag of lentils
- Vegetable stock powder
- Five packets of ramen
- 1/2 pot of instant coffee for special occasions
- Leftover instant soup
- Still an absolutely ridiculous amount of tea
- 2 bars of chocolate
- A tin of glazed pecans
- Still with those raisins
- 16 jars of peanut butter (I really didn't expect I'd come to appreciate peanut butter this much.)
- 2 frozen tubs of butter
- 5 boxes of mac and cheese
- 20 fruit cups (Does no one here eat fruit?)

- Sugar, salt, spice, all things nice
- 1/2 raccoon
- 2 fish
- 5 fresh carrots
- 3 withered wild garlic plants ←
- 13 old and wizened blackberries

How do you count wild garlic? In bushels? Leaves?

Phone call between Casey and his sister

ASHLEY: Hi, it's Ashley! I can't come to the phone right now, but leave a message after the beep. *Beep!*

CASEY: Ash, it's me. I've tried to call you a few times, but you keep going to voicemail, so I thought I'd leave a message. I wanted to hear your voice. I hope things are okay where you are. Things are rough here. I don't know if you know, I don't know if you get any news about me, but—

CASEY: I'm scared, Ash. I'm no doctor or miracle worker. I'm just a boy trying to keep his friends safe when everyone is dying.

CASEY: Did you know, Ash? Did you know that you can learn what it looks like when someone is about to die? Do you know that some of them gasp for air and others hallucinate and still others just let go?

CASEY: Did you know that muscles can still twitch after death? That some people still groan? I nearly screamed the first time it happened. I nearly broke down.

CASEY: Ah, you probably don't even know what I'm talking about. I'm sorry. I didn't want to burden anyone else, but I don't want to scare you either. Maybe I shouldn't have—I'm sorry.

CASEY: For what it's worth, despite everything...I'm *good*. As can be, in any case. I'm taking care of myself like you told me.

CASEY: I'm still here. And that matters.

This phone call has been disconnected.

sixteen
LOGAN

I HAVEN'T SEEN MY SISTER in over two weeks, and her absence is a wound that will not close. We've never been away from each other for this long. Even when she fell from the roof one summer and the hospital kept her overnight for observation, it's only ever been a day. Even when we were interrogated after the fire, we were together.

Every morning at breakfast, Casey tells me she's alive. She's alive, but she keeps having seizures. She's alive, but she's drifting in and out of consciousness. She's awake, but she's minimally responsive.

Casey thinks it may be a form of brain inflammation. Either because of the plague itself or because of how high her fever ran, but he doesn't know much more.

Every evening after dinner, Emerson waits outside the kitchen and confirms it too. They keep their distance, but they keep me updated.

Every day I ask them if I can go see her. I've passed by the outside window at least a dozen times, but it only makes it harder to see her so close but so out of reach.

Every night, in our room, I talk to her. I lie down on my bed, next to hers. I stare up at the ceiling. If I don't turn my head, and I don't listen too hard for her breathing, I can pretend she's lying in the bed next to me.

I tell her safe things. Gentle pictures, like Nia calls them. The way we try to make normal life go like it's supposed to, even if there's nothing normal about anything here anymore.

Like, "We took inventory in the kitchen and the pantry. I counted the bags of rice and weighed the bags of flour. We haven't had a food delivery since the start of this, and you can tell. Did you know they barely accommodated anyone's diets? We can't do anything but the minimum either, and it makes me feel bad."

And, "I taught Nia to sign. *Hello* and *how are you* and a few other words. She was the first to ask. She sketched me cutting my thumb on a can opener."

Or, "Isaiah is looking up recipes for raccoon. Granddad would be proud."

I don't tell Leah about the things that scare me.

Like how Isaiah hasn't been able to go online for the past

three days, because we've been having power outages and the phone lines are down.

Like how seven of us have died, and three others are still in the infirmary with her.

No one has recovered yet. Xavier and Isabella ran as high a fever as Leah's, and they're holding on like she is. Jeremy is slowly fading away.

It's only a matter of time before we all catch it, because despite all our precautions, we can't simply avoid each other. And maybe I want that. To be close to her. To be with her. Is that terrible?

I can draw out the plague's progression in everyone else. Someone starts to cough. It's so innocuous at first. Someone starts to cough, and sooner rather than later, they're coughing up blood. They collapse. They lose consciousness. And within a handful of days, they're gone.

I don't tell Leah about any of that though. What's the point of it, when she needs to focus on recovering?

What's the point, when she can't hear or see me anyway?

I talk to her every night, and in the morning, I wake before dawn to go to the kitchen. Familiarity is the only safety I have. I get there before Nia arrives. Because I'm the first, I'm the one who turns on the lights. I go through the kitchen to make sure everything is clean and nothing is weird, and clean our counters again. I collect the food we need for the day and mark on Nia's sheets what we are missing. What we *will* miss, in a day, a week, a month.

By the time Nia gets there, I've gone through all my motions. I am less overwhelmed and ready to share our work.

Then Elias comes in to prepare breakfast.

Or came in, anyway.

He started coughing three days ago. He died last night.

Today is different. I wake and get dressed and brush my teeth. I wonder how much longer we will have toothpaste.

Then I slip through the door, through the quiet east wing, through the dark. The sun isn't quite up yet, but the night lights are off. I don't know if it's another outage, but I keep my head down and keep walking.

I open the door to the kitchen, and the lights are already on.

Rather, one of them is. The other lamp to the back of the kitchen is flickering aimlessly, more off than on. The uneven rhythm bothers me. It leaves me feeling off-balance.

This is wrong. This is not what the kitchen should look like.

I breathe in, and against every instinct in me screaming to step back, I step forward.

Spoons cover the floor. Shards of a broken plate. A dusting of flour and bread crumbs. We baked massive loaves of bread two days ago, to go with the raccoon stew Elias taught us how to make. We saved the rest for breakfast and lunch, but the loaves we left out on the counter are gone, and the remainders are torn to pieces.

My heart crawls up to my throat and hammers loudly.

Wrong. Wrong.

Danger.

"Is anyone there?" Like they'd reply to my signs if they could.

Another step back mentally, a step forward physically.

Toward the pantry.

I reach for the door that stands slightly open. When I do, the door swings outward and slams into my face. Hot, overwhelming pain shoots up through my nose and everything goes red. It feels like my brain snags. A siren. A warning.

Danger. Danger.

Danger.

A figure shoots out of the pantry, arms full of food. A bag of rice tumbles in her wake, spraying the floor with grains. The food we need. The food we *counted*, bag by can by grain by bite.

Danger. Danger.

No.

I growl. I wipe at my face, and my hands come back red with blood. I'm not sure what is up or down right now, but I can see the figure—the girl—standing in front of me, her eyes wide.

Josie Watson. Who stabbed a girl. Who left with Hunter and his crew.

A shadow passes across her eyes when she sees me, and I grow cold inside.

"Leah? Or Logan? I'm here to—you have to let me—" She

snarls in frustration or anger, I don't know. "Get out of the way. I don't want anyone to get hurt." Her voice is as ragged as her clothes. She's not wearing a mask, and I've grown so used to every one of us wearing one that it looks strange. Her chestnut hair is matted around her face, and she clings to the bags she's carrying.

I shake my head, and my head pounds.

"Step away. Let me pass." Josie's voice sounds like she hasn't spoken in days. "I—I didn't take everything. Just enough. Look away. All you have to do is look away."

No.

Holding the bags close to her chest like a treasure, Josie brushes past me.

A feral growl escapes me. I stumble. I push myself forward in her direction—and we collide. I don't know what else to do but stop her. I was scared of her once, but I have to stop her. We counted all the food. We know exactly how much we have. She can't take it away from us. We need it.

The bags drop to the floor. I can hear something tear, and I want to look down to see how much more food we're spilling, but then Josie's hands are on my face.

I'm holding on to her shirt to stop her from stealing our food. She's clawing at my eyes to stop me from holding her.

I don't want her to touch me. I cannot let her go.

"You can't—you can't stop me. We have a right to the food too."

But she didn't *ask* for it. She could've come here and asked for it. Instead she tried to *steal* it. This isn't hers. It doesn't belong to her.

The tiny part of my brain that sounds like Leah tells me to figure out what's going on. To be careful of more danger. Is she here alone? What does she want? Is she sick?

Is she sick?

Let go. Let me go. Let go. I *can't.*

"I need it," Josie says. "*She* needs it."

We need it too.

I cling to her dirty shirt with one hand and raise my other to try to push her clawing fingers away. I can hear myself moan and keen. I don't mean to do it, but it happens. The sound is primal and desperate and full of rage.

My brain trips over the same messages over and over again. *Let me go. I can't let go. We need the food. Let me go.*

Josie lets me drag one of her hands down, and the moment I release it, she reaches up and smacks my arms away. She stumbles forward and something crunches underneath her feet. In one fluid arc, she brings her arm up to my throat and slams it against my windpipe, her forearm under my chin. She pushes me against the counter.

The edges of my vision grow dark. I claw at her. I keep clawing.

"You need to stop fighting it," she says. Her eyes are haunted, Granddad would've said. Angry. Hurt. Dangerous.

"It'll be easier if you stop fighting it. I promise I don't want to hurt you, but I can't have you stop me. This'll be fine. You'll sleep, nothing more. And I'll be long gone from here by the time you wake. It's the best solution for both of us."

Another tear trickles down my face, but this time, it doesn't come from me.

I stop clawing at her arm. I stop trying to push her off me.

I don't want to sleep. I can't sleep.

Leah needs me. One of us has to be awake. Always.

I spread my arms on either side of me and bend across the kitchen counter. I do the only thing I can. I reach as far as possible, until my fingers find the edge of the bowls Nia and I used for bread dough.

Josie leans in, and my field of vision narrows. Everything grows dark.

I whimper.

I let the last bit of breath escape from my lungs, overextend my reach, and shove the bowls off the counter so they go clattering onto the floor.

I close my eyes.

Leah.

seventeen
EMERSON

MY STOMACH CHURNS. IT'S FAR too early for anyone but the kitchen crew—and probably Casey—to be awake yet, but my room increasingly feels like a cell again.

When I started digging graves, everyone else in Hope found excuses to avoid me. I don't know if it's because they're worried I carry the plague with me or because they're uncomfortable at the notion of death. Maybe it's a bit of both. But the work needs to be done, and we need someone to do it. I *want* to be the one to do it.

It's far easier to be amid the dead than amid the living. I don't have to worry about trusting them not to let me fall. So I'll make myself useful—I'll grab my portion of food and spend the whole day outside preparing for more.

But when I walk toward the kitchen, the sounds of a struggle echo from within. I freeze. What is going on?

Someone grunts. Something metal goes clattering to the floor, sounding like an off-key cymbal. It sounds like someone is in trouble, and I can't just stand here.

I pick up my pace and slam the door open. There's food strewn out all over the floor. Torn bags and busted bowls rolling around. And one of the girls who left with Hunter is fighting with Logan. Or rather, overwhelming Logan—she isn't fighting back. Her hands are twitching, but she isn't struggling.

She's suffocating.

I do the only thing I can. I *move*.

I don't even stop to shout or to warn them. I have to stop what's happening. I put my head down and rush the girl to get her off Logan. When we collide, it's a tangle of limbs. Shoulder into shoulder. Equal parts tumbling and diving, my arms around her, and we're falling. Our impact with the ground rattles my bones.

Somewhere in my periphery, Logan gasps and coughs.

The girl I'm fighting is strong. I'm stronger. I've been building up muscle digging holes in the earth.

But she's desperate, and I don't know what I'm doing.

She snarls and sputters and thrusts to push me off, but I cling to her. We roll across the ground, across the sheen of rice grains that dig into my skull and my arms, then we twist and turn again.

When I lean over her, she brings a knee up to her chest and kicks out hard, wildly. Her eyes are frantic. Her foot connects with my abdomen and groin and pure, aching nausea surges through me.

"Get out," I shout to Logan.

The girl escapes from under me when I double over, but I push myself up again and cling to her. "No. Stop. Stay."

"Let me go!"

She kicks out at me again, and I struggle to hold on. I try to grasp at her hair, and she all but drags me toward the counter. Logan is nowhere to be seen. *Good. Smart girl.*

Get help.

"You have nowhere to go, stop fighting!" I shout.

"I have to get back to her." She reaches for the counter, and it occurs to me a second too late that she's near a kitchen block.

I reach for her again, but she has a head start on me. She can barely reach the smallest knife—a paring knife. But she gets hold and uses it to arc around her.

I let go immediately and dodge. I'm not trained to fight. My own instincts are all firmly on the side of flight and stumble.

The girl on the other side isn't trained either. She holds the knife like it isn't the first time, but she's breathing hard, and she's pale and sweaty. Her eyes dart over the absolute chaos around us: the floor covered in wasted food, the bags that lie torn outside of the pantry.

I can see the bread crumbs on her shirt. The stains from last night's stew around her mouth.

We circle, and she takes a step to the side, accidentally kicking a can of food to the side.

She raises a trembling hand up to push a strand of matted hair out of her face. Her shoulders drop, and she lets go of the knife.

It clatters to the dirty floor.

I leap forward. To stop her. To restrain her. This time, she's the one who dodges. She grabs my hand and uses the momentum against me, letting me swing past her, while my arm bends backward.

And two things happen.

My arm bends beyond the point of stretching, but I can't stop moving. At the very last moment, when I'm sure my arm will get torn in two or my shoulder will dislocate, the girl lets go.

I throw my free arm out, and the floor rises to meet me. I impact on my hand. A quiet but audible *snap* echoes through the room. It does nothing to slow my velocity.

I stumble forward across my broken wrist and slam headfirst against the wall.

Briefly, I see stars. I never thought that was real, but they're flickering in front of my eyes. Like needlepoints or pinpricks or pain. And time slows down.

Footsteps crunch past me.

A shadow creeps over me. It grabs at the floor. It grabs at the counter.

"I'm sorry."

Something hard and heavy comes down toward me, and I can't move.

Pain explodes behind my eyes.

Then everything goes dark.

New footsteps.

A scream full of rage and sorrow and anger.

Violin music echoes around me, that deep resounding echo that only comes from being in a church. But I never played at my parish. I didn't want to share that part of me with Father Michael or anyone aside from my teachers and my parents.

It's muscle memory, letting the bow dance across the strings, and it hurts to move my arm, to play, to be here.

It hurts.

It hurts.

Would I go home if I could?

Would I call home if I could?

No.

"It was Josie." A voice that I recognize but can't place comes through a fog.

"Why would she do that?"

"According to Logan and Nia, she wanted food. For her and another girl."

"So she figured she should steal it from us?"

"We're criminals after all."

"Shut up, Grace."

"It's true, isn't it? If we meant something, *anything*, we wouldn't still be here. We're a bunch of rejects left here to die. No one cares about us."

"Shut *up*, Grace. We're doing what everyone is trying to do right now. We're surviving. And though that may not seem like enough to you, it's enough to me, it should be enough to all of us. And not a single person among us deserved this."

"I wish it were that simple, Case. She *stole* from us, and we can't accept that. Because she endangered us, and I have to protect all of you. Logan offered to help you carry Emerson to their room. Please take care of them?"

"Where are you going?"

"To handle this."

It still hurts.

My bed isn't soft. It's lumpy and uncomfortable, and I moan. All my words and thoughts tumble together, because violin music still plays in the background.

Everything around me is muted and distant, like I'm floating.

I don't know if prayer counts if you're not sure you believe in anything. Maybe that's why I'm struggling. Maybe none of it matters.

My bed feels like a grave, but I hope the graves I dig are softer. I hope Serenity and Aleesha and Walker and Chloe and Elias and Faith and Mei are comfortable there. Even if heaven doesn't exist. Even if there's nothing beyond the peace of the garden. We all deserve a place to rest.

———

I'm nowhere, and the violin song won't stop, and the endlessness is absolute.

I'm scared.

No, I'm not.

———

I would go to Confession one last time if I could. Despite everything, I miss it. I miss sharing what is on my mind and in my worries, all the mistakes I made and all the things I would do different now. I miss the soft smell of incense and old stone buildings. I miss feeling lighter afterward.

But right now, I don't even know what I would say.

Forgive me, Father, for I have sinned? I have, I'm certain. I am—I was Catholic. I can feel guilty about anything without so much as trying, but I don't feel guilty about being here. I don't feel remorseful about being who I am, and I certainly won't repent.

We're *not* rejects. We deserve to be cared for and deserve to be remembered.

Forgive me, Father, for I have sinned. I believe the world—Your glorious creation—is broken, and when I'm not scared, I'm so angry, I could break it all further. I won't honor my parents. I won't forgive those who trespassed against me. I will not accept a single moment of this.

If You are love or mercy or whatever Scripture tells us, and Your will is being done, You have failed us. You have failed me, and I will not forgive that either.

———————

In the end, I sleep.

eighteen
GRACE

MY ANGER IS ALL-CONSUMING. IT darkens the edges of my vision, and it pounds in my ears. I thought we were safe. I didn't think anyone would come to aid us, but I also didn't think anyone would come to harm us. Let alone one of our own.

"You're this close to breathing fire," Sofia says from a few feet to my right. We're half a mile away from Hope, off the path that leads up to the building. Khalil saw a figure run away in this direction, so we're trying to find Josie's tracks, but the wind is rushing through the trees, and rain clouds are gathering overhead.

I can't laugh it off. I *am* this close to breathing fire. "She put all of us at risk," I seethe. "I can't believe she could be so selfish."

"She's scared," Sofia mutters. "We all are."

"And yet none of *us* have stolen food from each other."

"Because we have enough to get by. And that counts for a whole lot." Her words are soft and measured. She's tired. I've seen it happen to others these last few days, as the idea settles in that this is it now, that we're not going anywhere. Fear and anger get replaced by fatigue.

I need my anger to fuel me. Maybe Hunter was just trying to scare me when he said I'd be responsible for everyone, but that doesn't matter anymore. I *am*. I am the one constantly counting how much food we have—and I don't know how much we have left now. I'm running lists of the dead and the dying. I'm the person Isaiah comes to when the internet is gone again or when all he can find is news reports about rising death tolls and civil unrest and overflowing hospitals and mass graves.

We have to track Josie down. We need the food back she stole from us, because we have enough to get by but not for long. We need to take a stand to make sure nothing like this happens again. We need to—*I* need to make sure everyone survives.

Sofia kneels in the grass and runs her fingers over the muddy ground. She picks up something and smashes it between forefinger and thumb.

I scan the countryside and try to figure out where Josie might have gone. Toward the hills or the woods? Somewhere she can hide from us or the weather? Sofia and I will have to check our traps too, but we need to do that anyway.

"Are you certain you want to do this?" Sofia looks up at me with an unreadable expression on her face.

I let my rage burn hotter and brighter. "Yes, I'm sure."

"We could let her have this," she suggests. "It's only a few loaves of bread, and in the end, it isn't going to make a difference."

"But what if she comes back?" I demand. "It isn't just about the bread. It's about the food that got destroyed. It's about the fact that she nearly suffocated Logan. She broke Emerson's arm and bashed their head in."

She took our food and the one person brave enough to care for our dead. She might as well have taken everything.

It's about Josie attacking people I'm meant to protect.

If I think about it too hard, the fire that burns inside me is the same I felt when I pulled Ian off that girl in school. I saw her struggling. I realized he held one hand over her mouth and had the other pushed down her pants. I saw that she was hurting. And I hit him until my fists were sore. I kept punching and *kept* punching. I broke his nose. And his arm. My anger is a white-hot fire that will scorch everything in its wake, but I refuse to burn alone.

"So, what? We need to set an example?" Sofia very nearly hisses the words.

"Yes, is that so wrong?"

She spits on the ground. "You sound like the judge at my trial when you say stuff like that."

The words are a blow to the stomach. I don't have a response to it. I breathe out through my teeth. "It isn't like that."

"Isn't it?" Sofia holds out her hand, and I nearly laugh and cry when I see what's on her fingers. Bread crumbs.

"You've got to be kidding me," I say. "What a twisted fucking fairytale."

"Well, here's to living happily ever after, I guess," Sofia says.

We follow the bread crumbs. Sofia leads the way. The wind buffets us and the trees. What was a sea of gold and orange and yellow around us has become a monotone landscape of barren trees and undergrowth. It'll make our hunting and hiding all the more difficult.

We need to stock up on food—and protect it.

We turn onto the main road in the direction of the roadblock. None of us have gone here since the confrontation with the soldiers. Either Josie found a way past it, or there's another route out of here.

The bread crumbs are few and far between, on a blanket of muddy-brown fallen leaves. Off the road and on again, and the closer we get to the roadblock, the more anxious I grow. I don't want to be faced with the guards, with their guns or their determination.

I don't want to be reminded of how we're closed in and alone.

And with every step I take, that gnawing grows.

When we come up to the turn, I hold out my hand and brush Sofia's arm. She stiffens and halts immediately. "What?"

"Maybe we should leave the road," I suggest.

"The trail keeps going."

"I know, but…" I wince. A strand of hair flies into my face, and I push it away. "It's coming up to the roadblock where they killed Reid, that night when we all left the center."

Her eyes dart in the right direction. "Oh."

"Yeah."

Exhaustion crawls across her features. She scratches behind her ear and sighs. "So you want to keep going, but you don't want to follow the trail? No, I'm not here for that. If we get turned back, we get turned back. I'm not going to wander around like we don't have anything better to do. Emerson is hurt, Logan must be terrified. I'm not playing." Her voice takes on an edge. Finality, and worse, disappointment.

I duck my head and focus on the road. The bread crumbs are spaced out. Hardly enough to form a proper trail. They'll be covered or scattered if we leave the weather to toy with them. But are enough left to lead us to where Josie must be?

"Let's continue until we're turned away, then," I say through gritted teeth.

"*Fine.*" Sofia throws up her hands and stalks toward the turn in the road. Her voice echoes around me.

With that one word, she sounds like my friends from school. Like Ariana, my best friend when I stayed with the Marshalls, when she was particularly frustrated by my hardheadedness. Like Ruth, when I lived at the Podolskys. She could groan and grunt dramatically at anyone and anything, but especially me.

For the first time in almost two years, underneath the anger, underneath the humiliation, I feel an ache at the pit of my stomach, an Ariana-shaped hole, a Ruth-shaped hole. An emptiness where belonging is meant to be. I would have done anything to protect them too.

I push my hands deep into the pockets of my work pants, I push the loneliness away, and I follow Sofia in silence.

I'm sorry, I don't tell her. *I'm scared too.*

The silence grows until it envelops us both, but we keep walking.

Along the road, toward the narrow pass that leads into the nearest town. I wonder if the people of Sam's Throne know that we're here—if they think about us at all. Does anyone even know that we're left here?

With every step, my anxiety doubles.

We turn the corner toward the mountains and—

There is no roadblock.

No barricades. No floodlights. No soldiers.

No signs of blood from where they shot Reid, either.

I must've made a sound, because Sofia stops and turns to me. "Are you okay? Is this it?"

I open my mouth to speak, but my throat clogs up. They forced us to stay here, in Hope, *at gunpoint*. They told us it was stay or die, and when we were good and well forgotten, they left?

What even was the point of that, beyond sheer cruelty?

When I finally find my voice, it cracks. "I don't understand."

The only thing that remains from the roadblock is a truck lying off the road on its side. It looks torn and weathered, older than a couple of weeks. The tires are slashed and a few of the windows smashed in, but it still looks semifunctional. Its canvas flaps and billows. It looks like a good hideout.

The anger inside me has become fire and ice all at once, and it's devouring me. I raise a shaking hand and point. "Bet you anything that's where the crumb trail leads."

Even my voice is trembling. Sofia throws a worried glance my way, but I refuse to acknowledge it. Everything, *everything*—the anger, fear, betrayal—it's all wrapped up in that one wreck of a vehicle.

I stalk toward the truck and raise my voice. "Josie! Come out and show yourself!"

"Well, if she didn't know she was being followed..." Sofia mutters.

"Come on! Coward!"

My words are met with the constant roar of the wind and nothing else. We're out of the woods now, with no critters around us. No birdsong or the chirping of insects. No shouts from soldiers. No cars coming down the road. All that exists is the overcast fall sky overhead and the ice in my veins.

Sofia walks in the direction of the truck, her guard up, her steps careful around the shards of broken glass glinting in the pale daylight. "Josie?"

The canvas across the back of the truck moves again.

Sofia stalls, but I stomp toward it, crunching something beneath my feet.

Pushing the canvas aside, Josie appears. Her chin is held high, her hands wrapped around a crowbar. Her posture is proud, like she doesn't care about anything or anyone but herself. And right there and then, I hate her. I hate what she did to us, I hate where she stands.

I'm overwhelmed by the need to hurt her like *I* hurt.

I take another step closer, and she points the crowbar in my direction. "What do you want?"

I scoff. "What are you going to do? Bash our heads in like you did Emerson's?"

Josie changes her stance, pushing her feet wider, so she stands more comfortably.

"We want the food you stole," I say. "You have no right to it."

"We have as much right as you do," she snarls. Her shoulders drop, but she raises the bar higher.

"No, you don't. You left, you made your choice." From the corner of my eye, I can see Sofia circle around Josie, to get to the other side of her. It isn't subtle, and Josie must notice it too, but she can't keep her eyes on both of us. "You had a chance to stay and put in the same work as the rest of us."

"What, so we only deserve to be fed if we work hard enough? Is that what you're saying?"

"If you would've made an effort to help us out—" I start, but Sofia interrupts me.

"Who's *we*, Josie?"

She angles closer to the truck, and Josie swings in her direction. Seeing my chance, I dash forward. When Josie twists back to me, Sofia closes in on her like she's a trapped animal.

"Get back!" Josie moves the bar around wildly now, forcing us both to keep a distance, but we're close enough.

We both hear the coughing coming from inside.

And more effectively than any crowbar, that forces us back.

"What the *fuck*, Josie, you're with someone who is ill, and you still brought that plague back into Hope?" I would kill her if I didn't think she'd bash my brains in.

Her face crumples. "She isn't ill anymore. She reacts to my voice and to my touch. She'll let me feed her, but she keeps slipping away from me."

"Who?" Sofia asks, softly.

Josie pushes the canvas open and shows us the makeshift camp they've built inside. "Saoirse."

Saoirse lies on a bed of canvas and leaves. Her red hair lies in knotted strands around her face, and she's all elbows and hard edges. Her clothes are baggy and dirty. She is as pale as anyone in our infirmary. A cup of water sits next to her, as well as one of the loaves of bread, some late-autumn berries, and the remains of—something. The food they stole when they left? Something Josie scavenged? I don't want to know.

"She started coughing the day we left Hope, and Hunter and his cronies refused to let her come with." All emotion disappears from Josie's voice when she adds, "They suggested killing her, but I wouldn't let them. They thought it would be more merciful—and safer for them."

"That would be *murder*." I might be angry at Josie, but I'm horrified by Hunter.

"I chose to stay behind with her. To take care of her, but her fever ran so high... I didn't know what to do."

"It could've killed you too," Sofia says.

Josie juts out her jaw. "Yeah, well, I wouldn't have wanted to survive on my own. Alone is not worth living."

Behind her, Saoirse coughs and mumbles something.

Josie lowers her arms to glance back at her, and in the distraction of the moment, I dash forward and wrest the crowbar from her. She lets go of it with little to no resistance, and once I have it, she sits down hard. She glares at me with eyes as dark as the night. "We have as much a right to live as you do, you know."

"At any cost? At the cost of our food? Emerson's health? Do you even care what happened to them?" I drop the crowbar before I use it on her.

She shrugs. "I take care of my own. Isn't that what you're doing?"

It is, and I hate it. I hate how much I understand her, now that I know she's trying to keep Saoirse alive. It's far easier to simply think of her as a villain.

I grit my teeth. "Saoirse needs medical care. We don't have much to offer, but we do have some. We'll take you both back to Hope." I raise my voice before Sofia can interrupt me again. "We'll figure out what to do with you there."

Phone call between Mackenzi and her former best friend

MACKENZI: Look, I know this is awkward, especially after everything that happened. But...

MACKENZI: I can't get ahold of my dad? And I know he usually works long hours, but I also can't imagine there's a lot of demand for home improvement right now, you know?

MACKENZI: I just want to know he's okay. And yours is the only other phone number I still know by heart.

GWEN: *Fuck*, Mackenzi.

GWEN: I don't know what you want me to say.

MACKENZI: Tell me he's okay?

GWEN: I can't.

MACKENZI: Oh.

GWEN: For what it's worth, I'm sorry. [cough]

GWEN: He was a good man. He didn't deserve this. None of us do.

This phone call has been disconnected.

Phone call between Isaiah and Better Futures

———————————

BETTER FUTURES: You've reached Better Futures. Our offices are closed until further notice. Please leave a message, and we will try to get back to you as soon as we can.

ISAIAH: Hi, this is Isaiah Wood. I've called before from the Hope Juvenile Treatment Center. I've tried to email too. You probably won't hear this either, but...we're still here. Please don't forget about us.

This phone call has been disconnected.

nineteen
LOGAN

EMERSON MOANS IN THEIR SLEEP. They refuse to wake up. Too many people close their eyes and never open them around here, and I hate it. I *hate* it. I want my friends back. I want my sister back. I don't want to be alone here. I need them.

If I hadn't woken up early this morning, I would never have caught Josie. If I hadn't caught Josie, we would never have fought. If we hadn't fought, I would never have had to make noise for help. If I hadn't made noise, Emerson wouldn't have come, they wouldn't have tried to help, they wouldn't lie here like this.

Is this what it feels like when everything is crumbling? It's the same ache I felt before the fire. I hate it.

"Logan?"

Nia stands in the door to Emerson's room. She keeps her distance, which I try to do too, but someone needed to help Casey carry Emerson here. Someone needed to help splint their wrist.

Outside, rain's starting to tick against Emerson's window. Nothing more than a gentle trickle, and I stare at the patterns formed by the droplets.

"You need to eat. It's past lunchtime."

I half turn to her. Release my hands. "I'm okay."

Nia takes a tender step toward me. She's holding on to something in a paper napkin. "No, you're not. None of us are, but you need to eat. Did you drink anything?"

I wince. "You sound like Leah when you say that."

She frowns as she follows my signs, but I know she recognizes the sign for my sister, and she can figure out the rest from there. The corners of her eyes crinkle. "Well, she's right. And she would want you to take care of yourself too."

I scoff. "Fine. But we'll need to make more bread soon."

She holds out the napkin to me, and when I rise to grab it, she smiles. I unwrap it; it has a raccoon sandwich inside. The remainders of our meat with the last bread we have. Still, it smells good, and my stomach growls. I easily forget how hungry I am when my mind is occupied with other things, but when I take a bite, I don't know how to stop. I scarf down the food.

"Better, right?"

"Smells...good..."

I swirl around. In the bed, Emerson blinks. Their eyes don't focus on me, or on anything for that matter, but they turn their head toward the two of us—

And immediately wince. "Ouch. Hurts."

"Are you okay?" I step closer toward them.

They raise their hand to their head, and the movement alone makes them look a paler shade of green. I dash out of the way in time before they vomit on the floor. It isn't much—bile, mostly—but Nia immediately retches too. She says, "I'll go...grab some cleaning supplies."

Watching Emerson to see if they'll let me, I reach out and push their hair out of their face. I've done this for Leah before too, even though Emerson's hair is much shorter.

They moan. "God, it hurts."

They lean into my hand a little, and I can see them slowly registering my presence. It's different but familiar. They're out of it because they had their head bashed in, and they probably have a concussion. But I recognize what it feels like when the world is too much, too overwhelming, and when you can't connect with everything around you.

With their healthy arm, Emerson carefully reaches up to squeeze my hand and push it away.

"Logan... How are you?"

I crouch so I'm at eye level with them. I can't tell them I'm okay—or not okay, as Nia would tell me—but I manage a smile.

"What happened?"

I can't answer that with a smile. I don't know how to answer it.

"How do you feel?" Nia leans against the door opening. She's wearing bright-yellow gloves and carrying a bucket with water and cleaning supplies. She indicates with her head, and I get out of the way so she can move past me and clean up the bile.

She answers Emerson's questions where I can't. She tells them about Josie, about running into me when I went to get Grace. She tells Emerson what happened to them. I take over her place in the door opening, and I wish I could do all the talking for me. Or not even the talking, necessarily, but the explaining. I wish it were easier for people to understand what Leah does, what Nia does: there are many different ways to communicate.

Emerson clears their throat and catches my eye. "Thank you...for finding help."

"I'm sorry I couldn't do more. I'm sorry I—" I don't know what else to say.

Nia squints at me and shakes her head. "It wasn't your fault, you know?" She turns back to Emerson. "Thank you for helping Logan. I don't know what I would've done without her in the kitchens."

She's wrong. It was my fault. But her words feel good. They feel *right*. I've never felt wanted before, not by anyone who wasn't Leah, and she is a part of me. I *like* being in the kitchen with Nia. It may not be quite the same as a place to belong, but it's a place where I can make myself useful and where I understand the world around me.

I'm glad she feels the same way too.

Emerson lets themself lean back on their pillow, and they bring their broken wrist up to their chest. They close their eyes. "What about...the food?"

What about the fact that we were both near Emerson? If they were infected at any point dealing with our dead—are we too? What will happen then? With so few of us here, it's becoming harder and harder to keep our distance in times of need, but we can't afford to lose anyone else.

We can't afford to lose Emerson.

And I don't want to get sick.

Nia shrugs. "We'll figure something out. The most important thing is for you to feel better first."

And that is something I can help with. I tap the doorframe so Nia looks up, and I tell her, "I'm going to check in with Casey. See what we need to do to help Emerson."

She smiles. "Good plan."

———

When I leave Emerson's room again, I pass the common areas on my way to infirmary. It's busier here than it normally is at this time of day, though busy doesn't mean what it meant three weeks ago. All of us together can barely fill a room now.

I push my back against the wall to avoid bumping into anyone.

The hallway is alive with whispers and questions.

"Do you know what happened?"

"I hear she stabbed Emerson."

"She stole our food and destroyed the rest."

"She must have been working for Hunter."

To my side, obscured by the angle of the hallway, I overhear a conversation between Riley and Khalil.

"I always knew she was dangerous."

"Yeah, you're one to talk."

"Hey!"

"It's true though, isn't it?"

I stand on tiptoe and crane my neck to be able to look over and past them and Isaiah, though I know what I'll find.

Josie.

I expect to feel fear or revulsion, and I do. My breath catches. My hands go up to my throat to make sure no one is clinging to me. I don't want her to look at me. I don't want her to get close to me. I don't want to be a target.

But another part of me sees that her hands are shaking. She has her head down, arms wrapped around her waist. She has a few stray leaves in her damp hair. Her shoulders are pulled up almost to her ears, and she walks forward without looking at anyone. I can't tell if she's angry or scared, determined or desperate. Maybe she's all of the above.

She must hear the whispered accusations too, feel several pairs of eyes on her, because she stumbles.

"C'mon, keep moving!" That's Grace's voice, though it's slightly muffled. She sounds tired. When she enters through the door, Khalil and Riley immediately take a few steps back.

Grace is supporting a pale and coughing Saoirse. Saoirse's face is drained of color, and it makes her hair and her freckles only stand out further, and her head lolls back and forth. She doesn't seem to be particularly conscious, only propped up by Grace on one side and Sofia on the other. Grace and Sofia are pale too—and weathered.

Everyone steps back, but Mackenzi steps directly into Josie's path. She plants her fists in her sides. "You brought the plague back to us, you thief. They should've left you out there to starve."

"Get out of the way," Sofia grumbles. "Josie, keep walking."

Mackenzi doesn't budge. She faces off against Josie, while the others pass through to get Saoirse to the infirmary as quickly as possible.

I edge farther back alongside the wall. Riley looks furious. Isaiah clenches and unclenches his hands. Even Casey comes out to look, though he's tired and worn.

Josie pushes through, her face obscured, but Mackenzi steps in her path again and shoulder checks her. Josie immediately brings her fists up and pushes back. In return, someone else shoves her forward.

Grace shouts, "Stop it!" but it doesn't change anything. The hallways are narrow, and everyone is exhausted. Riley steps in to help Mackenzi, and everything escalates. Josie ducks her head to avoid the punches. Grace and Sofia push through with a sick Saoirse. Khalil tries to hold Riley back.

I don't want to be here.

We stuck together and managed to keep each other safe as much as possible over the past few weeks, more so than any of us could've hoped for, and I don't want to lose that.

Sofia whistles so hard, I flinch. "All of you, get back! Now!"

Khalil and Riley straighten, like it's one of the guards yelling at them. Isaiah holds Mackenzi back.

Josie ducks past everyone, her arms raised up to cover her face.

"We'll figure out what to do with Josie—with all of this—later," Grace says.

"Judge her?" Mackenzi demands.

Grace scowls. "Let us pass, and go do something useful."

"She brought the plague back to us!"

With four of us still sick, it never left.

This isn't it. We can't be the ones who judge Josie. We're all screwups too.

It's not like Leah and I meant to kill anyone either, but we nearly did. Out of fear and anger. Because we were lost and didn't know what else to do. Because we were fighting to protect each other, and how different is that for Josie, really? Especially if she was fighting to keep Saoirse safe?

It took me the better part of six months to get our own trip to the courtroom out of my system. Every night it would be the first thing I saw after I closed my eyes. The wood-paneled walls. The eyes of the guards on us. The whispers of the people around us. The feeling of dread and fear like an abyss inside me, and the knowledge that every single one of the people around us—from guards to visitors to journalists—judged us. Not by who we are or were, but by what others said we did. They judged us by the mistakes we made, the worst parts of us, the desperation that drove us, but not a single one of them listened to our full story. I learned that day that if there are many ways to communicate, there are equally as many ways to silence someone.

No one knew how afraid I was. How angry and hurt Leah was. No one offered us help when we had to leave Granddad's home. No one offered us help when we had no place to stay. No offered us help when we needed it.

I don't want to extend that same cruelty to others.

We should know better.

We don't have the moral standing to judge anyone.

I bow my head. I keep my gaze firmly on my feet and the little bit of floor in front of me, and I walk away from here. No longer to Casey, because Casey will need to help Saoirse.

Emerson needs me.

With so few of us left, we need each other. We all need each other. I'll find Isaiah when things quiet down and ask him if the internet still works. Maybe he can figure out what we need to do with Emerson's concussion or their broken wrist. Maybe there are things we should be mindful of.

Maybe I can't fix everything, but I want to find a way to fix something.

twenty
GRACE

AFTER SAOIRSE IS SETTLED IN the infirmary and we've found a place to keep an eye on Josie, everyone gathers in the cafeteria to discuss our options. It's full-on raining outside, the rain tapping rhythmically against the window and the wind rattling the roof as a constant backdrop to the conversations going on around me.

There are so few of us left. Casey. Sofia. Logan. Khalil. Nia. Riley. Isaiah. Mackenzi. Me. And Emerson, but they're in their own room, sleeping off their concussion. Logan and Nia are taking turns walking over there and waking them up.

Leah and Isabella and Jeremy and Xavier. All of them in various stages of consciousness and unconsciousness.

We count sixteen if we add Josie and Saoirse—sixteen out of

thirty-one—though goodness knows how long Saoirse will last. Or if we should add Josie.

I don't want either of them here. It's not right. But—

I hate how much I understand where she's coming from. It would be so much easier to act in anger and not consider the consequences of my rash actions. It would be so much easier too to let the collective frustration of the group deal with Josie.

"What do you want to do with Josie?" Nia asks me. She sits near the doorway, clutching her sketchbook. Her fingers are wrapped so tight around her pencil, I can see the outline of her bones underneath her skin. She's dragged a blanket to the room and has wrapped it around her shoulders.

"We need some kind of justice," Riley says. It's not the first time she said it. It probably won't be the last time. She has a cut over her eyebrow and a steely look in her eyes.

"What would that even look like?" Casey asks. He's leaning against the corner in the far side of the room. Everyone else keeps their distance from him, like they do from Sofia and me now. Effectively, we all keep our distance from each other.

Riley shrugs. "I don't know. We'll give her a chance to defend herself and then—"

"What?" Sofia has her hands wrapped around a mug of steaming-hot tea. For all the things we don't have, we have an extraordinary amount of tea from the guards' station. Hopefully that'll keep us going throughout the winter, especially since we're quickly running out of instant coffee.

"We'll throw her out, for all I care," Mackenzi's voice is low and livid. "She didn't want to be here, right? She can figure out her own way." She came up to me after we brought Saoirse to the infirmary, angry beyond words, and she hasn't calmed down yet. She's shaking.

I can feel a headache build behind my eyes.

This is neither a responsibility I wanted, nor one I know how to take. I stayed here to survive, and if any of the others survive too, so much the better. But this... They want me to do something. They're hurting. And I don't know how to make it better.

Khalil looks at me. "Why did you bring her back in the first place? What if Saoirse is still contagious or Josie's sick and her illness hasn't manifested yet?" His voice holds no anger, just a mild curiosity and a whole lot of fatigue. He's sustained a black eye from the hallway brawl.

Before I can even say something, Sofia answers in my stead, "Because in spite of everything, they're part of us. Saoirse is ill, and she needs care. Josie was hungry and desperate. We couldn't let her die outside, could we?"

It would've been easier. I don't say that. I didn't miss the edge to her words, and she may not be wrong.

Khalil nods. "I understand, but—"

"Josie can stick to her room. If she gets sick, that's the easiest solution." Riley raises her head, chin pointing out and a challenge in her eyes.

"No." Casey's voice is soft, but that one word hits like a thunderclap. He leans toward her, his arm muscles rippling and his hands clenched. His brown skin is near gray, and his shirt hangs loosely on his shoulders. "We're doing everything we can to survive. All of us, together. That's the only way to keep going."

"So we should accept that she stole from us?" Mackenzi asks, her voice faux pleasant. "It doesn't matter that she tried to suffocate Logan and harm Emerson? It only matters that none of us want to die?"

Logan narrows her eyes. She taps her foot. She signs something in Nia's direction, and the other girl nods. "We're not murderers," she says. "And not judges either."

"Then maybe we should figure out how to be," Mackenzi suggests. "Judge and jury."

"And executioner?" Casey demands.

"Calm yourself, doc," Mackenzi mocks. "We'll do this the proper way."

His eyes flash. He takes a step in her direction, then seems to think better of it. He pushes his hair back with his hands and stalks toward the door.

"Case, wait!" I call out.

"In case you missed it, I've spent the better part of three weeks trying to keep as many people alive as possible. So I'm going to check on my *patients*," he snaps, without looking back. "I want no part of this."

"Case…"

He slams the door closed behind him without another word, and it is irrational, it isn't about me, but it feels like it is. We used to be able to talk without talking. We used to be able to find comfort with each other. And now there aren't just doors but walls between us.

Alone is not worth living, Josie said, but I don't know how to keep all of us together. Maybe with all my anger stripped away, I still don't know how to make the right decisions.

"Protecting ourselves from intruders is a way of keeping ourselves alive too," Riley mutters.

Mackenzi smiles, her teeth bared, and it makes her look dangerous. "Imprison her. Leave her to rot."

"Throw her out. Let her figure out her own way," someone else says.

Sofia gets up and stalks past me too. Before she reaches the door, she turns around to all of us—but she looks straight at me. "Is this what has happened to us? Is this who we are now? Helping you find Josie seemed like the right thing to do. Now I'm not so sure."

Heat rises to my cheeks.

Logan demonstratively folds her arms, and she needs no interpreter to make it clear where she stands. She agrees with Sofia. Her words rattle my brain. No murderers. No judges.

Nia twiddles her fingers, then raises an eyebrow. "What Josie did wasn't right," she says softly, "but she did it to survive. She did it to help Saoirse survive. Doesn't that count for something? Are we going to punish her for trying to do good?"

Mackenzi audibly draws breath to speak, to interrupt, but Nia pushes on. "If we do, are we any better than the people who put us here? I'm not saying we all did…good…but I would venture a guess that we all feel mistreated. If only someone had listened to us, right? If only someone had given us a chance…"

Riley raises her hands. "Don't look at me, kid, I know why I'm here."

"Okay, fine." Nia rolls her eyes. "So you're the shining exception. But don't tell me you wouldn't've wanted someone in your life to see or hear you. Don't tell me that wouldn't have made a difference."

Riley shrugs, the very picture of a girl who's seen a world that doesn't care for her, so she doesn't care for it. I can't imagine how she feels. We may be both here, but our experiences are different because of the color of our skin. The hurdles we faced are different. We both may have had our own understanding of what difficult means, but our difficulties are impossible to compare.

"What if I don't care?" Mackenzi drawls. "I'm not here to find a moral high ground. I'm here to try to survive too. And she endangered all of us with her deathly ill girlfriend or whatever, so forgive me if I don't feel sorry for her. She chose her own path, she has to deal with the consequences. Right now, she's a waste of our resources."

And from there it goes in the same circle it did when we

started. Consequences versus empathy. I don't even know if they're actually opposites, and I don't see a clear path forward.

Did the judges who sentenced us ever feel the same way? Did they look at us and wonder why we did what we did? What could've been done to prevent it or to help us? Or did they want vengeance too? Not personally, like Mac and Riley, but revenge for the fact that we broke their sense of normal and acceptable. That we broke whatever social contract they thought we had.

If I'd known all of this would happen when I pulled Ian off that girl—perhaps the easier route would have been to simply let him assault her. That can't have been what they had in mind either.

I massage my temples. The dull, throbbing headache that's settled behind my eyes refuses to dissipate, and the conversations around me are still going. Everyone has an opinion, an ideal solution, an argument or five.

How am I supposed to make a decision? How am I supposed to decide what is right, when I'm torn between anger over seeing people hurt, fear that none of what we do will be enough—and the understanding that I would have done the same for Casey? For Sofia. For all of them.

Fuck, I would do the same for all of them. But I don't know how to make this decision on my own.

I clear my throat. "We're not going to solve this tonight."

The words are immediately followed by a barrage of protests. "We can't ignore what happened!"

"We have a solution!"

"We need to be able to talk about it."

I sigh and raise my hand until the silence settles.

One by one, they all focus on me, and I feel the weight of it in my bones.

"We'll vote on it tomorrow. Emerson should get a say too, and Casey, and everyone else not present here. We either do this together or not at all." Maybe that will help us figure out the right path.

The words are met with grumbling. Mackenzi and Riley share a look, and I can all but see the bloodlust between them. The anger too and the desperation.

I hesitate. "Khalil? Can you keep an eye on Josie until then? From a distance, of course, but to make sure she doesn't do anything foolish."

And to make sure we don't either.

twenty-one
EMERSON

I BROKE MY WRIST ONCE before. I was ten, and I went skateboarding with my best friend, Diana. It was a Saturday morning, and the streets in our upper-middle-class neighborhood were empty of cars, so we had the whole block to ourselves. Between the smell of baking drifting up from her house and the sensation of our wheels on the road, it felt like freedom. Neither of us could skateboard very well. We couldn't do the same tricks Diana showed me online, and I wobbled and balanced and overstretched continuously. We made our way down the streets, picking up the pace and egging each other on, and it felt like flying. Me on my pink board with purple wheels, and Diana on a beat-up, black-and-green one.

We'd been going faster and faster and faster. Our eyes

half-closed and our arms stretched wide. Neither of us saw the car pull up from the driveway until it was almost too late.

Di came to a screeching halt, her board crunching on the road.

And I swerved. I might have been successful if I had been better at keeping my balance, if I weren't already overstretching and overcompensating. But while I managed to avoid the car, my board snagged, and I went flying for real. I did the same thing I did during the fight: I stretched my arms in front of me to break my fall. I figured it'd be easy enough to catch myself, and I didn't want to hit my helmed head on the curb.

Pain shot through my arm like spikes of ice. I didn't hear the snap of bones breaking, but I felt it. Diana was at my side immediately, and one of the neighbors must have phoned my parents, because they showed up minutes later. I don't remember what they said, but I remember crying and my mother holding me, comforting me. My dad oh-so-gently carried me to the car so he could drive us to the hospital.

Diana brought my skateboard and helmet home so I wouldn't have to worry about those, and every one of them cared so deeply that, even though the pain made me sway, I felt rooted and protected. When I got back from the hospital with my wrist in a cast, Diana showed up with a bouquet of flowers her mother had bought for me. Dad cooked my favorite meals, and my mother bought me books to read while I recovered.

But oh, how I loathed the skateboard. I knew it was

irrational. It was the car and the maneuver and pure, bad luck. But I didn't care for a rational explanation. I didn't want to look at that skateboard anymore, and if I could have managed it, I would have found a way to snap it in two.

I asked Dad one night if that was bad. To think of violence against this inanimate object that had no blame in my spending six weeks with my arm in a cast.

He sat down on the edge of my bed and smiled. "I don't think it's bad," he said in that soft bass of his. "You are hurt, and that is understandable."

"But?" I prompted. Dad preferred to always look at both— or all—sides of a question. At least back then.

"But you may think of it as a learning experience," he said, with a hint of a smile.

Internally, I groaned.

"Practice forgiveness, Emmy," he said. He bent down and pressed a kiss on my hair and then left me before I could think of a counterargument. Before I could tell him that I was too old for his pet name. That I didn't care about forgiveness and I didn't want to practice it either.

I never broke that skateboard, and I went skating again with Diana in the spring, when we both turned eleven. I wore it down, not with anger but with play.

Now, I turn my splinted wrist back and forth to make sure it's supported as well as it can be. The splints are nothing like a cast. Not as stable, but not as itchy either. The bandages are actually quite soft, though the sticks hold my wrist and hand locked. Like the cast, they will prevent me from doing my work. I couldn't write with a broken wrist, and I certainly can't dig holes with one.

I still don't want to practice forgiveness.

I wonder how Diana is doing. If she's—how she's doing. When my parents kicked me out, I begged her to let me crash in her spare room for a few nights. She and I were best friends since our first communion, and we planned to be friends forever. We remained that way until she became concertmaster of St. Agnes's orchestra and fell in with the popular crowd at school—and I couldn't be who she wanted me to be anymore.

She closed the door on me too. I wonder if she's thought of me at all, these past few months.

I can't wish her well, but when I think of ten-year-old Di, on her black-and-green skateboard...I hope she's safe.

I stay in for a full day, and then I drag myself out of bed, though I have no idea what to do. My hand throbs, my head's still fuzzy, and the pain in my wrist is a dull but constant ache. I grab one of the few Tylenols that Mackenzi brought me when she also brought in dinner last night.

I stumble out of the room and nearly trip over Mackenzi, who for some absurd reason still sits outside. She looks up, dark circles under her eyes. Has she slept here? Has she been here the entire night, like my own personal guard? If not Nia or Logan, I would expect Grace to be here. Or one of the gardeners. Not her. And not like this either; with winter setting in, the rooms and hallways are getting colder.

Out of habit, I reach out a hand, then grunt when another flash of pain stabs through me. "Ouch."

Mackenzi pushes herself to her feet. "Don't worry, I—" She yawns. "I'm awake. I wanted to make sure you're okay."

I wrap one arm around my waist. "Why?" Mackenzi has never once spoken to me before. If there weren't so few of us left, she probably wouldn't have a clue who I am.

"Because you were hurt." She narrows her eyes. "Because *Josie* hurt you."

The slight inflection in her voice hints of trouble. At least she makes it clear that I shouldn't trust her. While she keeps her distance, she doesn't flinch away from me. She sets her jaw and waits for me to answer.

"I'm not okay," I snap. I can't remember ever having said those words before to anyone, not since that conversation with Father Michael. It makes me feel brittle. I don't like it. "I'm hurt and I'm lost, and unless you want to take over tending graves, I'm not sure what you can do to make it better."

I can't even play my violin like this.

Her carefully crafted frown flickers. Her nostrils flare. "Well, I can't make it better, but I can offer you something that might help."

I don't say anything. I cradle my arm.

"We decided—" She hesitates then amends, "*Some of us* decided that we can't let Josie get away with what she did. We've set rules to follow while we all stay here. She broke those rules, and she should be punished."

I tilt my head. A part of me aches to point out that Josie *wasn't* staying here, so she can't be bound by the same rules. But I don't. I don't want to. "What do you have in mind?"

She shrugs, but she keeps looking at me through her lashes. "We'd have to talk about that, of course, but I wanted to make sure you're on board with it. With consequences. Grace wants to vote when we're all present, but that doesn't seem right to me. Seeing as how it was *you* who Josie hurt. You should have the first say in what happens next."

I can't deny the glint in Mackenzi's eyes. The edge to her voice. The way her words seem cautiously chosen to lure me in and trap me. This is what temptation looks like, and Saint Jude, forgive me, I want to be lured in.

Maybe it will make me feel better to have something to focus on. Something to distract me from the pain inside and out. If I'm hurting, I don't want to hurt alone. If we're hopeless cases, we might as well act like them.

Before I can respond to Mackenzi, footsteps echo in the hallway. Grace walks toward us, her hands in her pockets and her face set to thunder. Her hazel eyes flash. "Fuck off, Mackenzi."

I cringe. I wish I could turn my pain into anger as easily as she does. It may not be healthy either, but it can't be worse than this emptiness and this loneliness.

Grace turns from Mackenzi to me, and something flickers behind her eyes. "I'm sorry Mackenzi jumped on you, Emerson. We made plans, and she had no right."

"Plans, huh?" I take a step back with my back against the door.

"Yeah."

"What kind of plans?" Does she not trust me in the same way I don't trust her?

Grace grumbles, "Look, we can talk about that later. How do you feel? How's the arm? Do you need something?"

Cold determination settles inside of me. I need lots of things, but above all, right now, I need an answer to my questions. "Why later? She's not wrong, is she?" I ask. To my own surprise, my voice sounds soft and reasonable, the exact opposite of how I feel.

Grace blinks. "What do you mean?"

"Josie may have put us all in danger, but she did hurt me. Me and Logan. We should have a say in what happens to her."

"And you will," Grace insists. She looks tired. "You'll get a vote, like everyone. I'm trying to do this right. I don't want to make the mistakes that the people who put us here made."

I snort; I can't help it. "We're all dying, Grace. Isn't it a little late for that?"

"Besides, it isn't just about revenge or about community," Mackenzi says. She turns back to me, ignoring Grace. She smiles, though it doesn't reach her eyes. "It's about justice. Don't you want justice?"

Grace might be shooting daggers at the other girl, but Mackenzi doesn't flinch. She holds out a lifeline to me. Something I can understand and cling to.

Because here is the awful truth of it all.

I do. I *do.*

I want justice for being dumped here.

For being left here.

For being *hurt* here.

If I could've gone to my small patch of garden, to our own cemetery, maybe it would've been different. If I could've cared for the graves and the memories, and felt my peace there, maybe I wouldn't be so torn up inside. If I could talk to the dead and remind them of their stories, maybe I could remember myself. If I could find myself in music.

But even that was taken from me.

So, yeah, I do want justice. I want to taste revenge.

I don't want to practice forgiveness ever again.

twenty-two
LOGAN

MY BRAIN IS BUZZING AFTER the meeting in the recreation room, so I have to rest before I find Isaiah. But in the morning, I track him down in the warden's office, where he spends most of his time these days. He's even brought his breakfast here.

He goes online when I ask, and I pass him notes I prepared ahead of time, the writing marred by the trembling of my hands. I sit by his side and watch him search and figure it out. It takes the better part of an hour for a single page to load, while the connection keeps disappearing and rebooting.

Isaiah opens his own notebook and writes down any details he finds. Of still-rising death tolls and ghost cities. Of states in disarray and people going hungry. Of food supply lines and production grinding to a halt. Watching Isaiah work, I realize with certainty that no one is coming for us. Everyone is too busy trying to make the best of a terrible situation.

And aside from making our own version of a cast, there is very little we can do to make Emerson's life better. Fractured wrists have no easy solutions. Unless it's a very clean break, Emerson will be cooped up for at least six weeks.

Isaiah frowns. He pushes papers back and forth as rhythmically as when I tap my fingers against my leg. "We could all be dead in six weeks."

I try not to think about that.

Then it occurs to me—Emerson might need other things. Painkillers. Distractions. Better food than we have available. Grace and Sofia went out hunting again early this morning, but we can only survive on raccoon for so long.

I wait until after preparing lunch—with all of us sitting around three tables now, and Emerson sitting next to Casey out of habit. Until after clearing the plates and washing the dishes.

And then I walk out.

All casually, like Leah once told me. Pretend to know what you're doing, and people will let you go about your business, she said, the first time she stole food and pads for us.

I keep my head high. I wrap myself in one of our work coats, though the weather is soft and gentle. I pick up an abandoned backpack from the guard station. I use a scarf as a face mask. And I walk like I know what I'm doing. Like I know where I'm going.

I do. One step at a time. I remember the way from our unfortunate nighttime walk. I remember the way from the guards driving us here in the first place. It's one of the upsides of the way my brain works. I understand how patterns work, and I can remember them.

So I keep walking. One step and then another.

When I'm out of reach of Hope, and no one has come to take me back, I drop my shoulders and lower my head, and I look down at my feet. At the ground, covered in orange and red and brown leaves.

Hope may seem silent at times, especially now that it's so much emptier, but it's nothing compared to the stillness outside. It's not completely desolate. The wind rustles through the trees, and the foliage on the ground crunches and whispers. I know absolutely nothing about birds, but I can make out three or four different calls.

Still, there are no voices, no footsteps—and especially no one who's coughing.

I can breathe here. I feel at ease here.

And I keep walking. One foot in front of the other.

"This may be the only way in which we've ever been different," I tell the Leah in my head, the Leah I'm always talking to. "You always hated the outdoors, and I loved it. I like how the leaves and the grass bounce beneath my feet. I like the breeze on my skin. I could grow to like the quiet too. It reminds me of me."

Leah would laugh at that. I miss hearing her laugh. No

matter how bad things were, that always made me feel like everything would be all right.

I reach the corner in the road that leads to the mountain path and the roadblock. I heard whispers last night that the soldiers are gone and Josie and Saoirse hid out here in a tent or a cave or something.

When I near the roadblock, I find nothing there but the empty corpse of a truck. The rough patch of road is overgrown with weeds and grass, and the wheels are completely flat. I crawl a little closer. A dark shadow rises from the canvas cover, and I scramble back.

Two large birds take flight from their comfortable hideout.

I push myself to my feet again and wait to see if I disturb anything else. If I can see any movement. Then I do what every sensible person would do in my situation. I take a deep breath and run past the truck with all the speed I have, and I don't look back.

I have to keep going. One step at a time. For Leah. For Emerson. For myself.

One step. Another. And another. And another.

Along the mountain trail, past the red trees and the yellow trees and the orange trees and the stubborn green ones.

On.

I reach the outskirts of Sam's Throne by late afternoon. A small town with exactly one post office, one convenience store, and an elementary school—or at least, that's what I remember from when Leah and I were transferred into the care of one of Hope's guards here.

We weren't even supposed to come to Hope, but our court-appointed lawyer—like Hunter—was obsessed with my special needs. She argued that I couldn't and shouldn't be held responsible for what Leah did. That it would be better for me to go to some kind of care facility.

I tried to explain to her that she didn't understand me. My needs aren't any more special than anyone else's are. I want my sister and a roof over my head and to not go hungry. I don't want to be scared. I do want to be loved. I want to live long enough to be an old cat lady, like Granddad's friend down the street.

Leah snapped, like she had only done a few times before.

By the time we settled things, we were here, together. It felt lucky, then.

I don't know if it still feels lucky now.

Dashing from one street corner to the next, I sneak my way to the town center. When we were transferred through here, Sam's Throne certainly looked a lot more alive. People wandered the street to buy their groceries, to pick up their mail, to take their kids to school. An elderly man walking his dog passed us by and muttered something about kids these days.

It doesn't look like that anymore. All the doors are closed, the windows are curtained. The main street—or whatever passes for that here—is utterly abandoned. The few parked cars have gathered dirt and dust. It looks like a scene from an old Western. All it needs is a tumbleweed or an old newspaper flailing in the wind.

Scarce lights peek out from behind some of the curtains as the sun goes down, and there are barking dogs behind some front doors. I wonder if that means anyone's still alive—or the exact opposite.

Several of the doors have stripes of white paint of them. Or markings drawn in chalk.

Plague crosses.

Other homes have candles in front of the windows, along with flowers. Children's drawings of rainbows, stuck to the glass for the whole world to see.

The elementary school has lights on inside, without curtains to block my view. The classrooms aren't filled with desks and chairs but with stretchers and people coughing and people under blankets and people under sheets. The front entrance is obscured by large military tents.

I keep my head down and walk farther. One step. Another.

I'm drawn to the building like a moth to a flame, but I force myself to keep to the shadows. I don't want to get caught. Would anything have been different if Leah and I had gone somewhere else? If we'd been separated?

I don't know, and I won't ever find out. I have to keep my focus on the solution, as Granddad would say. *Figure it out, kid. That's all we can do.*

So I walk until I find the small convenience store. The windows are boarded up. I don't look around me to see if anyone's on the main street. I dash toward the door, which swings on its hinges. A bell jingles when I push forward. Get in. To safety.

Run.

This is what would help Emerson: better painkillers. This is what would help all of us: food, whatever I can carry. Whatever is left.

The shelves of the store are almost empty. Some of them have toppled over to make a mess in the aisles. There is no toilet paper and not a lot of food left. Bottles of juice and beer have shattered on the floor, making a sticky, disgusting mess. The built-in coolers are open and empty. The little produce that's here has rotted through and probably attracted pests, but I try to ignore that and go aisle by aisle to figure out what I need.

I stuff pads and Band-Aids and a few bottles of painkillers in my pockets. A small bottle of hand sanitizer that's been opened and used, but it isn't entirely empty yet. I wish stores carried the antibiotics Casey told us about, the ones that could maybe help with the plague, but I wouldn't even know what to look for.

I swing the backpack off my shoulder and shove in all the over-the-counter drugs I can find. I move to another aisle and add anything that seems useful, in the small quantities that are still here. Shampoo and soap bars. Toothpaste in small traveling packs. A single box of cereal, half-open—but it's still food. A jar of peanut butter. I stand on tiptoe and tease a chocolate bar from the farthest edges of the shelf and a granola bar as well. Herbs and spices that no one wanted to take, for whatever reason. A spilled bag of rice. I scoop up what I can and seal it into the bag.

And then I see it. Underneath a toppled over shelf, all rolled into a corner out of sight, almost a dozen cans of food. Some of them are busted open, but most look salvageable.

I cling to my backpack and drop to my knees.

I reach for them, and I nearly sob in relief when my fingers manage to curl around the cans. This may not keep us fed for weeks, but I have canned meat and vegetables. It will help us restock what we've already eaten.

I push all the cans into my backpack until it's so full, it might burst at the seams, and something to my right crunches.

A soft click. The unmistakable sound of the safety being disengaged on a gun.

I slowly turn my head and stare right down the barrel. A bulky man wearing a face mask over his nose and mouth glares at me. His bushy eyebrows have almost grown together, and underneath his blue cap, his hair is peaky blond. He wears a stained fleece shirt. "Looks like I've caught myself a rat. Hands where I can see them. Do not come any closer. Tell me exactly who you are and what you're doing here."

Some problems call for drastic solutions, Granddad said. But I have no idea how to solve this.

I shake my head.

"Filthy thief." The man leans toward me, though he still keeps a careful distance between us. He doesn't have to come closer to be threatening. "Kick your backpack over here, then we'll figure out what to do with you."

twenty-three
GRACE

FUCK.

I don't know how to help Logan without endangering myself. I saw her walk out, so I followed her. I wanted to make sure she wouldn't do anything irrational. Anything like this. Why can't any of them just follow my rules?

I don't want to make the situation any more explosive than it already is.

I need something I can use as a weapon—or a distraction. If we can get out of here, I doubt the guy will follow us. Or maybe he will? The soldiers shot on sight without hesitation. What is to say it won't be any different for him?

If there's anything I've learned these past few weeks, it's

this: fear does strange things to people. In some ways, it's more dangerous than anger.

I need a weapon.

"Speak up, girl! Hurry with that backpack!" The store guy's voice has a ragged edge to it, and he coughs behind his mask.

Logan's response is immediate, instinctual. She pushes herself back farther against the shelves. She's trembling. Her hands reach for purchase or something to shield herself with. A can of beans rolls away from her.

The guy scoffs. "It's just a cough, girl. The only thing that bloody plague left me."

As soon as the words leave his mouth, a shiver curls up my spine. I breathe out hard. By the way Logan's eyes widen, I can see she heard it too. He had the plague—and he survived it? How is that possible? Everyone we know who's had it died or is lingering with long-term effects. Is there a cure? A way to heal people?

Logan opens her mouth behind her own face covering, but she can't say whatever she wants to say. She balls her fists, and the pure frustration that courses through her is almost tangible.

"One step at a time," he growls. "Keep your hands where I can see them."

Logan still hasn't moved.

The guy uses the gun to beckon her. "Come on, now. Don't think for a moment I won't shoot."

Here's the thing though, I don't think he will. With every

second that crawls by, their standoff lengthens, and he does nothing but threaten. If he wanted to shoot her, he would have done so already—right? He's threatening her to get his way. The gun may not even have bullets in it.

Maybe we can make it through this after all.

The mere thought of it leaves me dizzy. I'd nearly given up on the idea of a future, but this makes it sound possible. Tangible. If we can make it through, I want all of us to survive. I'll hold our entire small family together by my fingernails if I have to.

Before the rational side of my brain can stop me, I dash forward, past the guy with the gun, in Logan's direction. The doorbell jingles when I cross the threshold.

"Mia! There you are!" I try to communicate to her with my eyebrows that she should play along. Her eyes are wide with terror.

I half turn to face the guy, who has a quizzical look on his face. "Oh my goodness, I'm so glad you found her!" I lay it on thick. All the charm that doesn't come naturally. All the innocence I lost two years ago. "*Thank you.* I don't know how to thank you."

I get to my feet again, so I can effectively block Logan from view—and from the line of his gun. I raise my hands in an excessive shrug, like I'm apologizing for her. "My sister is *special*. She's meant to stay home with me and our aunt, but our aunt got sick, and I lost sight of Mia. She went wandering. I think she wanted to find some food for us, because you know how it goes.

We don't have much. If our aunt's illness is"—I drop my voice but continue to ramble—"If it's the plague, we'll have nowhere to go. I think she was worried that there wouldn't be any food left. We've been hungry before and she doesn't understand it."

At my barrage of words, the guy slowly starts lowering his gun. I hope we look harmless to him. Two white girls, underfed and fearful. We wouldn't hurt a fly, right? I hope he isn't the type of guy who knows everyone in a small town.

I reach out behind me to give Logan a hand up. She clings to me with one hand and to her backpack with the other. Her expression is one of determination and hurt.

"We promise we don't want to be difficult. She definitely didn't mean to steal. She just…" I wince like I'm uncomfortable. I lean toward the guy again, like I'm letting him in on a secret. Logan squeezes my hand. "She doesn't understand the difference. She doesn't mean any harm, but she's been so scared. We all are. And I'm so glad that you found her and she's safe. I wouldn't know what to do if she fell ill too."

The guy opens his mouth and closes it. The way his eyes dart back and forth now, he's deciding we're far more trouble than we're worth. But he's still holding on to the gun, and he's still dangerous.

In the silence that follows, Logan coughs. It sounds so natural, so real, that even I freeze up. The guy does the same. He takes a step back, despite his claim that he's already survived the plague.

"Mia! Are you okay?" I swing to her, like the worried older sister that I pretend to be. I reach out a hand to touch her face—though I don't quite get close enough to do so, because it would make her uncomfortable. Out of eyesight from the guy, though with a shadow in her eyes, Logan very slowly and very purposefully winks.

"I don't know what game you're playing"—the guy clears his throat—"but I want no part of it. Get out. Get out of here. Don't let me see you do this again."

"Oh, thank you, sir," I gush. "Thank you."

Logan coughs again, and he takes another step back, opening enough of an escape route for the two of us. And we run. I grab Logan's arm and pull her along with me. She's still holding on to the backpack, and when the guy notices that, he *roars*. "Leave the backpack! Thieves!"

"Sorry!" I shout, feeling weirdly giddy. "I wasn't lying about the food!"

We dash out of the store, dodging rubble and shelves and torn boxes. Logan lets go of my hand, and she swings the backpack on her back. She's quick, and she motions for me to follow her. It's our speed that saves us, I'm sure. It takes the store guy a second or three to realize what's happening, and by the time he's screaming at us, we're already halfway through the door.

From there, Logan takes the lead. She guides us away from the store and into a narrow side road, so even if the guy follows us, we won't be in his immediate line of sight.

Another corner, another side road. Past half a dozen homes with white marks on their front doors. Past a church where light is burning inside and the lawn is covered in tiny wooden crosses. Some with colored yarn or fabric knotted around them, others with necklaces and bracelets draped over them, still others that are painted in bright colors—even if the painting seems childish at times. Another road. All the way until we're deep in a residential area and I'm the one to call for a halt. "Logan! Give me a moment to catch my breath."

She skitters to a halt, but she keeps glancing around us like she expects someone else to get the jump on us. I rest my hands on my knees and struggle to catch my breath.

Logan pulls at my sleeve and indicates her head.

"I know." I gulp a breath. "We have to keep going. How come you're in better shape than I am, anyway?"

She grins, and the backpack bounces on her shoulders.

It reminds me: "You found food! I could kiss you!"

She immediately takes a step back, and I can't help it. I laugh. It feels weird and uncomfortable, like my muscles have forgotten how, but it makes me feel lighter too. It makes me feel more human.

Food. We have *food*.

Logan's eyebrows pull together in a frown, her nose scrunched up in a way that's adorable.

"I won't *actually* kiss you," I say. "But whatever made you decide to come here… I'm glad."

Logan starts walking again, head down, and apparently incapable of waiting around any longer. But she extends her arm and points at her wrist. Her hands flap, and it's a comforting sight.

Emerson. Of course. "You thought you could find better drugs?"

A curt nod.

I pick up my pace to catch up with her. "You dislike the idea of voting, don't you?"

Another, more empathic nod.

"Yeah." I mull it over in my head. Her comments during our meeting. The weird, uncomfortable, intoxicating spark of hope in the store. They're more important than the rage simmering beneath the surface. "I'm scared of making the wrong call though."

She glances at me through her eyelashes.

"And we can't let Josie do whatever she wants either."

Logan snorts. She reaches behind her and pats the backpack. I wince.

"Fair point."

She swirls toward me and raises her hands like she wants to sign something more, but then she throws them up in clear frustration. I wouldn't understand it, and we can hardly stop to find paper and pen in the middle of this neighborhood.

"I'll listen to what you have to say when we get back," I promise. "We all owe you that."

Logan slows down her pace, and she tilts her head, mulling over the words. Then she shakes her head.

"We don't?" I take a stab in the dark. "Or that isn't why you did this?"

The look she gives me makes it clear it was a nonsensical question to begin with. Of course, she didn't do it because she wanted gratitude. She did it because she feels responsible for the others. I'm not the only one who does.

But that responsibility means we need to take care of each other. And I can't let anger—or worry—guide me.

I breathe out hard and run a hand through my hair. "Do you know what I dream about?" I ask Logan.

She shakes her head.

"I dream about Paris." Paris is an ache that's settled in my bones over these last few weeks. It's always been that during the hardest times. When I wouldn't feel at home somewhere, I would take books about Paris out of the school library, and I would pore over the unfamiliar names and places. The Arc de Triomphe. Les Invalides. The Panthéon. The Place de la Concorde and its guillotined ghosts. I was convinced that even if I couldn't find my own history there, I would go there and still find some sort of roots. "When I stop worrying about all of us, I wonder what the city looks like now. I want to cling to the idea that it's still there, you know? With the Eiffel Tower lit up at night. And tourists, still sitting on the steps and the benches in front of the Sacré-Cœur, like nothing bad has ever happened. Because someone ought to live."

I rub at my neck. "But I realized, it isn't about Paris. It's about finding something better than this place. It's about wanting somewhere to belong."

Logan nods.

"Maybe...maybe that's what I want to do when I grow up. Be that person for teens like us who have nowhere else to go to either."

She smiles, and then, with a slight roll of her eyes, she lowers the collar of her shirt and points at her throat. The bruises from Josie's hands are still visible, and her message is clear.

We ought to live too.

We're reaching the edges of Sam's Throne, and Logan's eyes flick toward every home we pass with a white dash of paint on the door. Like she's noting and marking them.

Personally, I'd rather avoid them all. The plague is real in Hope, but it's overwhelming here. It's everywhere. And this side of Sam's Throne might well be a ghost town. Though whether it's died out or abandoned, I don't know.

On the other hand...there might be food here. "Can you mark the homes we passed on a map?" I ask, so quietly, I'm not sure Logan could even hear me.

After a while, she nods.

And something of the heaviness returns.

———

We pause again once we're off the mountain path and past the abandoned truck, where dusk creeps in. We sit in the fallen leaves between the oak trees, and my stomach is growling. Logan sorts through her backpack and tosses me the hand sanitizer after she's used it herself. She takes off her mask and pulls up a box of cereal. It looks like some kind of off-brand frosted Cheerios.

She tears open the box further and holds it out to me. I cup my hands, and she pours the cereal in them like gold coins. It feels as precious. I take the first tiny grain circle and let it melt on my tongue. It's stale and sweet, and I might be crying.

Logan munches down an entire handful of Cheerios all at once.

And then she laughs.

Her laugh is warm and bright and full of crumbs.

She reaches her fingers up to the corners of her mouth in wonderment.

We eat with handfuls at a time, but it doesn't take long before we both slow. We have to be careful with what we have—and save it for the others too. Logan's food will give us all a few days of variety. It will give us time.

"I'm sorry for calling you *special* back there," I say softly, before we get up to make our way back home. It's been weighing on me. "I know you don't like it, and it isn't an excuse, but I needed a story. I wanted to make sure he wouldn't feel threatened by us."

Logan packs the box away in her backpack and bites her lip. She gestures at the cans and the other spoils of her trip with an almost apologetic wince.

I don't have to guess at what she's saying. "It worked, and I'm glad. We both made it work. But I also think it hurt you, and I'm sorry about that. I should've thought of something else."

Logan stills and considers it. Then she nods. The corner of her mouth pulls up into a lopsided grin, and I want nothing more than to know what she's thinking. She reaches for my hand and squeezes it, and I smile too.

"When we get back, please teach me—and all of us who want—more signs? We have to find better ways to communicate."

In all ways.

twenty-four

EMERSON

WORD SPREADS THROUGH HOPE LIKE wildfire. Both Grace and Logan are gone, and no one knows where. The afternoon fades to dusk to nightfall, and everyone is distracted by it. At least the others have their assigned duties. Isaiah wrestles with the computers to find the latest news on the plague and doesn't say much else. Mackenzi tries to call home—even though the phones haven't worked for the past few days, and while she may be our handyman, she has no way to fix it. Khalil protects Josie from our righteous indignation. Riley works in the garden. Casey tends the ill.

Nia prepares the fish that Sofia caught in a nearby creek, with the last few potatoes from storage. The spuds were all sprouted to be little gardens on their own. The ones she didn't cook, she gave to Riley to try to plant.

No one eats well. Casey and I sit in silence away from the others. My wrist aches, and it makes me feel faint.

Everyone gives me a wide berth, like no one quite knows what to say to me. Mackenzi smirks in my direction once or twice.

After dinner, I lean against the serving counter and cradle my arm against my body. The pain is a constant, dull throbbing, with stabs whenever I move too much. It spreads through my body like restlessness, like wanting to do something. I want to talk to Grace about what will happen to Josie. Not later. As soon as she's back.

It's why I stayed in the cafeteria, despite it being almost an hour past dinner. I can't face the emptiness of my room with the emptiness inside of me.

"It's different when we know you and Grace are out hunting," I say to Sofia, who is cleaning up the room with intensity.

She grunts. She's usually one of the ones who avoids me.

Nia echoes that from the kitchen. "Logan never leaves. She would want to stay close to her sister."

Sofia shrugs. "They must have had a good reason, I'm sure."

I don't want to go back to my room. "We could play cards in the recreation room, while we wait for them?" I suggest.

Nia scrunches up her face. "I want to prepare tomorrow's food."

"I'm not done here yet," Sofia says, though the cafeteria looks cleaner now than it did in the weeks before we were abandoned.

"Never mind," I say.

Sofia runs her hand through her hair and sighs. "Maybe after. I want to stay up until they get back anyway."

"Or you can help us unpack?" Grace says from the doorway.

We all swirl around, and a sharp pain shoots through my wrist again. It leaves me dizzy, and I bite back a hiss.

Grace and Logan walk into cafeteria, making a very odd couple. Logan has dirt smeared all over her face, and Grace has crumbs in her hair. They're carrying a backpack between the two of them, and they both look exhausted—but happy.

The sight of it is so foreign, it leaves me breathless.

"We went shopping," Grace says, raising one shoulder in a half shrug.

"You went *what*?" Sofia leaves the rags behind and stares at her friend incredulously.

"It was Logan's idea, actually. She wanted to help Emerson get painkillers." At this, Grace throws an undecipherable look in my direction. The type of look that promises, *We'll talk later*. "She ended up in Sam's Throne, and we also…found more food options. It isn't a lot, but we'll enjoy them while they last."

Only then do the words really settle in.

I say, "Logan. You went to get painkillers for me?" at the same time as Nia shouts, "Food?!"

Sofia rushes forward to grab the bag, and Grace plops onto one of the seats. Logan stands a little awkwardly in between them, moving her weight from one leg to the other and back, but she's smiling too. When Sofia overturns the bag on one of the tables, grains of rice and Cheerios spill out, followed by cans of food. They all *ooh* and *aah* like this is a treasure they've never seen before.

Nia grabs cleaning products to wipe down all the cans and boxes. No one knows if it makes a difference, but she'd rather be safe than sorry.

Logan comes to stand by me, and she takes a small, blue bottle out of her pocket. When she hands it to me, I can read the label. Advil. Hopefully this'll help with the pain.

She smiles so hesitantly, but it feels like a gut punch. "You went into town, for me?"

She nods, and I don't know how to wrap my mind around that kindness.

"*Thank you.*" It hardly feels sufficient.

Grace looks up from the can of tomatoes she's holding. "It comes with conditions though."

"Such as?"

To my right, Logan raises her eyebrows, and Grace nods at her.

"We're not going to vote on what to do with Josie," Grace says, determination in her voice. She pulls herself up taller and folds her hands behind her back.

I cling to the bottle in my hand and feel that pit inside my stomach grow again. "Don't you know—"

"You weren't the only one she hurt," Grace interrupts me.

"She attacked Logan too. Logan, who, by the way, risked her life to get you those painkillers. She faced down a guy with a gun for you."

My mouth clamps shut.

"What Josie did was wrong, but can you honestly say you wouldn't have done the same thing for someone you cared about? Someone you loved? She wanted to survive. *We* want to survive. We're *all* making hard choices."

"I never hurt anyone," I snap. Her questions sting, and it's the type of pain that Advil won't cure.

Grace tilts her head. "So she'll take over your job. If you want her punished, that's fitting, don't you think?"

I open my mouth to comment, and she holds up a hand.

"I don't know about you, but I don't want to be the type of person who decides whose life is valuable and whose life can be discarded. I don't want to be like the people who locked us up here and then forgot about us. I want no part in that." She takes a deep breath. "I don't expect you to forgive her, but Josie can work to repair what she did."

"So what?" I demand. "We're just supposed to trust her to be better?"

"Yes." She says it so simply. She lowers her voice. "I know you don't trust me, Emerson. I know you'd rather not trust anyone. But we're all trying."

"Maybe that isn't enough," I say. "Not when mistakes get people hurt."

Grace colors hotly. "I'd like to think not all mistakes and faults are unforgivable."

"Some of them are."

She doesn't deny that, but she glances at Logan, who nods encouragingly.

Grace swallows. "If you don't trust me, that's fine. But there are people here who care about you. I hope you can find a way to trust them. Here or when we get out."

I scoff, too raw to be polite. "*When* we get out of here, sure. Do you even hear yourself, Grace? Miss me with your fairy tales."

Of all the things I expect Grace to say or do in response to my anger, she does the absolute unthinkable. She *laughs*.

"The store guy who threatened Logan? He told us he *survived* the plague. He had a bad cough still, but that was the only thing. Can you imagine? There are people out there who still thrive. All we have to do is make sure that's us."

Her words hit me hard, and I stumble back to sit down. "He *survived*? Are you sure?"

"Yes! He said so!" Next to Grace, Logan is nodding vehemently. "And I've been thinking. We're not sick yet. Maybe we won't get it. Not everyone gets sick; not everyone is infected. Even Isaiah will tell you as much. All we have to do is keep it that way."

"All we have to do..." I shake my head. I feel faint. "I admire your optimism."

"I need something to keep me going," she admits, and briefly I can see the pain beneath her anger.

Logan pulls at Grace's shirt and signs something. From the other side of the table, already writing down a list of our new haul, Nia interprets. "Elias was the last of us to get sick five days ago. We haven't gone more than a day or two without anyone coming down with it since the start."

Sofia narrows her eyes. "Are you sure?"

Logan shrugs but nods.

"We'll have to make sure none of us catch the plague from Saoirse then," I snap.

Logan flinches, and guilt flickers through me.

Grace stares at me with steely eyes. "We'll have to make sure of that. Logan and I will be extra careful these next few days too. But we *will* survive. And while we do, Josie will take over your duties."

"Fine." I pocket the bottle of Advil. I'll give Casey the ones I won't need, but for now, I need them. "Thanks for the painkillers, Logan. I appreciate it."

With that, I stalk out. Away from them. Away from it all. Away from that dangerous sense of hope, because it hurts more than my wrist does. It's harder to bear than hopelessness.

Leave Grace to sort it all out, because she will anyway.

———————————

She does. I don't know how she convinces the others that this is how we do things now—I don't even know *when* she does it. But after breakfast, Josie follows me out. She's shadowed by Khalil, and her steps are marked by Riley and Mackenzi's glares. She looks pale and tired but determined.

She doesn't say a word, so I don't either.

Grace's question last night rattled me. I understand Josie. I *would* have done the same for my friends, once upon a time.

But that doesn't mean I have to like her.

We pass through the garden to the other side of the fences. Riley and I cut through the fence to create a better passage after only a couple of days. It was too much of a fuss otherwise—and cutting through all that wire was cathartic.

When we get to our small cemetery, I point to the oldest grave. It's the only one that's slightly overgrown. Weeds more than flowers, but I've come to like it. It makes it look like she's still part of us here.

"That's Serenity." I clear my throat and add, "Hi, Serenity." I always greet them all, one by one. I promised them I wouldn't forget them, and I intend to keep that promise.

I count them off. "Aleesha and Walker and Chloe and Faith and Mei."

One grave looks freshly dug, with the ground only settling now. The smell of newly turned earth still lingers in the air. "That's Elias. He came down with it five days ago and died within a day. We've never lost anyone so quickly before. I didn't... No one anticipated it."

Josie sniffs, but she turns away before I can see her wipe at her eyes. "I don't know how you do it. I don't know how any of us are supposed to. When we left with Hunter... Saoirse wasn't the only one. Others started coughing too. Some of them must have gotten sick, but I don't know anyone who died. We were abandoned before..." She draws a shuddering breath. "I need to know. Has anyone ever died after being sick this long? Did anyone hold on for weeks only to die after all?"

It's the first time she fully looks at me, and there's so much heart in her eyes that I have to close mine. I don't want to answer this question, because that's a type of cruelty that goes too far, even for me. But to not answer would be crueler still.

"Yes."

Josie's shoulders drop. "Oh."

She angles her face up toward the pale, autumn sun, barely cresting the trees around us, and she doesn't speak. She shivers. In the silence we hear birdsong, and Khalil and Riley, arguing.

"When we don't need new graves to be dug, I tend to the ones we have. I help out in the garden. You can figure out where you're useful, I'm sure." I keep my voice as level as possible. I don't want to feel bad for her. I don't want to see how much that one word impacted her. I want her to get to work.

"I'm sorry," she whispers.

I cradle my arm close to my chest. "I don't care."

FRAGMENTING FOOD SUPPLIES

- An already fragile food supply chain is forming tears under the weight of plague spread and lockdown restrictions.
- Meat processing plants have been shut down following outbreaks, farmers have been forced to dump milk and destroy potato stockpiles, and transport has come grinding to a halt.

It's going to be a cold and lonely Christmas.

With hospitals overflowing and death tolls continuing to rise, another challenge is already presenting itself. It's not connectivity—while phone and internet networks have been straining under the weight of increased traffic, network providers claim they can handle increased demand for the foreseeable future. It's a far more basic problem: food. Fragile food supply chains are being disrupted across the country due to movement restrictions of food workers, vulnerability in food processing, and missing links in logistics.

"Many stockpiles are going to waste because we simply have no way to process them," says a spokesperson from the Department of Agriculture. "High mortality rates have caused sourcing issues too. Even in those situations where supply lines function as intended, stores are understaffed and, in many cases, have shut down completely, breaking the chain right before food reaches the consumers."

A secondary presidential task force has been called into

existence to discuss potential solutions for supply problems. In addition to the consequences of the outbreak, food insecurity could cause massive civil unrest. It also goes to show the fragility of the system; if these essential supply chains are breaking down, what will be next?

But even in places where food supply chains are still functioning, Christmas is going to be a solemn affair. Governor Brooks (AR, D) has explicitly called for people to respect lockdown measures during the Christmas period and stay at home instead of traveling or visiting other households. "I expect everyone to understand and respect the severity of the situation," she says, following an outbreak in Faulkner County that was traced back to a megachurch service.

Hope for Better Futures: A History
By Isaiah Wood

This is not a proper introduction.

Once all of this is over, someone needs to know what happened here. If we're the ones to tell the story, that would be best, but human memory is fallible. I don't know when this will end or how long it will take. I don't know if we can remember all of it.

So I'm writing it down now. All of it. The internet is slow. The phones aren't working. We thought it may have been Better Futures at first, deciding not to pay the bills. Especially since they haven't responded to our messages. I can't get through to anyone. But outages appear to be the case everywhere. Network congestion, according to one of the news sites.

This is the best thing I can do until I find other ways to make myself useful: record who we are and what we've done and experienced, for posterity. They call me the Professor. I can act like it.

This is what you'll find in here:

- A timeline of the events. I've done my best to be precise and truthful. I'm starting three weeks too late, so I'll do best to reconstruct those weeks carefully.

- Our personal files. All of us. Our criminal files. Our psychological reports. You should know who we are.

- All the logistical information I've managed to recover from Warden Davis's computer. The guard assignments, from the weeks leading up to the outbreak to the first days after the initial outbreak, when our guards were still here. I don't know if any of them infected us, but I want to be as complete as possible. The last head count he did the day before the staff left. An email he sent to Jemma, Hope's resident therapist, to tell her not to worry about the teens, that we'd be taken care of. Emails from Better Futures's management.

- Everything the others will give me. Notes, drawings, memorials. Recordings of phone calls. We've all found different ways to cope.

Phone call between Riley and her best friend

RILEY: Hey. You still alive?

SAPPHIRE: Yeah. You?

RILEY: Yeah.

SAPPHIRE: Good. It sucks out here.

RILEY: It's not much better inside either.

SAPPHIRE: Wouldn't think so.

RILEY: God, I'm terrified.

SAPPHIRE: You? Scared? Hell must have frozen over.

RILEY: Oh, fuck you.

RILEY: Yes, I'm scared. I haven't been this scared since... Well. That day.

SAPPHIRE: That day you decided it was enough and you had nothing left to live for, and I ended up sitting by your unconscious side at the hospital in full drag? That day?

RILEY: Yeah, that's the one. I'm sure you looked royal.

SAPPHIRE: Honey, I always do.

SAPPHIRE: You better not be calling me because you're sick now.

RILEY: I'm not. I promise.

RILEY: I just really wanted to hear your voice.

RILEY: Do you know what the absurd thing about this whole shit show is? I'm terrified because I don't want to die. I'm still fucking afraid of living too, but I don't want this plague to kill me.

SAPPHIRE: What scares you so much about living?

RILEY: For everything to hurt and nothing to get better.

RILEY: And don't you dare tell me it gets better.

SAPPHIRE: I wouldn't, because neither one of us can know that. But I do know that one day, this plague will be over. This pain will not last.

SAPPHIRE: Now, life may not get easier. The world will not suddenly be fair. All those things require work and struggle, and I know you're tired.

SAPPHIRE: But one day, there'll be other things than pain.

RILEY: Like?

SAPPHIRE: Like joy and love and people who care for you. Like peanut butter cups and drive-in movies and candlelight at midnight and the sound of wind rustling through the trees. Like friendship. You have me. I'll always be here to listen to you when you're hurting and to ride out the storm with you.

RILEY: Candlelight at midnight? I never pegged you for a romantic.

SAPPHIRE: I'm not. I'm just desperately clinging to the idea that one day, the things that make life worth living will balance out the things that are too hard to bear.

RILEY: I'll see it before I believe it.

SAPPHIRE: As long as you stick around until you do.

RILEY: Is it enough if I promise to try?

SAPPHIRE: Honey.

SAPPHIRE: Of course it is. It's everything.

This phone call has been disconnected.

Phone call from Sofia to her brother

Attempt #1

SOFIA: Luca? The phones have been spotty here, but—

We're sorry, you have reached a number that has been disconnected or is no longer in service. If you feel you have reached this recording in error, please check the number and try your call again.

Attempt #2

SOFIA: Come on, pick up—

We're sorry, you have reached a number that has been disconnected or is no longer in service. If you feel you have reached this recording in error, please check the number and try your call again.

Attempt #3

SOFIA: ...

We're sorry, you have reached a number that has been disconnected or is no longer in service...

WHAT IS PLAGUE MENINGITIS?

- Neurologists are reporting a complication in the treatment of plague patients: the occurrence of plague meningitis.

- While incidence of plague meningitis is low, it adds complex and ethical questions for hospitals that are already struggling with offering the care needed.

- Plague meningitis predominantly shows up in younger patients who have survived the initial few days of infection, with clinical signs and symptoms developing between 7 to 14 days after the onset of illness.

- With limited treatment options, it is currently unclear how well this type of inflammation responds to antibiotics or what its long-term effects may be.

Exact numbers aren't available yet, but it's becoming increasingly clear that this continued outbreak of Y. pestis is a health danger on multiple levels. A growing number of patients—predominately teens and young adults—who have survived their first days of infection are showing signs of plague meningitis, an inflammation of the meninges (the protective membranes covering the brain and spinal cord).

Signs and symptoms cover an array of possibilities, from neck stiffness and photophobia to high fever and loss of consciousness. Where standard treatment consists of a high dosage of antibiotics, it's unclear whether those are effective given the bacteria's resistance. In coming days and weeks, experimental treatment with various broad-spectrum drugs will hopefully be able to provide more than mere anecdotal evidence.

Meanwhile, the Health Department has requested a selected task force of ethicists to advise on treatment protocols, especially with an eye toward survival rates and lasting side effects. "No one officially wants to be the one to make the call, but with a limited number of hospital beds available, prioritization of patients has come into question," said Mr. Warbler, one of the members of the task force. "It is only rational to consider quality of life as part of that equation and whether or not it's better to let some people die."

Disability justice organizations across the country have responded with outrage, rightfully calling the discussion an unacceptable step toward eugenics.

Frequently reported side effects of meningitis infections include focal neurological signs, hearing loss, and epilepsy. Focal neurological signs comprise a wide spectrum of potential phenomena, including but not limited to unsteadiness and weakness of limbs, partial paralysis, dyslexia or dyspraxia, amnesia, aphasia, seizures, and loss of smell.

twenty-five
GRACE

SOFIA AND I GO BACK to Sam's Throne three days later. Late at night, when the overcast starlight won't give us away. The faint light of the coolers gives the store an eerie glow. We find nothing new in the aisles of the store. What little was left has been scavenged and put to better use.

But I expected that to happen. I brought Logan's hand-drawn map with me, where she drew all the abandoned houses we saw. All the houses with plague signs and warnings. We follow the same route, and Sofia is quiet when she sees all the reminders of illness and death.

I don't say anything—I don't know *what* to say—but I reach out and brush her fingers with mine. It sparks like touch always does.

"It's one thing to know that this is happening to us," she says, eventually, softly, when we walk past the church and its countless markers for the dead. "It's something else completely to see it happen to everyone."

"It's hard to wrap your mind around the scale of it, isn't it?" I ask, though it's more of a statement than a question.

"Hope is such a small world," Sofia says. "Between what happened inside those walls and our hunts outside, I never thought about anything else. I tried to call my brother again, but he never picked up. And I...I compartmentalized, right? Easier to imagine everything's okay if you don't linger on it too much."

I nod. "I thought about the good foster families a few times. The friends I made when I stayed with them. I learned not to grow too attached. It's the easiest way to survive."

"When you think about it, probably the worst too." She winces. "Luca has a wife and two little girls. Before I got sent here, I was supposed to go live with them."

"Maybe you still can? Once this is all over?"

"Yeah, maybe." The wind picks up around us and yawns through the street, the sound a soft, distant cry. Sofia turns to one of the houses with a bright-white stripe across the door. "I'm afraid of what I'll find."

I brush my hair back. "Yeah. I wish I knew how to make that better."

"You can't," she says simply. "We'll hold on, and we'll make it through. As many of us as possible."

It's all we have. I take a pen out of my pocket and fold open Logan's map. I mark the door with the new plague cross. As we walk, I note the changes we see. The new slashes on doors. The worn, old ones. The houses where flowers and plant have rotted and dried out without anyone replacing them. The houses that look completely abandoned.

I pause in front of one that looks particularly empty. It looks like it was once a comfortable middle-class house, with flowery curtains in front of the windows and a potted plant near the front door. But the plant has dried out, and the white slash across the door has cracked and faded. One of the small windows on the second floor is broken. Inside is completely dark.

"We should take a look," I say. I take a mask from my belt and gloves from the infirmary that Casey gave me. We still don't know for certain if the plague spreads by touching the same surfaces. We deal with it by not taking any chances.

Sofia hesitates. "Here?"

I ball my hands to fists to keep them from shaking. "Here."

"Didn't we have anyone left who got convicted for burglary?" she asks, and it's clear she tries to make it sound like a joke, but it lands like a gut punch. Sofia sighs. She reaches for her own supplies. "Never mind. Window? Door?"

"Let's try the door first." I walk over and half-heartedly give it a push. I expect it to be locked, but it creaks and swings open to a darkened living room. The little bit of light filtering in around me and through the windows illuminates the shapes of furniture. I hold my breath, waiting for any sound to come from the inside, but what greets us instead is a deep silence.

My nose itches.

When my eyes adjust to the darkness, I can see the chaos in front of me. The sofa has been overturned, and what must have been once a coffee table is cast aside and has a crack down the middle. Everything else looks normal enough. The cabinet along the wall hasn't been opened. The drawers are all where they're probably supposed to be. No one stole the TV off it either.

But someone pushed their way in and had to make room.

I take a deep breath and step in, and the second thing that hits me is the stench. The putrid, sweet smell of rotten flesh. I gag, I can't help it. Behind me, Sofia makes a muffled sound then dashes out again and vomits. I want to gulp in fresh air, but I'm terrified of opening my mouth. The smell is so heavy, I can *taste* it.

I manage another minute of edging my way in, but by then, my stomach is protesting so loudly, I dash back outside like Sofia did and retch.

"We can find another house," she hisses, while she's still wiping her mouth.

We could. But the trouble is, "I don't know which other ones are safe yet." We could keep mapping. Give it another day or so, but I'd feel far more confident if we could stockpile extra food now. To be safe. To be sure.

"I'll try again," I manage. Trembling, I reach for the small bottle of water in my backpack and use it to soak my mask. I don't know if that'll be any better, maybe it'll make it worse, but I hope the layer of cold will protect my nose.

I take as deep a breath as I can, and then I run. Through the living room, toward the kitchen. I have my backpack open and I open cabinets, shoving in what I can. I stay far, far away from the fridge, because I can't imagine that'll be in a much better state than the rest of the house.

When my lungs feel like bursting, I dash out again, retch, and repeat.

Eventually, over the next week, even raiding dead people's houses becomes easier. We keep the food as cold as possible and as far away from the kitchen as possible until it smells edible. Dry food is better than fresh. Canned and bottled is best of all. We take everything we can find. We run and hide when we see other humans, but that's rare. Some days, the food we find offers us a reprieve from worrying about our inventory. Some days it's barely enough to keep us fed.

But while it's possible to grow used to almost anything, I can't grow used to the smell. It's everywhere. It's worse in houses that haven't been cleared at all—and we do avoid those. It clings to me, like ghosts. No matter how hard I try, I can't get it off.

No one else notices it.

———

The days are easier than the nights.

In the morning, before I go see Isaiah, I spend time with Casey. We both stay on either side of the hallway, but spending time together matters. We take every precaution we can, though it seems to me that if he were going to get infected, it would have happened already.

Maybe Logan is right. Maybe we're all safe now. Maybe we're the lucky ones.

No one else has fallen ill since Josie and Saoirse came here. We're all painfully aware of it, but no one has dared to mark the days yet. We're too scared to jinx it.

Isaiah's tiny little snippets of information, those few things he manages to scrape off the internet, tell us that the world is falling to pieces. But Casey tells me Isabella is recovering. It's slow, and she would be our first recovery. It would mean everything.

The world may be ending; we find ways to live.

"She sat up independently today," he says with a smile that's never quite as wide anymore, but it's still genuine. "She was still coughing, and she couldn't say much, but it's progress. I didn't think, after a whole month…"

"Me neither."

He licks his teeth, like he's embarrassed. "You know, I started carving the days into the small nurse's desk in the infirmary, to keep track of how long it's been. It feels like every day is a week, and every week is at least a month."

I nod. Time seems to pass differently here. I forgot about Christmas entirely until Isaiah reminded me, and even so, I didn't celebrate beyond going into town to steal food. I lit a candle in one of the empty houses.

"If she recovers, there may be hope for the others too." Jeremy slipped away, but Saoirse is still holding on, and so is Xavier. And Leah, of course. The first to fall ill, and somehow, she's still here. Maybe she can't leave Logan any more than Logan can leave her.

At least we have a term for it now. Plague meningitis. It explains why both Xavier and Leah kept having seizures.

Casey nods. "I'll take care of them as best I can."

I smile. "You will. It's what you've been doing. It's what you've always done for me."

A shadow flits across his face. It's there, then it's gone. It may be exhaustion, like the circles under his eyes—and mine too.

"Let me know if anything changes, okay?"

He's already turning back to the infirmary. "Always."

Isaiah has nothing new for me. The internet is completely down, and the phone lines only offer white noise. This time, he's quite sure they're not outages. We've been disconnected. He's in the warden's office regardless. It's his HQ now—and his safe space too. He's collected folders from the guard station and the therapist's office. Those official-looking manila folders and large stacks of paper. He keeps moving them back and forth. He's restless.

Presumably, he's given himself access to our personal files too. That possibility only fully occurs to me now, but I can't seem to care. The people we were don't matter that much anymore.

I lean against the doorframe. "What are you doing?"

"Making a file of all of us here. Of everything that happened.

Of everyone we lost." He has placed different stacks of paper across the desk. "I talked to Emerson about remembering. Nia may let me use some of her drawings. I have all the notes from all the days we've been here."

He doesn't look up to me, but his voice holds a determination I've rarely heard before. "It's important. I don't want someone to just remember the dead. I want them to remember us too."

We all want to be remembered. I want to keep remembering.

"Can I help in some way?"

"No." Isaiah isn't rude, he's clear. I appreciate that.

"If there's anything I can do, let me know." I leave him to his work, but I make a small note to myself to ask him about his progress later. And Emerson about their graves. And Nia about her drawings. While I knew all those things were happening, I never really cared about it until now.

Truth is, something has changed in Hope since Josie and Saoirse came here. Since Logan found her way to Sam's Throne and we stole into the town the first time to get food. Between what she found and what Sofia and I have been scavenging, it's given us the space to breathe. It's a reminder that the world outside still exists.

And that may be terrifying—but it's exhilarating too.

But at night, I can't sleep. The smell of death clings to me. The lists of names bounce around in my head. I know that every time we go into town, we put ourselves at risk, and it's worth it to be able to eat, but I worry. We still have water and power, but I worry we'll lose those next now that internet is gone. I worry constantly.

In the end, I roll out of bed again and get dressed. I pull my hair into a messy braid. I reach for one of our makeshift masks out of habit. And I sneak out of my room.

Wandering through the empty hallways offers me a strong sense of déjà vu. It's colder. It's different. But it's also exactly like I did that night we found out what's going on.

So maybe it's meant to be that when I wander out into the garden, desperate for fresh air, I'm not the only one there. Emerson is sitting on the ground between the graves, a blanket around their shoulders, their violin resting on their knees, and a distant look in their eyes.

I can't help but smile. "Weird."

twenty-six
EMERSON

I BREATHE IN DEEPLY. GRACE is quiet enough when she walks up to me, but everyone else here is quieter. I've spent so many nights in the garden, I've learned to separate the ghosts from real life. I play for them, sometimes, as quietly as I can. Other nights I let the silence be its own tune.

I wonder if any of this was meant to be. Us being here. Or me being me.

"What is weird?" I don't bother to turn around.

Grace steps closer. "I was curious if anyone here sleeps at night anymore."

"Probably not." I wander around enough to see lights on in the rooms, hear the scuffling of feet, feel the restlessness of all around me. It's why I come here now. The dark of night is peaceful. The air smells cleaner. The distant calls of birds and wildlife remind me that the world keeps turning. I spent Christmas Eve here, on my own, and I tried hard to ignore every second of it.

Grace doesn't come closer, but she doesn't turn around either. I want to tell her to leave me be, but I'm aching for conversation too. We haven't really talked since the first time she came back from Sam's Throne, and I've had ample time to think about her words.

I reluctantly pat the ground next to me. "Join me? No one else here says much."

She huffs. "I would imagine not."

Grace crouches down next to me, and after a moment's hesitation, she folds her legs under her and sits. She hisses.

"I hope you brought a warm coat. The ground gets cold in the middle of the night."

"I didn't," she admits.

"Amateur." With my good arm, I hold open the blanket and let her get closer.

She moves with the same hesitation, and I understand why. It's uncomfortable, at first, to be this close to another person. I breathe out hard when her arm brushes mine, and she laughs.

"This is strange too, isn't it?" She purposefully bumps her arm against mine a second time. "That isn't the broken arm, right?"

Something bubbles up inside of me. I *giggle*.

"I don't hate it," I admit. "But it's probably dangerous."

"It probably is." She doesn't move away. "But so is freezing to death."

"I'm not sure Arkansas nights are cold enough for that, even up here in the mountains."

"Hush, let me have this. Besides, hypothermia is still a risk."

Truth is, I don't want her to move either. I want to reach out my hand and curl my fingers around hers and hold on for dear life. Two months ago, I didn't even know who Grace was. In the first few weeks of being here, our paths barely crossed, and in our past few conversations, I wanted to strangle her on a number of occasions. But tonight, when she's close enough that I can feel her breathe in and out, she's my tether.

We sit in silence for a while, and then she asks, "Why did you do it?"

I frown. "Why did I do what?"

She opens the blanket enough to let the cold in, and she waves at the graves. "This. Dig graves. Spend time with them." She pulls the blanket to her chest again and huddles closer. "I know you think it's important to remember, and I agree. It's also a whole lot healthier to bury them. But...why you?"

"Because it needed to happen." I opt for the easiest answer first, but Grace's question sets the cogs in my head turning. I've barely answered those questions for myself.

"Sure," Grace says, "but we could have found an alternative."

"Such as?"

She pulls her knees up to her chest and rests her chin on them. She's turned toward Aleesha's grave, though I doubt she's aware of that. "I don't know," she admits. "I guess we could have taken turns?"

"Someone had to do it, and we don't know if it's dangerous. Better if it's just one of us."

"Aren't you scared?"

I lean into her. I don't do it on purpose, but the warmth draws me in. I can count on the fingers of one hand the times someone has touched me this past month. Only by accident or for aid, and I'm starved for it.

"I'm terrified," I admit. "I don't have a simple answer for you. I *do* think it's important. To have our todays, tomorrows, and our yesterdays. I want someone to remember me. I don't want any of them to be alone." I weigh my words. "But that wasn't what convinced me."

Grace waits, but when I stay silent, she asks, "What did?"

"I wasn't meant to be here, you know? I got kicked out of my home, and my parents didn't want me back when I got arrested. Those first few weeks, every morning when I woke up on my raggedy bed, I had the same words running through my mind. *I don't belong here.* I thought it would get easier. I thought maybe working in the garden would change things, but the truth is, I *still* don't think I belong here." I never said any of that out loud, and the words weigh heavy, but speaking them makes me feel lighter. I pull my shoulders up to my ears, and a flicker of pain trails through my arm. "And I don't know where I *do* belong. I don't know who I am. I'm still figuring that out."

For the first time in a long time, my hand goes up to my neck, to reach for a necklace I no longer wear. A small, jeweled cross on a golden chain that my parents gave me after my confirmation. I broke it after that botched conversation with Father Michael, and I never picked it up again. I miss the feeling of the sharp edges underneath my fingers. "Are you religious?"

Grace considers it. "Some of my foster families were. I don't know that I am. I never really thought about it."

I huff out a laugh. "It's always been such a big part of my life that I feel lost without it." I realize that's the truth the moment the words leave me. "It's not just that I don't belong here or that I miss my parents or my home, though those things are true. But I've lost all my certainties. I loved the feeling of being part of something greater."

Even though our parish was small, the voices echoed through the church and lifted me up.

"That's why it's so hard for me to trust anyone," I say. "You were right about that."

She nods silently.

"It made me feel like the world had a purpose to it, and a kindness too. It made me feel like there was nothing I could do that wouldn't be forgiven." My voice is hoarse, but my hands are steady. "I lost that. I lost…knowing what the world looks like. I lost love and community, and I lost God."

I gesture at the carefully tended graves. It's too dark for either of us to see, but Josie took over my work with care and determination. She's gathered rocks from all across the garden— and the other side of the fence too—and she's been using them to cover the earth. She's been trying to find ways to make markers. Gravestones. I hate to admit it, but she's made this place better.

"This is the closest I've come to finding that purpose again. Bits and pieces of me."

"Bits and pieces of God, too?" Grace asks. She clears her throat, and her eyes are suspiciously bright.

"I don't know," I answer truthfully.

She tilts her head a little to look at me. "Would you like to find God again?"

"Yes." To be angry. To hurt. To be accepted. To come home. *God, yes.*

Grace takes my hand and holds it.

When I wake, my body aches like we stayed up all night, though Grace and I both went to our rooms in the early morning.

But I feel lighter, despite the achiness.

"You look horrible," Josie says, when she sees me in the garden after breakfast. Her hair has grown past her ears, and she's tied it back in a small ponytail. She hasn't mellowed. She's still all angles and anger. But she's gentle with the garden and with the graves. We understand each other quite well these days.

"Still better than when you choked me."

We're even working on something that resembles banter, though it's harsh and sharp, and it cuts. It seems to make us both feel better.

And to her credit, though I hate to say it, Josie works hard to make amends for what she did.

"We could try to burn names into wooden markers," she says, when she spreads new stones around after carefully cleaning them. "Crosses too, but I'm not sure everyone would be as comfortable with that."

I would be. I would be okay without one too.

"Wouldn't carving be easier?" I lean against the fence and watch her work. She tells me she hates how I watch, but the first few times when I tried to walk away, she halted me with a question. And a second. And a third.

"I don't know if anyone knows woodwork. Luke did, but he left with Hunter." She swallows. Awkward, like every time Hunter comes up in conversation. "And to that point, I don't know if we have the tools for it."

"Khalil may know."

"I'll ask him, but I think wood-burning is better."

"I don't think we have the tools for *that*."

"Khalil may know." She lobs the words back at me with ease, and I scowl.

She draws breath to speak when someone shouts her name. "Josie!"

We turn and find Grace walking up to us. I raise my hand in greeting. We haven't really spoken since last night, but that tether is still present. Like with Josie, we're connected, somehow. But this morning, she's pale, and her eyes are distant. She acknowledges me with a slight nod before she turns to Josie.

And her shoulders drop.

We've been here before. I know what she's come to tell us.

"I wanted you to hear from me," she says. She clenches her hands at her side. "Saoirse died."

Josie drops the rock she's holding. She tenses all over. "No..."

"I know you were hoping she would pull through. We all were, but—"

"Were you?" Josie interrupts Grace, hard. Her voice has a razor-sharp edge to it. Anger. Grief. Hurt. "I've heard the others talk. The whispers that I'm a waste of resources, that I only made life harder for all of you." Josie shakes her head. "Can you look at me and tell me that you spared us a moment of thought? *Us*, not what we did. Not the trouble we caused you. Can you tell me you ever saw us as part of your little community?"

Grace breathes out hard, like Josie punched her. "Of course..." she starts, but her voice trails off. Her mouth works, but no sound comes out.

And Josie does the worst thing she can do. She laughs. "That's exactly what I mean."

"I do." The words leave my mouth before I really think

about it, but Josie turns to me with a hunger born from starvation. So I push through. "See you as part of our community. I won't lie to you and tell you it's easy. I'm still furious with you for what you did to me. But I understand it too. When you're here with me, to tend the grave and the garden, I can forget it. I can look at this place and see that you made it better. I can't speak for anyone else, but you belong here. I will help you dig a grave for Saoirse so she belongs here too."

With that, Josie drops to her knees, hides her face in her hands, and she sobs.

Hope for Better Futures

A Timeline

Day 33: Every time someone coughs, we all jump. Not literally, but it sometimes feels that way. It's been two days since Saoirse died. We're all keeping count.

Day 37: Khalil cut himself with a garden saw today. No one knows quite how it happened, but he was trimming the trees, and he must have slipped. It's a bad wound, but it's not life-threatening. Casey tried to patch him up as best as he could, but we don't have a lot of medical equipment here, so it didn't look very neat. Khalil jokes he's going to have a cool scar along his arm, but until it heals, it's going to keep hurting.

Casey keeps us all together with the handful of Band-Aids and painkillers he has left. I don't know how he does it.

He shouldn't be responsible for us. He's not a doctor. He's sixteen. But we trust him.

Day 46: We're hungry. Logan brings me the inventory lists to keep with all these files. I know we have beans left for days. And small portions of rice. We have whatever the hunters find us, including raccoon and possum. Oyster mushrooms we think are safe. We can eat three meager meals, but never enough.

I worry that we'll become careless and make mistakes because we're all tired and hungry, and I worry it will only get worse. We try to take care of ourselves, but it's hard to think straight. It's harder every day. Without any perspective, what are we holding on for?

BURIAL RITES FOR SAOIRSE SULLIVAN

HEY.

EMERSON OFFERED TO HELP, BUT I NEED TO DO THIS ON MY OWN. I NEED TO SAY GOODBYE TO YOU BY MYSELF. WE'VE SPENT ALL THAT TIME ALONE TOGETHER, AND I WANT TO TELL YOU—

I HATE YOU. I'M SO ANGRY AT YOU. I NEARLY DIED FOR YOU, I STOLE FOR YOU, I HURT FOR YOU, AND NOW YOU LEAVE ME? YOU PROMISED TO STICK WITH ME, AND I WANT TO HOLD YOU TO THAT PROMISE, BUT I CAN'T DO THAT NOW. I DON'T KNOW HOW TO GO ON WITHOUT YOU, BECAUSE YOU TOOK A PIECE OF MY HEART, AND MY CHEST FEELS EMPTIER.

I DON'T KNOW HOW TO KEEP SURVIVING WHEN I KEEP LOSING, AND YOU'RE NOT HERE TO TELL ME.

SO I HATE YOU. I HATE THE FRECKLES ON YOUR NOSE. THE SPARKLE IN YOUR EYES. ALL THE TROUBLE THAT FOUND YOU AND ALL THE TROUBLE YOU FOUND.

I HATE HOW YOU WERE THE ONLY ONE TO MAKE ME FEEL LIKE I MATTERED. LIKE I COULD BE SOMETHING AND MAKE SOMETHING FROM MY LIFE. I HATE THAT YOU PROMISED ME THE WORLD AND THEN LEFT ME. I HATE THAT I CAN'T HOLD YOUR HAND ANYMORE OR BRAID YOUR HAIR OR TELL YOU RIDICULOUS STORIES. I HATE THAT YOU'LL NEVER GET TO SHOW ME YOUR GRANDPARENTS' FARM OR THE TREASURES YOU HID THERE. I HATE THAT I'LL NEVER BE ABLE TO BRING YOU HOME.

I HATE YOU.

FUCK.

I'LL MISS YOU.

twenty-seven
LOGAN

TODAY IS THE FIRST DAY Isabella leaves the infirmary. She sits on a chair, and Casey and Josie carry her into the garden. She's growing stronger. She can speak a few words. She can't manage more than a few steps on her own. But she's sitting up, wrapped in blankets, and everyone shows up to watch her breathe in fresh air again for the first time since she fell ill. We keep our distance. I lean out of a window. Some of us peek out of doors. Khalil and Riley stick to the garden shed to give Isabella her distance. Everyone wants to be present.

The sight of it is magical. One girl, on a chair, in a garden. We stare at her like someone uncovered a treasure chest or a magic sword. Isabella is paler than she's ever been, and she's fragile. She's lost her hearing, and no one is quite sure if it's permanent. She wasted away during her illness, and Casey told us it would take a long time for her to recover.

Leah is wasting away too. I want to see her sitting here in the chilly winter air. I want to see her up close. See her breath form clouds. Casey says she wakes up regularly now, though she's fragile, and she's struggling with her memory and her speech. She doesn't even have to speak at all. We've always found ways to communicate without words before. I just want her here. Or be with her.

But Isabella's presence means there's hope for her and Xavier.

No one has died since Saoirse. It's been four weeks since Josie and Saoirse first came here, and no one else has fallen ill.

Despite the cold, fresh, green plants are popping up amid the straw-covered vegetable beds. The feathery, bright leaves of tiny carrots. Fluffy clouds of kale. It's not much. It'll be months before we'll be able to feed ourselves. It's barely enough now for a scarce meal, but it lives. My stomach growls at the sight of it.

I turn away from the window and grab my backpack to meet Grace outside the gates. At first, she and Sofia did the hunting and scavenging, but at the turn of the year, Mackenzi suggested we change the work schedule. Unexpectedly, Isaiah was the first person to back her up. With no internet or working phones, he asked for Mackenzi's job of "fixing and cleaning things," while he kept building his collection of files and thoughts. Mackenzi joined Sofia hunting. It's the only attention anyone's paid to New Year's. Food is our main priority right now. Keeping the plague out matters only if we don't succumb to hunger.

Both Riley and I asked to help Grace with her scavenger runs to Sam's Throne, and so we're alternating. Today, it's on me. I need it.

I'm happy for Isabella, but it's hard to see her sit up and smile. It's far easier to follow Grace along the now-familiar path through the woods, where the trees look stark and cold. It's easier to walk the mountain path with a comfortable silence between us and the quiet where I know myself.

When we near Sam's Throne, and the light around us turns a burnt orange, a familiar nervousness settles in my stomach. That bottomless pit of not knowing what we'll find on the other side. Or perhaps the gnawing is hunger too. The traps didn't produce anything yesterday or the day before, and we've all but run out of our own supplies. Every successful trip into town gives us enough food for a day or two at most.

I nudge Grace carefully. "What do we need?"

Nia helped her to learn my signs. Enough to get by.

She frowns. "Food. Information. An updated map. Food."

I pat the pocket with my copy of the map and the pencils I brought. Since Grace asked me to draw a map, we've been updating it with notes about abandoned houses, plague crosses, and more. It helps us figure out which houses to avoid and which houses to enter. None of us want to accidentally break into a house where someone inside is ill. Especially now that we may have managed to keep the plague out of Hope.

"I don't know why some of us fell ill and others didn't.

Maybe there's a good reason for it, but I don't want to gamble that it was anything other than luck," Grace says.

I can't—I don't want to imagine any of us carrying the plague back to Hope.

"I also don't know how we'll get information," Grace admits, "but I'd like to know what's going on in the rest of the world."

"How?"

"One of the oldest houses, maybe? The ones we know have been emptied? We can try to see if any of *their* computers will work. They usually have better food stocks anyway."

In many of the newer houses, hunger has taken hold too. Or other thieves have.

I pull a face, and she raises her hands. "I know it's not ideal, but I don't know what the best alternative is. We can't very well walk up to people to ask them what's going on."

I raise my hands to sign then think better of it and pull the map out of my pocket. I point at the store and the area around it. It has a post office somewhere in the vicinity, probably a town hall too. Central gathering points. We can't be the only ones angling for information.

Even the school or the church, from a safe distance. If we—

Grace shakes her head. "No, too dangerous. I don't know if I can talk us out of another confrontation with Store Guy. Or anyone else for that matter."

I nod. "I understand."

I don't agree, but I understand. And Grace won't be able to see the nuances in my signs. The hesitation that must show on my face.

"We'll start with food and go from there. Once we have a good house, I'll do the runs, and you map the street, okay?"

I nod again. With the map still in my hands, we cross into town, and I immediately begin to mark the changes. The houses with new plague crosses, the houses with shattered windows, the houses where light is still burning. Grace and I stick close to each other, trying to not attract attention as two girls wandering a mostly deserted ghost town. She continuously scans the streets too.

When a dog barks, she pulls me behind a tree before either of can pinpoint where the sound is coming from. Two streets down, a door opens and closes, we both freeze. Later on, I grab her sleeve and pause her when I'm certain I hear the squeaks of bike wheels. My heart continues to hammer in my throat even when no bike ever shows up. The shadows around us lengthen.

"Do you think children still ride their bikes here?" I sign at Grace.

She frowns. "I'm sorry, Logan, I don't know what half those signs mean."

I shrug. "Never mind."

One house has a wind chime hanging from its porches, and its eerie melody crawls up my spine.

Eventually, we find one of the houses on our list. It's dark and empty, and the white slash across the door is faded away. The door swings back and forth on its hinges.

"Fuck," Grace whispers. "Someone may have cleaned it out."

I edge closer and glance in through the window.

"How does it look?" Grace whispers.

I catch a flash of color on the living room floor. A pink-and-purple dollhouse, with doll-size furniture spread out in front of it. It even has a tiny cup on a tiny table, like someone was playing with it only hours ago. I turn back and swallow hard.

"Logan?"

I sigh. "It looks empty."

She steps up next to me regardless, and she breathes out hard when she spots the play set. "Oh."

Yeah.

"I hope they left for somewhere safe."

"I hope they're alive." I try not to think about it too hard, because it's the only way I can keep going. Leah and I used to play with a dollhouse Granddad had in his attic. He once let slip that it was our mother's.

"I hate this," Grace mutters under her breath. She pushes her hair back and sets her jaw. "I'll go in to search for food. You go update the map, but don't stray too far."

She doesn't wait for a response, but instead she dashes into the house. And I'm grateful she's gone. It's easier to lie with signs, but I'm still a terrible liar.

I don't want to update the map. I want to keep going, now

more than ever. I want to know, I *need* to know that the rest of the world is better than this.

I understand Grace's hesitation. We *can't* bring the plague back to Hope. But we can't forget the rest of the world or be forgotten either.

So I pull up the map and my pencil and walk the street like I'm taking notes, but when the house disappears behind the trees, I put them back and keep walking.

We're nowhere near the school, but our map has grown after nearly a dozen runs. I've been studying the quickest route while we walked here. I walk from streetlamp to streetlamp. I know where I'm going.

The main street is as empty as the town itself, with everyone keeping to their houses. Locked down, or following a curfew that we're unaware of, or simply afraid. The store is boarded up now, and the post office a few doors down is too. It means I have to keep walking.

Until a low whistle echoes against the store fronts.

I freeze and push myself against the closest wall, already scanning the streets for escape routes.

"Hey, psst."

Twilight has made way for dim nightfall, and I can't figure out where the sound comes from.

Then someone moves from the shadows.

"What are you doing out?" A girl's voice, soft. She sounds unthreatening, but I can't be certain.

She steps into the light, and she's my age, perhaps a little older. She has long black hair, light skin, worried eyes. She holds her hands wide in a gesture of goodwill. Her clothes are dirty but whole, and she wears a jangling bracelet around her wrist. I drink in her presence. It's so strange to see someone outside of Hope that my brain latches on to every single detail. The mismatched shoes. The slight scars on her forearms. The hint of sadness in the lines of her face.

She keeps a careful distance. "Are you okay?"

I open my mouth. I try to dislodge my jaw and shape my tongue around the right words in an effort to answer, but like so many times before, the words exist in my brain, but I can't speak them. I cannot will them into being.

She takes a step back. "Are you sick?"

I shake my head.

"Are you alone? Are you a survivor too?"

Nod.

"Do you need a place to spend the night?"

I hesitate. I don't. I want to go home when I've got what I need, but does it look weird if I say no?

As if she read my mind, she says, "You don't have to answer if you don't want to. Quite a few of us have no one—have no home to go back to, and I don't want to make you uncomfortable. If you need shelter, the town hall is set up for us lost and lonely." She points down the road, to the right. "It's a bit chaotic, so I usually walk around until I'm tired, but they're good people.

They may even have some food rations left for you. They try to divide those as equally as possible."

I try to not look confused.

"We're all we have now, right?" The girl can't suppress the sorrow in her voice, but I hardly notice it.

I hold my hand over my heart. "Thank you."

Before she can say anything else, I step out of the light and into the shadows. She mutters something. I don't listen. My heart hammers. I follow the route she pointed out, and my feet march to the beat of her most important words.

Food rations. Food rations. *Food rations.*

She might just mean they rationed food like we have, but if the town has actual rations... Could we get them too? It would mean the world. The winter. Our lives. Grace will hate me for disappearing on her, but this information would make up for that.

We wouldn't have to steal from dead people.

I turn the corner, and the town hall appears in front of me. Brightly lit, like a beacon in the night. Yellowed light shines out through the tall windows, and the porch is lit up too. A young Black man sits on the steps. He's humming a song and doesn't react to my presence at all. He may not even see me, as bright as his surroundings are.

I cling to the shadows and circle around the building. Pieces of paper hang on every door and every entrance: NO PLAGUE. NO SIGNS OF SICKNESS. All of them have words scribbled on them too.

I dash closer. They're messages from survivors who hope to

find loved ones ("Elin Newberry was here. Find me, Ray." "If Kirsty Jameson reads this, I'm sorry. I can't stay here."). Notes of remembrance ("Miss you, Dad.") and grief and anger ("The government is lying to us. All of this is a hoax.").

Underneath is another note, on crisp paper. It has an official-looking letterhead and a lot of fancy words. I glance at the header then snatch it from the door and stuff it in my pocket. It crinkles and tears, and I pause to make sure no one is reacting to the sound.

If they even heard it, that is. When I push myself against the outer wall and inch toward the nearest window, a constant hum of voices drifts out. Discomfort crawls up my spine. So many people and so much louder than what I've grown used to.

I find the darkest corner and glance in, and what I see takes my breath away. It's crowded. As crowded as the school was when I first came here. People are lying side by side in the big, open room. Some are sleeping on stretchers and pallets with blankets pulled over their heads. Others are sitting up and talking or playing cards. In the farthest corner, a young boy and a young girl are bouncing a ball back and forth between them. Along one of the walls, Christmas lights are strung, though it's well past Christmas. Almost everyone is wearing masks here too.

It's overwhelming.

A community of survivors, like Hope. But we number just over a dozen, and I guesstimate at least a hundred people here. Together. Safe.

I hate it, and I long for it.

In the center of the room, a lonely boy turns and looks at the window. He sees me. I know he does. My heart skips a beat, and I push back, into the night. But when he gets up to walk to the door, the light catches his face, and I pause.

Andrew?

Andrew who left with Hunter. Andrew, who is *one of us*. What is he doing here?

I stand frozen, questions swirling all around me, and before I find a place to escape to, he steps out. He's wearing a torn and patched-up outfit that makes me aware I'm still wearing my uniform.

"Logan?" His voice is as soft and careful as I remember. He's fighting back a smile that doesn't reach his eyes. His hair has grown out, and he has a scar along his palm. "Are you okay? What are you doing here?"

I point at him.

He pinches the bridge of his nose. "I need a place to stay after—are you still at Hope?"

I nod.

"Is everyone okay? Did anyone fall ill?"

I bite my tongue and try to figure out how to respond to that, but he keeps talking.

"I'm glad we left, you know? Even though Hunter's plan was a disaster. I'm the only one left. Everyone else died. Guess we didn't leave the plague behind."

I wince. He isn't the only one, I want to tell him. Josie is with us.

That's not the point, I know.

He shrugs. "At least I'm alive." He narrows his eyes and evaluates me. There's a calculation to him that's never been there before. "What about you? Are you safe? Come in."

I shake my head. Gesture at him to follow me instead. He could come back with me. He could come home to us.

His smile fades. "To Hope? Why, so I can feel locked up again?" He scoffs. "No, thanks. Never. You'd be far better off here too. We have food, although it isn't much. The government rations everything. We aren't forgotten. I have friends who can gather extra meals for you. Find medication if you need it. The people in charge can't know we're from Hope, but it's not like you'll say anything anyway." He tilts his head. "We do have to do something about those clothes."

My stomach whines at the thought of food, my head spins at the thought of medication. But something about the way he turns toward me and scans the area around me reminds me of Hunter. Andrew may not have been anything like him when he left, but he is now.

I take a big step back.

In all the time we spent together in Hope, I never saw him as violent, merely quiet and intimidating. When he smiles and his teeth bare and he follows me, I know better.

"I insist, Logan. The people here have forgotten about you.

They've forgotten about Hope. I can't have you wandering around to remind them."

He reaches out and grabs for my arm. I bend backward to stay out of his reach and almost tumble over. I don't wait for him to make another move. I won't stay here. I won't. I have to go back.

I push myself forward, and I run.

PUBLIC NOTICE

In light of our continuing state of emergency and lockdown measures thereof, and in light of the disturbed food supplies, the government of the State of Arkansas will continue to provide households with food and medicine rations, pursuant the same rules and regulations as prior distribution.

"We cannot combat one public health crisis by creating another," said Governor Brooks. "Food insecurity cannot be a reason that our upstanding citizens put themselves and their loved ones at risk. The only way to ensure people can stay safely at home is by not giving them unnecessary reason to leave the house. At least until such time that a cure can be found."

Rations will be provided at predetermined locations in every city and every town, every month at the below dates, until further notice.

Handouts will be overseen by the National Guard. All necessary safety measures—including masks, distance, and shielding—will be in place to ensure distribution without transmission.

twenty-eight
GRACE

"WHAT DO YOU MEAN, THEY forgot about us?"

"*Everyone* but Andrew died? Are you sure?"

"How do we get food rations too?"

"How could they forget about us?"

The recreation room is a cacophony of questions and comments once Nia has helped tell Logan's tale. Logan keeps her distance from all of us. She's regained some color, but she still looks pale, and between signing her story, she's picking at a peanut butter sandwich and sipping from a steaming mug of tea. She avoids the stares of the people around her. Of *me*.

I lean against the cabinet, arms folded over each other, and try to get my breathing under control. With every incredulous response, the pain and anger inside me grow. When Logan returned to Hope, I walked away to the privacy of my own room and punched at the wall until my knuckles were sore, equal parts furious that she left me and relieved that she was safe.

But that felt like nothing compared to this. We *were* left here to die.

"They're all trying to find ways to get by," Nia translates for Logan. "I don't think they did it on purpose."

"I'm not sure that makes it better," Khalil says.

"We have a right to survive as much as anyone," Josie says. She rarely speaks up in these gatherings, but today, nothing can stop her. She has her fingers curled in such tight fists, I can count the bones, and the muscles in her arms flex. "Upstanding citizens. Ha. If they're handing out food rations, we deserve to get them too. If they're keeping people safe, we deserve to be safe. If they have medical supplies—" She chokes on the last word.

I place my hands on the cabinet and launch myself forward with a big step to get the restless energy out of my body. "Josie is right." I grab the torn pamphlet from the table and crumple it in my hand, but I manage to keep my voice from cracking. We need to make this work, all of us. "We deserve a chance. We deserve to live too."

"So we go get it." Emerson sits on one of the tables, and they tap their foot against its leg. With their free hand, they're plucking at their splint. "It says households have a right to rations, doesn't it? We're technically a household. If we show up, they can't send us away."

"Can't they?" Riley asks, before I can. Riley's hair has grown out, and she's bound it back in a ponytail. She still has dirt underneath her fingernails from today's work in the garden, and she picks at it. "Might be me, but in my experience, they can, and they will. They're the ones who write the rules, Emerson. They don't have to abide by them."

"What can they do?" Mackenzi sneers. "Arrest us?"

"Shoot us," Riley throws back. "They can shoot us. Remember? They've done it before."

"I remember," Emerson says. "I was there. But that's exactly why we *should* try. Things were different back then. The military was under orders to confine everyone to their houses. They were scared. This is a different assignment. They'll want to help us."

I haven't heard them so full of trust in a long time, maybe ever. And I wish I could believe it isn't actually naivete. A reminder of the life they once had. Nothing that happened so far indicates the authorities will want to help. But... "We'll have to try."

"They don't want us there at all," Riley retorts. "Andrew said so himself!"

"Then it's a good thing Andrew isn't in charge, don't you think?" Casey frowns. He leans back in his chair, balancing precariously on its hind legs.

Riley scowls. "We're doing fine. We don't need any more help."

Logan signs something, but I pause Nia's translation with a hand gesture. Everyone immediately quiets, and I sigh. "I would love for that to be true. We're doing far better than anyone might expect, but we're not doing fine. We're holding on by threads. If we fail to gather food for a week, if the garden doesn't pull through the winter, we're immediately vulnerable. If one of us falls or breaks something or cuts themselves with a saw *again*, we have no way to treat the wounds. If anyone falls ill, we can't do anything." My words are met with absolute silence. "I don't know about you, but I'm hungry and tired."

My shoulders drop. "The fact that we're here at all is a miracle, and I have to imagine you're scared, because I am. If we could keep Hope to ourselves and never depend on the outside world again, I would feel better. But we can't pretend we don't need this. We do."

"We could use a stocked medicine cabinet," Casey adds. "Painkillers. Antiseptics. Antibiotics, just in case. It may take a long time before they have a cure or a vaccine or whatever. With the right supplies, we can keep ourselves safe."

"So you would risk our lives to hypothetically save our lives? Does that make sense to you? What if they do get violent? What if anyone there is infected? What if—" Riley's hands tremble with anger or perhaps fear. And I understand it, I do, because it is terrifying. I want to go there and prove to them all that we belong here, but I'm also terrified of bringing the plague back to Hope.

"We can prepare for that. Make a plan and a contingency plan," Emerson says, not unkindly. "It doesn't have to be dangerous, and if it is, we can always turn back. All I'm asking is that we don't give up before we try."

"According to the sign, rationing is done carefully," I say. "With masks and distance and other forms of protective shielding, though I'll admit I don't quite know what that means. We can send two people in on behalf of all of us, and they can isolate once they come back, to make sure they weren't infected. Like Logan will isolate now too." I can't help it that this last sentence has a bit of a bite to it. But I can't let my anger make this decision. It needs to be done by all of us.

"We've gone into town plenty of times before," Logan signs with a wince, though she and I are the only ones who've ever met others there. "You too, Riley. You know we can get out again if we have to."

"What if they won't give it to us though?" Riley asks softly, and the moment she does, a chill settles over the room. This is the question that's on everyone's mind but no one wanted to ask. Not: *What if something happens?* Not even: *What if they did intentionally skip over us?*

What if it happens again? What if we show up and we're turned away? What if we can't count on *anyone* anymore? Why ask for help, and let yourself be vulnerable in the process, if you know it won't be given to you?

Every face in the room reflects the same worry, and the worst thing is—it never even crossed my mind. Not like that. Not like the existential dread of being both abandoned and denied.

What if they leave us again?

"We go anyway," Emerson says. They swallow hard, but they sit up straighter, and they stop tapping their foot. "We try. We try, because I want to believe not everyone will turn us away. I'll be the one to get in line if you want me to."

"At least you don't look threatening," Josie says, her words snide and teasing all at once. "They may even take pity on you."

Emerson raises their splinted arm and gives her a one-finger salute.

I slowly breathe out.

Casey chokes back a laugh, and someone else giggles. It defuses the tension enough for the undercurrent of conversations to start up again, but Riley and Mackenzi are still scowling.

"We'll come too," Nia says loudly. She nods at Logan, who smiles wryly and signs, "Maybe they'll take pity on *me*."

"I think Emerson is right," Casey says, adding his voice to the chorus. "We need to try. I would come if I could."

"You're not going anywhere," I say immediately. I narrow my eyes at him. He's not. Not if I can help it. We can't spare him. He's no more a doctor than any of us, but by this point, he's the closest thing we have. And I don't want anything to happen to him.

Casey scowls, but I'll deal with that later. I continue. "As for the others, how about this? A plan and a contingency plan. We send Nia and Logan, if she feels up to it, as representatives of Hope, on behalf of all of us. Emerson can pretend they're one of the townspeople, in case the authorities are difficult. And Riley and I follow the three of them from a distance to keep an eye out for trouble and escape routes if we need them."

I turn to Riley, who jiggles her jaw and sucks in a breath. Then she nods. "Yeah, I can do that."

"Good." I don't even have to pretend to smile. "*Thank you.*"

"We're going to have to find you some decent clothes, Emerson," Riley says, eyeing me. "If you want to pass as a normal person, that is."

Emerson wrinkles their nose. "Normal?"

"A baby-blue polo shirt and slacks," Mackenzi suggests.

"A three-piece suit. Someone's holiday outfit," Josie smirks.

"A jacket made from raccoon pelts," Khalil throws in. "Thematically appropriate and all that."

"Whatever people in the real world look like," Isaiah says solemnly, and it's so well meant and absurd that we all laugh. It lightens the mood for the rest of the night, while we plot and plan increasingly ridiculous scenarios. It takes the fear out of the situation, but the weight on my shoulders grows heavier.

We need the food. We need the supplies. But most of all, we need this to go right.

If it does, we stand a chance.

———————

We talk until deep into the morning, until everyone flags with fatigue and filters out. Everything feels like a responsibility now in ways it never did before. I beckon Logan and pull her aside before she can leave for her room too.

Logan reddens, and when the hallway around us quiets, she starts to sign, but I cut her off.

"Logan, wait. I need to get this off my chest." I'm so tired, my voice is trembling, but I force my temper to stay down and keep my anger in check. "I didn't get to chance to say this before, and I want to. I know why you left me behind in Sam's Throne. I understand it—hell, I'm *glad* you did. Obviously, the risk paid off."

Logan nods, tentatively.

My hands clench. "But it was thoughtless and dangerous. Not just for you, for both of us. When we go hunting and gathering, we go in pairs so we can keep each other safe. I was terrified and exposed out there. I had no one to keep watch for me. I didn't know where you'd gone to or how to get you back. All I could do was imagine coming back here to tell your sister and Nia I'd lost you, and it damn near broke me."

Logan's shoulders drop at those words. Something in her face crumbles. "I'm sorry," she signs. "I didn't mean to hurt you."

I reach out a hand to her, but I wait for Logan's nod of permission before I squeeze her shoulder. "It's okay, it all worked out. But I need you to know I was worried about you. And I will be worried about you when you go into town for the food drop. You and Nia and Emerson. You matter to us, you're a part of us, and I want you to be safe." I sigh, and midway, it turns into an exhausted yawn. I frown at my hand. "So, next time you feel the need to go investigating in spite of my disapproval, please tell me. And when you go with Nia, please be careful."

Some of the tension leaves Logan's stance, and she nods.

I let go of her shoulder. "Thank you."

Logan signs a goodbye and makes her way back to her room.

I don't follow. I step closer to the wall and lean my forehead against the rough stone. I close my eyes and breathe in deeply. Once. Twice. Several times. I clench and unclench my hands by my side, but the tension that courses through me refuses to leave my body. It simmers right below my skin, and it settles around my spine.

When I shake my arms out and push myself up again, I spot another figure just around the corner to the room. Emerson leans against the wall, their brow furrowed but a soft smile around their eyes. "You didn't explode at her."

"Go do something useful, Emerson," I grumble, though their words warm me.

"I believe this will work," they whisper.

I shove my hands into my pockets. "You sounded convinced in there."

"I want us all to survive, Grace," they say. "I want us all to live."

I sigh deeply. "Yeah, me too."

"Grace?"

They wait for me to look up.

"I trust you to protect us."

With that, they smile and walk away.

Dear Leah,

I know you hate letters, but Casey promised to read this one out loud to you, so I hope you don't mind. If you do, get up and come tell me.

We're going into town to try to get food and other things. The roadblock has been gone for a while now. I haven't had a chance to tell you yet, but we've been stealing from empty houses to refill our own supplies. It's the same thing you told me once, right? I know we're not supposed to steal, but we're not supposed to starve either. We should all be able to eat when we're hungry.

So I've been going out with Grace every five days. And I take inventory with Nia the next day. We plan out food and meals as best as we can. You should see some of the recipes we think up.

What we have is barely enough to eat. I'm worried that it will run out. I don't want to starve before we can survive.

But this is different. They're handing out rations, and if we can convince them we deserve to eat too, we won't have to worry anymore. You can come back to us. I know you think I jump to conclusions sometimes, but it's true. If we have a steady supply of food, we can survive this. I'm sure of it.

And if something does go wrong after all...I want you to know I'm proud of what I did here. And I would take

this chance a thousand times over if it meant saving you.
Because I know you would do the exact same thing for me.
I miss you. I love you. I'll see you soon

LOGAN

<u>Kitchen Inventory List, Again</u>
Or: How do we feed fourteen people with this?

- 1/2 bag of rice (50 lb)
- 1 bags of beans (50 lb)
- 1/2 bag of lentils
- 2 loaves of bread
- 1 pan of fish soup
- 2 cans of chicken
- 1 can of peas
- 1/2 box of cereal
- 2 jars of peanut butter
- 1/2 container of trail mix
- 3 glazed pecans
- 24 bags of tea
- 1 possum
- 3 fish
- Dreams of cakes and pies
- And cookies
- And pancakes

  Stop it, you're making me hungry.

  I am hungry.

  I know.

twenty-nine
GRACE

WE SPEND SEVERAL DAYS PREPARING for our food run. Riley stole a fancy button-down shirt and pants for Emerson, and they couldn't stop stroking it. Nia and Logan went over their story at least half a dozen times. We planned our trip to the very second. We ate a full meal tonight so that we're all focused and attentive.

We'll leave tomorrow before sunrise.

I pace in the hallway for a bit, my heart hammering, and my hands cold. The temperatures inside are rapidly dropping with the change of weather, and I should ask Isaiah or Mackenzi to figure out the central heating of this place. Tomorrow. Or the day after, rather.

Tonight, I have other things on my mind.

I pause in front of Casey's door, raise my hand to knock,

then turn back again. I don't understand why this is so difficult. We've kept our distance so carefully, and perhaps that barrier extends to our everyday now.

Three more steps, pause.

Another step or two.

The door opens.

I freeze.

Casey sighs. "You shouldn't be here, and you're driving me up a wall. Either come in, or get back to your room, please."

I push my cold hands into my armpits and let my hair fall in front of my face, suddenly self-conscious. This is who we used to be. It's not who we are. I'm trying to mesh together the me from several months ago with who I am now, and the pieces won't fit.

"*Grace.*"

"I'm trying to be strong for everyone else," I admit. "Tonight, I don't want to be. But I don't think that's fair to you either."

I don't have to see Casey to know he's shaking his head. "Come in, you."

"Are you okay with that?" My voice is so much smaller than I hoped it would be, but I'm tired and lonely and scared out of my mind.

"It's been weeks since the last infection. I don't think either of us is ill, and if we are, well..." He doesn't finish his sentence. I turn to him, and he rubs his hands over his face. The circles under his eyes are constant, and his shirts hang loosely around his shoulders. We should steal clothes for all of us at some point.

He pushes his door open farther and beckons me in.

"Fuck it." I stop resisting, duck under his arm, and enter. Casey's room is as threadbare as mine in its own way. He's added a second cover to his bed and an extra pillow, which he probably grabbed from one of the empty rooms in the west wing. The wall facing the door has a large water stain on it from a semifixed ceiling leak, while the paint on the window frame is peeling off. Instead of graffiti, his room has names and lewd messages carved into the door.

He steps in and closes the door behind him then leans against it. "What's up, Star Kid?"

His voice is so familiar, it undoes me. I plop down onto the bed and put my head in my hands. "I'm scared, Case. I'd like to go back to being angry instead."

He doesn't move, doesn't come closer. His dark eyes soften. "Do you want to talk about it?"

I almost laugh. "No."

"This is it, isn't it? Our best chance?"

It might be. I won't admit that out loud. "I want to be here with you. I want to remember what life was like before all of this."

He looks at me through his lashes, with something like relief in his posture. "The good old days?"

"God, no. They were absolutely terrible. But a different type of terrible." I hesitate. "And a different type of good, maybe." I reach out to him. "Sit with me? You don't have to come too close. But I figured we could both use a break."

He sags down onto the floor. His shoulders drop. The tension around his jaw dissipates, and he rests his arms on his knees. "I'd like that. I'd really like that."

"Have you slept at all lately?" I cling to the side of the bed to stop myself from joining him on the floor. From letting our shoulders touch and our fingers intertwine. I hunger for his touch so badly, it's like a physical ache, a gnawing inside me.

He smiles crookedly. "I've finally learned to fall asleep when it isn't quiet outside. Apparently the trick is to exhaust yourself beyond measure. I've slept. But I dream about those soldiers and their guns. I have nightmares about the people I've lost crawling out of the graves we dug."

I don't know what's worse. Not sleeping enough or dreaming too much. I try to steer the conversation in another direction. "What do you think the world will look like when all of this is over?"

"If there's a world left by the end of it, you mean?"

"Wow, bitter much?" I'm not used to that. Not from him.

He closes his eyes and doesn't speak for such a long time that I worry he's fallen asleep. When he finally does answer, his voice is distant. "I hope there are still ice cream parlors. Do you know that's what I miss most? Before I ended up with my foster family, I lived with my sister, Ashley, in a small apartment above the pharmacy where she worked. It was barely big enough for her and too cramped for the both of us, but we made do for almost a year. She wasn't great at taking care of me, but every Friday after work, she'd take me to this tiny frozen custard place. Each week, we tried a different flavor. Vanilla custard. Birthday cake. Mango gelato. Mint chocolate chip. We had three flavors left on the menu by the time I was taken away from her. Those first few nights in foster care, I repeated the flavors to myself, over and over and over."

"How old were you?" I ask softly.

He scrunches up his face. "Six."

"What were the flavors?"

"Lime. Toffee. Stracciatella." The words have a singsong quality to them, and I wonder how often he still repeats them. My stomach growls at the thought of it. "If the world ever goes back to normal, I want to go back to her. And taste those flavors of ice cream."

"Do you know if she's—" I stop myself. "That sounds good." I rock back and forth on the bed, my fingers still clutching the edge. "I'd like that for you."

"I also want to graduate," he admits, after another bout of silence. He doesn't answer the question I nearly asked. "Find a way to work in a hospital."

"Go to med school?" I ask.

He raises his eyebrows. "Got a problem with that?"

"No." I tilt my head, considering. "After all of this, I wasn't sure that's what you wanted to keep doing."

"It's because of all of this that I do." He settles in a bit more comfortably. He folds his arms behind his head and leans against the wall. "I don't know if med school is for me. I don't know that I'd want to become a doctor or anything, but maybe I could go to nursing school. I want to learn how to care for people. I want to be able to help."

"I respect that."

"Hope for a Better Future, hmm?" He smirks.

I scowl. "You're hilarious."

"I know." His grins softens to a real smile. "I like the idea of a *brighter* future though, Grace. Something to work toward. One day, this plague will be over. You read the notice; they're working on medication. If we get the rations, if we can survive that long, we can endure whatever comes next."

"I know," I say, plucking at the hem of my shirt. Something of that same fire from before settles inside me, but it's not anger this time. It's fierce determination. "But it has to be more than that. You told me yourself. Survival alone isn't good enough."

"So we live," he says. "We thrive. We eat ice cream. We travel the world. We chase our wildest dreams and our most impossible fantasies. We wish on every falling star, and we love with abandon." He changes position to sit a little straighter. "And whether that happens once the plague is vanquished or we are free again, I don't care. It's enough to know that it will. It must. For ourselves, and for the people we carry with us. Everyone who should still be with us, if only someone had cared."

"We can't live for them," I say.

"No one can, but we can remember." Casey balls his hands

into fists. "We can remember that every single one of them deserved to live as much as we do. Nothing we did out there merited being abandoned and left to starve. Nothing we did merited a death sentence, and we *will not forget that*."

"So, do you want to work in a hospital or overthrow the government?" I attempt to jest, but Casey's steely gaze sobers me.

"Both, if I have to." He shakes his head. "Food and medicine, Grace. What on earth did we do that means we don't warrant that? Aren't we human?"

It's on the tip of my tongue. To ask him why he got sent here in the first place. He's one of the few people in Hope who's managed to keep his secrets close to his chest. It cost him quite a few cuts and bruises from the west wing.

I bite it back, but his eyes darken anyway. He was always too good at reading me, and it seems unspoken words can still hurt. He rocks to his feet.

"Does it matter, Grace? Maybe I shot someone. Does that mean I don't matter anymore? If I did what your foster brother did and assaulted a girl, would I deserve this? Maybe it was armed robbery or murder that got me sent here. Would that be enough to let me die in an outbreak? Where do you draw the line?"

I narrow my eyes. "None of us are that bad. Remember? We're here because the state and Better Futures believed we could be rehabilitated and turned into productive members of society."

"God, yes, *productive*. Because that's all we should care about." He grimaces. "Is bad the opposite of human, Grace?"

I hesitate. "I don't know."

"The twins were convicted for arson and attempted manslaughter. Are *they* bad?" He breathes out hard. "Besides, if *we* are left to our own devices, do you think it's any better in detention facilities? This is supposed to be a *good* place."

"I guess not," I admit. I hadn't thought about it or about anything else beyond these walls and this community. I couldn't. I can't.

Casey does the unthinkable. He grabs me by my shoulders and pulls me to my feet. He wraps his arms around me and holds me so closely, I might suffocate. He holds me close enough that I can smell the citrusy shampoo we stole and the scent of musk and detergent. He holds me until I stop resisting, stop shaking, stop tearing up.

He holds me until I cling to him in return and everything is *right* and the world may stop turning around us.

"We can't forget, Grace. Promise me you won't. We are the only ones who can save ourselves."

My voice is muffled. "I promise."

I won't.

I'll save them all if I have to.

I'll carry his words with me when we go into town tomorrow, like a shield, an anchor, a guiding light.

Like a memory of who we were and who we will someday be.

thirty
LOGAN

FIVE OF US LEAVE HOPE. Almost half of everyone who's left. The others, minus Leah and Xavier, come to see us out. Over the past few days, the importance of this trip has grown, and it makes me nervous. I don't want us to fail. I don't want us to be disappointed.

We walk to town together but split off before we get there. Nia and I in our cleanest and best, with surgical masks that Grace stole from one of the houses. I try not to think too hard about who wore them before us. Emerson wears their Sam's Throne disguise uncomfortably. Their shirt is a little too small, the jeans a little too wide, and they keep rolling their shoulders. When they put on the woolen jacket that Sofia found, they complained that it itched. But they don't look like they come from Hope, and that's what matters.

Grace and Riley keep some distance behind us.

Nia nearly rubs elbows with me while we walk toward the town center, her eyes darting around. Her breath catches several times. "It's so empty here. Where is everybody?"

"At the town hall," I sign. "Or dead."

She swallows hard. "Do you think this'll work?"

"I think it's worth a try."

"What if it doesn't? What do we do then?"

"We let Emerson try. If they don't succeed either…"

"We'll figure something out, though I don't know what yet." Nia spends all her time in the kitchen. She knows how empty our stores are.

"Exactly."

"This is our last chance, isn't it?"

The reality of that set in for all of us over the past couple of days. From good chance, to best chance, to last chance. I don't know what to say.

"Stay close to me, will you?"

I reach for her hand and squeeze her fingers. I keep my eyes on the street in front of me and refuse to count the plague signs for a change. Instead, we follow the easiest route toward the main street. We avoid the church and the school. The house with the dolls inside and the last one we cleared. It had an unfinished painting of a father and his daughter at a carnival on an easel. The picture used as reference leaned against it.

When we get closer to the town hall, other people join us

on our route too. Some glance in our direction, but most keep their heads down. They're alone. As hesitant as Nia and me. As scared too.

I try not to stare, but I need to be aware of them. Where they are, how they walk, how close they might get. It's why Leah would ask me to stand guard when she went out stealing.

The door in the house to our right opens. A young woman walks out with a toddler in her arms. The girl has blue ribbons in her hair, and she's wearing a cute, yellow dress that's too large for her. The woman's gaze meets mine for a second, then she immediately looks down. She clings the girl closer to her.

On the other side of the street, a boy in a wheelchair makes his way down the street. He's wearing headphones and a mask, and he pays attention to nothing and no one but the empty road in front of him. He speeds past us.

"Do you think any of them survived the plague?" Nia whispers. "Do you think they are still waiting for others to recover too?"

I shrug. I don't know, but it's the nightmare that haunts me. The idea that there are people like Leah out there, not surrounded by friends or family, but in marked houses. Alone.

The closer we get to the center, the busier it gets. Occasionally people shout across the street and greet each other, though they keep a careful distance.

The first time it happens, Nia tenses up completely, and I freeze in my tracks.

She tugs at my hand. "Come on. We've got to keep going."

By the time we turn onto the main street, the silence I've grown used to here has made way for a soft buzzing of voices, the occasional shout, and once, children laughing.

Nia starts at that, before she laughs too. "Wow, that's different."

"Everything is." Everything is different, and I wish I could show Leah this. She'd like it. She'd appreciate that people still manage to find ways to live.

She'd appreciate it and wouldn't have a clue what it means, because she never saw any of this. The mere thought of it hits me hard. Leah still lives in another world. She wouldn't understand it.

Three trucks are set up at the parking lot near the town hall. In front of them, tables are covered in large boxes of food and whatever else is handed out here. Soldiers with guns guard both. They're all wearing masks and face shields and gloves. This must be the protective gear the note mentioned.

People form long lines in front of the tables, but no one hands out parcels yet. I assume it's because it's nowhere near noon yet, but the lines are growing. One or two people stand close together, with masks and hungry expressions, then there's a gap of a careful distance followed by people. And so on, until the line turns the corner.

I nudge Nia. "We should get in line."

She nods, speechless. Her hand goes to her pocket, and she

takes out a torn piece of paper. On it is the story we wrote, the one we rehearsed until we know it by heart. She'll have to do the talking, but if it's necessary, I will be able to prompt her.

When we get in line, the people in front of us turn and stare. An elderly Black lady with a big, plaid scarf around her shoulders and a mask to match nods at us, but the ginger-haired man behind her scowls. He clings to a plastic card the way Nia holds on to her speech.

He mutters something, but I strain not to hear it. This is nerve-racking enough without people like him making it worse.

"Granddad wasn't completely right," Leah told me once. "It isn't just good people and wolves. There are also people who assume everyone else is a wolf, and that makes them dangerous too."

Granddad thought we were wolves.

A teenage boy with light-brown skin and sandy hair gets in line behind us. He doesn't even spare us a glance. He has a phone in his hands, and his thumb is rapidly moving across the screen.

When Nia notices it, her eyes widen. "Wonder if I could borrow that for a bit…"

I wince. "Probably not."

"I know, I won't ask. I don't want to make a fuss, but… I would like to know how my family is doing." She scrunches up her face, like she has so much more to say but doesn't.

We haven't had working phones for weeks, and it's sometimes

hard to imagine things going on as normal—or as normal as can be—in the outside world. If anyone were to come and tell me a year had passed since this whole mess started, I would believe them in a heartbeat.

The line continues to grow, and it makes me feel restless, this many people in one place.

In the distance, church bells echo, and as if on cue, our line moves. The line adjacent to us is half a pace slower. A girl clutching a bag nearly drops it when she rushes three steps forward.

She sees me look at her, and color rises to her cheeks.

It becomes a dance for all of us. A few steps forward and wait. A few steps more. We crawl closer to the corner, and with every step we take, my heartbeat kicks up a notch. I want to be able to flap my hands, or pace, or tell Leah what's going on. Anything to distract me from the restlessness building up inside of me.

Nia has found her own way to cope. She crumples the piece of paper between her fingers, straightens it, and does the same all over again. If I lean in close enough, I can hear her whisper the words we agreed on.

On my left, the girl with the bag reaches into her pocket and produces a similar card to the one the guy in front of us has, and my breath lodges in my chest.

I elbow Nia. "I think they have ID of some sort."

She pales. "We don't."

"I know. Maybe we'll get it if we make our case?"

"If we don't, Emerson has a problem too."

"Yeah."

Emerson hasn't joined a line yet. They're holding back to keep a good distance between the three of us so no one can accuse us of colluding.

The nervous excitement makes way for ice-cold fear. It makes every step feel like a mile, and as the time crawls by and the sun arcs across the sky, the only option I have is to follow Nia's lead and go through our text line by line.

Until we're there.

The soldier behind the table does not show any recognition. He doesn't look like he was at the barricade when we first escaped. But he raises his head and holds out a gloved hand. "Ration card please."

Nia clears her throat—and clears it again. "Sir, we're from the Hope Juvenile Treatment Center, several miles up the road from here. There are fourteen of us left, less than half of who we were. We're in dire need of food too."

With the masks and face shields, it's hard to tell if the soldier shows any reaction to Nia's story. But he's still holding out his hand. "Do you have a ration card?"

"No, sir. We weren't offered—" Nia clears her throat again. "We weren't informed of the rations. We weren't given any cards, but we believe we have a right to—"

"No cards, no rations," the soldier interrupts her.

Nia wavers, and I reach out to steady her. "Sir, you don't

understand. We are all minors. There are fourteen of us left, and we're hungry."

Her words are met with murmuring from the people around. The girl in the line adjacent to us is staring from us to the soldier and back, her eyes hard. The man who left the line in front of us has crossed the street and glowers. Someone behind us tells us to stop holding up the distribution.

Another soldier jumps off the truck and walks toward us. She glances at her colleague. "Any trouble here?"

Nia is full on trembling now. "We don't want to cause any trouble, we just want food. We want to find a way to make it through this too."

The soldier looks down on both of us. Her voice holds an indifferent edge when she says, "This food is allocated to Sam's Throne and the people here. If you want to claim rations, I suggest you contact the state officials or private company in charge of your care."

"We have no working internet or phones," Nia throws back. "How are we supposed to do that?"

"That is not my problem. Perhaps you can come into town and find assistance here." The soldier gestures vaguely at the people around us, who are either staring or have taken a step or two back. The guy across the street is joined by another familiar face—Store Guy, gun and all. He's talking and gesturing, and his face is turning a threatening shade of red. Wolves, the lot of them. I'm sure they'll be dying to help us.

She turns on her heels toward the trucks, and the other soldier shoos us to the side.

"No card, no rations. Clear the line, please."

My heart sinks, and my shoulders drop. Next to me, Nia's breath hitches.

No cards, no rations.

We're so hungry.

The soldier is resolute, and someone behind us grumbles for us to hurry, and we may be surrounded by more people than I can wrap my head around, but I've never felt so lonely and so forgotten before. I reach for Nia's sleeve and pull her away, because it's the only thing I can do. Because it won't make a difference to them to see us crying.

That's when Store Guy and the guy across the street take a step in our direction.

Without taking my eyes off them, I nudge Nia and sign, "Careful. They're dangerous."

I've barely finished the thought when Store Guy points at us. At me. "Thief!"

One of the veins at his temple throbs, and his neck bulges.

The voices and murmurs of the crowd around us become a tidal wave, and my breath catches.

"We gotta go!" Nia shouts. And we don't hesitate for a moment longer. We *run*, while the other man shouts, "Someone stop her! Stop them both!"

I glance behind me to see that he's grabbed his shotgun, but his eyes are darting between us and the soldiers who are making their way toward them. No one responds to his call, though everyone's turned to look at what's happening.

We duck and weave around people in their endless lines and the trees that line the pavement, trying to get away from the street as quickly as possible, but it's crowded enough that it's hard to put distance between us.

And Store Guy has his gun too. He doesn't seem to care about the soldiers or the eyes on him. He seems to be breathing hard, and if possible, he's even redder than he was before. He tracks me with his barrel, closes an eye, and lowers his shoulders.

I turn away and keep running.

Bang.

thirty-one
GRACE

THE GUNSHOT ECHOES ACROSS THE square. There are screams everywhere. The lines for the food move as if simultaneously, with everyone jumping back and cowering. I can still hear the echo of Reid's words.

We're too close now. Don't you see? I can't go back. I can't. I can't. I have to try.

Riley stumbles to her feet from our hiding point, and I leap forward to grab her leg to stop her. My ears ring. My eyes burn. Riley trembles under my grasp. "Grace! Logan! We have to—"

"No!" I don't want to lose anyone else. I *can't*.

"I have to get to them. This is exactly why I hated this plan!"

"We can't."

Riley reaches out to me and turns my face in the direction of the trucks. "We *can*."

Store Guy has dropped to his knees, and he is cradling his wrist. His gun lies a few feet in front of him. Three soldiers circle around him, their own guns at the ready. Another two have grabbed the other guy by the soldiers. "Violence will not be tolerated," one of the soldiers says loudly, for the crowd's benefit as much as the men, it seems. "Open carrying is in direct violation of the rules of distribution and—"

I stop listening. I crawl forward out of our hiding space and attempt to locate Logan and Nia. They're both huddling against each other but pushing themselves to their feet again.

I breathe out hard. I want to vomit. I want to curl up within myself and stay here and let the world be the world and just forget about it. I want to cry. I want to sleep.

I want to go home.

"*Now* you should go to them," I manage. I force my hand to let go of Riley's leg and allow myself a second or three to breathe, to push through the fear and the fatigue.

Riley massages her leg, and she nods. "Yeah, I should."

"Is Emerson still in line?"

Emerson joined the line when Nia and Logan reached the front of it, to keep as much of a distance between them as possible. Riley stands on tiptoe and points. "There."

I follow her mark and find Emerson being shuffled back and forth along with everyone else while soldiers shout orders at them to line up properly. Their shoulders are up to their ears, and they fidget with a sleeve. They don't have a ration card or ID either.

Fuck. I hate it, but we're still here on a mission. We still need the food. We need a ration card, and there's only one thing left to do. I know what I have to do.

"Can you watch them too?" I ask.

Riley nods. "Where are you going?"

"I'll be back soon."

She frowns. "Grace..."

"I'm going to try a thing, but I have to do it alone." I rub my eyes. Riley would hate it if she knew, and for all the right reasons too.

"Promise me you'll be careful? We may not agree on much," she says with a rueful smile, "but Hope needs you."

I can't promise that. "I'll do my best."

She stares at me like she's trying to read my mind. I don't look away from it. I don't wince.

Eventually, she shakes her head. "Fine. Do what needs to be done." With that, she turns and darts out of her hiding place, toward the girls. I give it a moment to make sure no one sees her or attempts to stop her, and then I turn away.

I take my copy of our carefully constructed map out of my pocket and backtrack our route into town. When I leave the main square behind me, the crowd's voices dissipate too. The only thing I hear is the pounding of my heartbeat in my ears, the echo of the gunshot, and the yowling of an angry cat a few blocks down. My legs feel like lead, and my head is spinning. Every time we try to find help, someone shoots at us.

I can't get Casey's words out of my mind. We *are* the only ones who can save ourselves.

I find my way back to the church, with all its small remembrances, and from there I turn toward one of my familiar routes. I know all the houses by heart here. The ones we've cleared out, the ones on our list as maybes. The ones that have been cleared out by officials, though those are few and far between.

And the ones with new slashes on their doors. Markings that weren't there two days ago. On "my" block are three new houses. I pass them by twice before I make my decision. Not the bright, two-story house with the two pink bicycles lying on top of each other outside the garage, where a young girl stares out of the window but doesn't see me pass by. Not the single-story bungalow with all the curtains drawn and an angry slash on the door.

I stop in front of a house with a chaotic lawn and meticulously landscaped plants outside the door. The plague slash across the door is shimmering.

We never found ration cards in any of the other houses. We didn't know to look for them, of course. But if what the letter says is right, they've handed out rations before, so the cards would only be in new houses.

Plague houses.

Here.

We can't wait another couple of weeks.

I fold the map and put it back in my pocket. I've entered houses like this before, so I know the way, but I hate it. No one in their right minds would enter a plague house. I breathe in deeply and grab my mask, and I circle around the house. I find my way in through the kitchen window...

And enter a house that doesn't reek of death. Not yet.

Instead, it looks clean. Pots and pans hang from a rack above the counter, and the kitchen spoons and utensils peek out of a colorful ceramic jar. I'm not entirely sure what it's meant to portray, but it looks like a child's school project. A kitchen towel with lace and flowers hangs from one of the cabinet doors.

I ball my hands into fists and push my fists into my pockets. My instincts tell me to run and not look back. To raid the fridge and the kitchen cabinets and leave the rations card. There may be enough to keep us going for another two days, and who knows what the world will look like then.

I shake my head. The world will still look the same in two days. Lonely and hungry. And the next rations delivery won't be for another month. I tenderly walk toward the living room. The house is quiet. Quieter than I would like it. It makes me feel like everything around me is holding its breath and the walls themselves have eyes.

Then the floorboards creak.

"What are you doing here?" a voice rasps from directly behind me.

I want to spin around, but a stabbing sensation in my back prevents me.

"Answer me, girl."

I slowly raise my hands—and all my words flee.

"Are you ignorant, or do you have a death wish? Is that why you entered a plague house?" the person continues. The voice is so raw and croaking that it's impossible to tell anything about the person speaking.

"May I turn around?" I ask, with my hands still high.

After some hesitation, the stabbing sensation disappears. I take that as agreement and ever so slowly spin to face the inhabitant of the house. I keep my hands visible and make no sudden movements. And my breath catches in my throat.

In front of me stands an elderly woman, probably in her early eighties. She has long, silver hair and cold, blue eyes. Red blotches mar her face, and she has blood splatters on her blue woolen cardigan. Her hands are frail and her posture unsteady.

I take a step back right when she starts coughing, and my heart sinks.

"Speak up, girl," she says, when she's regained her breath. "Do I need to call the police?"

I laugh. I can't help it. I'm terrified and tired, and this is absurd. Are there even police officers anymore? "My name is

Grace," I say. "I live at the Hope Juvenile Treatment Center, and we're hungry."

The woman lets the kitchen knife she's holding drop an inch or so. "Yes, and?"

"My friend is lining up for rations today, but they need a rations card. No one will give us anything otherwise."

"So you thought you'd sneak into a plague house and steal a card for yourself?" Contrary to her angry words, the woman lowers the knife farther. "What an absurd idea."

"I know," I admit. I didn't even let myself think about it too hard. "But I don't know if I could find a card anywhere else, and I'd hoped, since your sign is still so recent…" I stop when I realize how that must sound.

She has no such qualms. "You hoped I'd be dead but our food and our bodies not yet looted."

I don't—I *can't* deny it. "Yes."

She doesn't shout at me. She doesn't tell me to get out. She doesn't have to. I'm here already, aren't I? "You weren't given any food?"

"No food. No care. No way to contact our families." I keep my voice as steady as I can.

"And you didn't get sick?"

In the back of my mind, a small voice is shouting at me. Telling me to leave the house, get away from the woman, run while I still can. But instead, I sag down on the nearest chair— one of those old, leather armchairs—and I tell her. I tell her everything from the first night until now, like a waterfall of words and stories that needs to make its way out of my brain.

The old woman walks to a chair opposite mine with considerable difficulty and sits down. "And so you thought it would be better to die trying to find a solution than go back empty-handed."

Yes. I promised Casey that too, though I didn't say it out loud. "I may be lucky."

"You may be." She doesn't sound convinced. She wavers back and forth on her chair. She opens the drawer of a coffee table and pulls out two cards. "One of these belonged to my children. My Marcus went to get it when they—" She swallows. "The other one is ours. You should take both, for as long as they'll work. I'll have no use for them soon."

My breath catches. I feel faint. "Are you sure?"

The woman smiles, and it makes the coldness in her eyes thaw a little. But then she coughs again, and when she holds up a handkerchief to her lips, I can see the blood spatters. "I'm certain."

She hesitates then pulls out a cell phone with the charger still plugged in. "Take this as well. Some of you should be able to call home. Some of you should be able to contact your families before this is all over."

I'm too tired and relieved to be emotional, but I reach out to her regardless. I cover her hand with mine before I can think better of it. "Thank you. *Thank you.*"

She looks at my hand over hers and shakes her head. "I'm sorry."

I'm blocks away from the house before I realize I don't even know her name. I cling to the cards and the phone like they're made from solid gold. They're as valuable.

I make it back to the line well before it's Emerson's turn. They see me coming and frown. "Grace?"

I turn one of the ration cards in my pocket over between my fingers before I take it out. I hold it up. "You forgot this."

Emerson's eyes widen, but to their credit, they don't say anything to give the game away, and I ignore the question in their eyes.

I keep my distance. I have to. Just to be sure. I focus on what matters: one card for Emerson and one card for Riley.

I bite my lip. "Find the others on your way home? I still have to collect something for Sofia." I hope they understand my flimsy excuse. The traps seemed like the best reason to leave the others for now. Just until I know I'm safe. Until I know they are too.

Emerson takes a step toward me, but I shake my head. "Stay in line, please."

"Grace…"

"*Please.*" I toss the card in their direction.

They snatch it from the air and immediately wince. "I will. I—"

"I'll see you back home."

thirty-two
EMERSON

WE HEAD HOME WITH TWO boxes of food, medication, and other essentials. Logan helps me carry one, pulling far more of the weight than I can, and Nia helps Riley. She's laughing at something Riley said, and despite the fact that the boxes are heavy, the return journey feels lighter than it has...ever since I arrived here, probably. Today, it feels like we're walking home with our future in our hands.

Logan is the only one who looks around her with a kind of frown, and I know what—or rather, who—she's looking for.

"Grace will find her own way back to Hope," I mumble.

Her half smile doesn't reach her eyes.

"I'm worried too," I admit.

The ration card burns a hole in my pocket, and I don't want

to know what she did to obtain it. I can guess, and that's bad enough. My Saint Jude medal bounces against my shirt, and the sensation fills me with emptiness and comfort and resolve. *Pray for us. Pray for Grace.* I cannot lose someone else. Not again.

When we get back to Hope, Josie is the pacing in front of the entrance. She all but jumps when she spots us and immediately runs back inside to call out our arrival. By the time we actually reach the gates, every single person who can be outside to greet us is.

We place the boxes on the grass in front of us and collectively take a deep breath. The boxes aren't too heavy, and the trek isn't too long, but the combination is absolutely exhausting, and while my wrist is improving, this *hurts*. I waver.

Casey is the first to walk out to greet us. His eyes dart from the boxes to the four of us, though he keeps a distance, like we agreed.

"Where is Grace?"

"She went to check the traps on the way here," I tell him. I hope to God my lie isn't as obvious as hers. "She isn't back yet?"

"She isn't." Casey sighs, and I can hear him think and worry. "What happened?"

"We needed ration cards," I say. I outline what happened in the broadest strokes, and Casey grows paler. "I don't know about Grace, but we didn't get into contact with anyone but the soldiers. Everyone else kept a careful distance, and they all had protective clothing." I raise my voice on that last sentence, loud enough that Mackenzi can hear from the door opening. She nods.

"We'll all keep to our rooms for a couple of days," Nia says. She leans against Logan, who doesn't appear to be bothered by it. "Like we agreed. But I'd like to see what's in the boxes before we all go our separate ways."

Logan signs something, and Nia laughs. "Someone will need to take inventory too. And cook for us."

"Let's take the boxes to the cafeteria. We can unpack them there," Casey says.

"Perfect. You can do the unpacking. We'll eat and watch," Riley grumbles. But she smiles. We all smile when we grab the boxes and follow the others into the building. Several times I catch someone else glancing back at us and smiling, whispering excitedly.

It sends a thrill up my spine. We come bearing gifts, and this feels like Christmas in a way even Christmas never did. Gold, incense, and myrrh have got nothing on the promise of food when you haven't had a full meal in several weeks.

We place the boxes on the center table inside the cafeteria, and then the four of us withdraw to one of the farthest tables in the room. Casey retrieves a knife and cleaning products from the kitchen, while Josie places meals on another table. I can't help but laugh when I realize it's pieces of toast—from the slightly-moldy-but-not-quite-off bread we found in town—and what remains of the fish Sofia caught earlier this week. Bread and fish. How appropriate.

Casey surveys the room while we tear into the food like hungry wolves. "Should we wait for Grace?"

The four of us nod, but everyone else thinks differently.

"Open it up!"

"We've been waiting all day!"

"She'll be back soon enough!"

"Maybe there'll be chocolate!"

I can't pinpoint who says that, but Riley snorts.

Casey still hesitates.

"I don't think she would want us to wait," Sofia says, and that's what convinces him. He takes the knife and carefully slides open the packaging tape around both the boxes.

And when he unpacks, the rest of the world lies forgotten. Even Isabella, who is bundled up and propped against the wall, cranes her neck to see everything.

Heavy bags of rice and pasta. Flour and sugar. Two boxes of cereal elicit the first *oohs* and *aahs*, even if we have no fresh milk to go with them. But there is powdered milk. Bags of lentils and beans too. Boxed mac and cheese. Two jars of peanut butter. Mayonnaise and ketchup and pancake mix. Never before has canned meat looked so good, not to mention pasta sauce and canned vegetables. Granola bars and dried fruit. Both boxes have canned peaches too, and when Casey pulls out the first can of condensed milk, Mackenzi *whimpers*.

"I could make peach cake." The words are filled with so much longing, and they're so blatantly absurd coming from her, that we all laugh. Isabella giggles and coughs and giggles again. It's relief and hope and *joy*.

"Let's make sure we have enough first," Casey says, attempting to remain practical.

But, of all people, it's Isaiah who opposes him. "We could make something special since we didn't collectively celebrate any holidays. We could celebrate our own."

"Food day?" someone suggests.

"Peach cake day!"

From there, everything else we unpack is magic. No chocolate, unfortunately, but animal crackers and a carton of fruit juice in each box. Enough for all of us to have a sip. Toilet paper, soap, and toothpaste. The soap is of a better quality than anything I've ever seen here. Laundry detergent and hand sanitizer. Even pads and tampons for those of us with periods. Mine is infrequent at best, but it's good to have the option.

Finally, inside both, a smaller box: supplies for our medicine cabinet. Casey clings to those a second longer than he needs to. He has Tylenol, Advil, Band-Aids, antiseptic solution, and bandages. Other pills in marked bottles.

When we're done unpacking, the ration card still burns a hole in my pocket, and Grace hasn't returned. We have two standard family rations of food and pills. It looks like riches.

The cards will ensure we can get more, and that's a gift of immense value.

Mackenzi is holding on to the canned peaches like she uncovered a diamond the size of her fist. Isaiah is petting the instant coffee.

A weight I didn't know I was carrying drops from my shoulders. Nia and Logan smile while they look at the stack of food, like they're already mentally adjusting their inventory lists. Isabella shares a few tender, careful words with Isaiah. She's grown pale and weary, but she's glowing.

"Will the cards keep working?" Mackenzi asks, once the four of us have finished our food and our new supplies have been transferred to the kitchen. It's clear she's asking Riley, though why she would know anything is beyond me.

True to form, Riley shrugs. "Probably. As long as they don't know the original owners are gone."

"It's been a while since they cleared out houses too," Logan says, with Nia interpreting. "As long as we keep using the cards, they will just assume everything's okay."

Mackenzi laughs. "Well, in that case…"

"An endless supply of food!" Khalil grins, and his words are met with cheers.

Logan tilts her head, and I wink. It's technically not endless. We'll need to be careful and continue to ration properly. But that's splitting hairs. It's endless in all the ways that matter. It's certainty, when we haven't had that in months.

Only Casey frowns. He gestures for me to step away from the others, and I do, but we keep a distance between us, so it's not like we can have a very subtle conversation.

"Where's Grace?" he asks again.

"She'll be back soon, I think." I hope.

He scoffs. "She did something foolish, didn't she?"

I shake my head. I have a decent idea of where Grace got those cards and the risks she must have taken. "She did something right," I say. "She may have saved us."

He winces. "That's exactly what I'm worried about."

Perhaps, in a way, I am too. I stack the plates we used and put them on a table between the four of us and the rest of the group. Josie collects them and brings them to the kitchen. "Don't worry, I'll take note of the inventory," she says, as Logan and Nia filter out.

Logan narrows her eyes, but she nods. She isn't as used to working with Josie as I am, but I can only imagine she will be soon enough. Josie's mellowed—or maybe we all have.

Everyone gives us wide berth while we move to our rooms. By chance more than purpose, we're the only four left in the east wing, so it's easy enough to quarantine. Now that we've done what we needed to do, Nia is yawning, and Riley is flagging too. Logan doesn't show fatigue, but her gaze has turned inward.

I don't want to go back yet. With the adrenaline rush of this entire endeavor well and truly gone, my arm is screaming at me, and it's making me restless.

"I'm going for a stroll in the garden," I say to no one in particular before I get to my room.

Riley narrows her eyes, but nods. "Make sure you avoid the others."

"I *know*."

She waves her hand at my annoyance. "Good. Because we're going to have to get back for more supplies in another couple of weeks." She walks to her room with a smile and an uncharacteristic bounce in her step.

My feet drag by the time I get to the garden. I cradle my wrist to my chest, using the gap between the buttons on my shirt to support my wrist, like I'm some eighteenth-century lord instead of a tired, hurting teenage gravedigger. Definitely don't remember seeing that on my high school career test.

I circle around the vegetable garden toward the graves, when someone coughs.

I freeze, out of habit. Out of fear. My mouth goes dry, and my palms are sweaty. "Who's there?" The words are soft even in this silent winter night, so I clear my throat and try again.

No response but another bout of coughing.

I take a step toward the sound to see if anyone needs help. I take a step back to stay out of range. I'm torn within myself.

We've kept the plague out of Hope for weeks. Did any of us bring it back?

Oh.

My heart sinks.

No.

I lean forward and manage to make out a shadowy figure sitting against the fence. She's a shadow against the star-filled, moonless sky overhead. She's huddled up and has her shoulders pulled up to her ears. She's breathing hard, and she's ghostly pale.

"Grace?"

She lifts her head to face me, and her eyes are nearly black in this light. "Emerson. No. Go away."

I don't. Of course I don't. I don't ask her what happened either, because the answer is painfully obvious. "You should come in. Casey can take care of you."

"No." She shakes her head. "I'm not going to be responsible for another outbreak in Hope. I just... I wanted to be close, you know? Nowhere else to go and all that."

"I can go get him," I say. "He can help you here. We have new medication thanks to the rations. Nothing to help with the plague, but perhaps he has something to ease your throat. Make you more comfortable. It isn't much, but—others have survived, Grace. It's going to be okay." I'm rambling, I'm all too aware of it. But she looks smaller than I've ever seen her, and I can't get closer to offer any comfort. She risked her life to get us those ration cards, I know she did. And now...

"Can I at least get you a blanket?" I suggest weakly. "You need to stay warm."

She laughs, and when she breathes in, she wheezes. "I'm okay. I'm not too cold."

"Grace..."

"You shouldn't be here," she says. The words obviously take effort. She swallows hard and groans. "Go away. Please."

"Neither should you, but here we are," I counter. I keep my voice in check as best I can. "So I'm going to find you a blanket, and I'm going to warn Case. We'll keep our distance, I promise. But we won't let you be alone."

I run, don't walk, back to the main building and whisper a prayer with a fervor I've never felt before. To God, if he's out there. To the world around me. To all of us.

Please. Please. Not Grace.

Phone call between Grace and Mr. Podolsky

PODOLSKY: Hello?

GRACE: Mr. Podolsky? It's Grace. I don't know if you remember me but—[cough]

PODOLSKY: Grace? Of course I remember. You were a young child—young girl—when you lived with us. You were... What do they call it? A bright young thing.

PODOLSKY: Why are you calling?

GRACE: [cough]

PODOLSKY: Are you ill?

GRACE: I'm okay. I—I wanted to call to say thank you.

PODOLSKY: For what?

GRACE: ...

PODOLSKY: Grace?

GRACE: Are you and Baba all right?

PODOLSKY: We're fine. What did you want to say?

GRACE: I'm glad.

GRACE: I...

GRACE: Do you remember you taught me how to build snare traps? I didn't think they'd ever come in handy again, but they did. [cough] It helped us survive.

PODOLSKY: You were a survivor from the moment you came to us. Elena saw it too. I only gave you tools to make it easier.

GRACE: That's not true. And that's not why I wanted to thank you.

GRACE: You gave me a place to belong. You gave me a place where I felt safe and cared for. You gave me a universe that felt endless and timeless. You gave me dreams of Paris. *That's* what made me a survivor.

GRACE: That's why we're all surviving.

PODOLSKY: Grace—

GRACE: I gotta go. I...[cough] I needed you to know that.

GRACE: Thank you.

This phone call has been disconnected.

thirty-three
LOGAN

GRACE EXPOSED HERSELF TO THE *plague to get those ration cards.*

We all know what happened. Word spreads, whether Grace wants it to or not. She doesn't want to come in. She doesn't want anyone to get close. And it's not how it's supposed to be. She's supposed to go to the infirmary and allow Casey to treat her. She's supposed to recover and be a part of this—this weird family we've built.

But I don't think she will. Everyone in Hope goes to see her at some point during the day. Riley and Nia and I keep ourselves away from the others and stick to our rooms as much as we can, but we do too. It's Grace. We can't just ignore her or what she did.

When I walk over to the garden right before lunch, Emerson

is standing near the fruit trees. They keep an eye out to make sure no one gets too close—including themself. They're fiddling with the necklace around their neck.

Grace is bundled up in blankets. She's sitting in the shade of the shed, sheltered from all the things that can't harm her anyway. She has a cell phone lying in her lap. She looks at me with bloodshot eyes and determination and something so close to anger.

I don't know what to say to her. I have to figure something out.

I take a step back and nearly collide with Casey, who is running back and forth between the garden and the infirmary, between the people he's forced to protect and the best friend he has to let go. He swerves at the last possible instant, taking care to keep a distance between us. "Sorry, Logan."

"It's okay," I sign.

He's holding a plastic water bottle in his hands, and he seems intent on rolling it in Grace's direction. To take care of her, even if she won't allow him to come close enough.

It's *not* okay. He's grieving and hurting, like all of us and more. He needs to be with Grace, especially now.

I narrow my eyes and clear my throat.

Grace shakes her head. "What do you want?"

I need her to look at me, otherwise I have no way to tell her what I want to say. I tap my fingers against my leg and wait.

She sighs but turns. "What is it, Logan?"

"Tell Casey to stay here," I say.

She coughs, and a little trail of blood trickles down her chin. "No. Absolutely not."

"He needs you, and you need him. I'll mind the infirmary today."

"I need him to go inside and stop hovering around me. I need all of you to go back inside."

I don't point out the obvious. If she didn't want us to care for her, she shouldn't have come back here. Because I get it. When everything is too scary and too overwhelming, we all want to go home. That's why we're together.

Casey tries to figure out what's happening between the two of us. "What did she say, Grace?"

"Nothing."

"*Grace.*" The pleading in his voice is sharp and painful.

"*Fine.*" Grace takes a deep breath, and she immediately starts gasping for air again. "Logan says you should stay here. She'll keep watch at the infirmary today."

Casey's breath hitches. "I couldn't let you…"

"Think about it," Emerson says, with a dark look in Grace's direction. They've knelt next to the vegetable beds and are pulling out stray weeds with their unbroken arm. "It may be the only place we could safely go while we wait out if any of us—if anyone else picked up the plague. If we're infected—or infectious—it's not like Leah or Xavier would care, right?"

"I don't *know.*" His eyes find mine, and they're so full

of doubt and uncertainty. "I don't know if they can be infected again. I don't know if they're still infectious. I don't know if they're strong enough. Are you willing to risk it?"

That's one of the main reasons why he always kept me—and all of us—out. This disease has always been too serious to gamble on a what-if. Am I willing to risk it? We need each other, now more than ever.

"You don't know if *they're* still infectious?" Emerson shakes their head. "After two months? Be reasonable, Case."

"He's right," Grace croaks.

"He's not, but even if he was, it's the same risk we already took when we went into town," Emerson says. "We won't leave you here to die, Grace. Not alone."

"Please." Casey's plea isn't directed at Grace but at me, and I take that as all the permission I'll need.

I nod at him. I nod at Grace. I don't know what else to say but simply, "Thank you," and with that, I run.

I hesitate in front of the infirmary door. I've wanted to go in here countless times. Some sleepless nights, I made plans to steal in to see Leah. Other times I hoped I would fall ill too, just to be with her. I tried to convince Casey to let me in approximately ninety-seven times, and while I understand why he said no every time, I didn't like it. I even stopped asking for a while, when she began resting easier, because I was terrified to somehow jinx it. I collected glances and moments, from the door opening, through the window, through the letter that Casey read to her. I saw her blink. I saw her seize. I saw her sip from a cup of water Casey held for her.

But now I'm here. I'm finally here.

I take a deep breath, flatten my fingers along my leg, and immediately start tapping again.

I push the door open.

The infirmary is one of the brightest rooms in the building, with light filtering in through the window and white sheets on the beds. Or off-white. They've been washed and cleaned of blood too many times to count. Casey has food and water set up on the nurse's desk, and next to it lies one of the torn-up books from our little library. It's dog-eared and dirty, and he's used a pencil as bookmark.

It's hard to imagine this place was overflowing only a couple of weeks ago. Now, three of the beds are cleanly made, and only Xavier and Leah are in here.

Leah.

She lies on the bed closest to the door, farthest from the window. She's all wrapped up in her blanket, like she's been tossing and turning. Her hair falls in strands across her face. It's longer than I remember. Her face has fallen in, and it's more angular. She looks older.

Or perhaps I feel older.

She has one hand above the blankets, clutching the fabric,

and I can't stop myself. I all but dive for it, my fingers curling around hers. I don't even have eyes for Xavier, who lies two beds down. I want to stand by my sister, be close to her, feel complete again for the first time since the world ended. She's warmer than I expected, because she looks so pale. At least she isn't burning up like she was the night they carried her in.

I have so much to tell you.

With my thumb, I rub circles across the back of her hand. I wait for her to open her eyes, but she doesn't. She doesn't turn to me.

Leah.

I need to be closer, or I might burst, and the only thing I can think to do is crawl beside her. Careful, balancing on the edge of the bed so I don't jostle or overwhelm her, but close enough that the warmth her body radiates mingles with mine. Close enough that we're whole and complete together. It's intoxicating and *right*, and it makes me feel like my skin can't contain me.

I wrap my fingers around hers again. I could fall asleep like this. No matter what happens outside of this room, no matter what happens tomorrow or the day after. It may be selfish, it may be horrible, but I could fall asleep now and feel safe in the knowledge that I'm home with her.

Inside my hands, Leah's fingers twitch.

I pull back so hard, I nearly tumble out of the bed again.

"Leah?"

She turns her head to me ever so slowly while I teeter on the edge, and I forget how to breathe. To be here with her is every-thing, and it would be enough. But to see her, to *talk* to her...

She squeezes her eyes shut, like she's flinching away from something. Her lips are dry and cracked, and a few strands of hair tumble across her face. With a trembling hand, I reach out to push the hair behind her ear.

That's when she opens her eyes.

Hazel eyes and so many questions. Her gaze wanders the room before it settles on me. She frowns. She doesn't push herself up into a sitting position. She stares at me for a long time before I see the recognition click. She opens her mouth, and no sound comes out.

But she opens her hand and reaches out to me, and nothing else matters. There are so many different ways to communicate, and this is our language. She's my person who understands all the things I can't say or write or even sign. And I'll be hers.

Our fingers entwine, and once she feels them, she pulls our hands up to her cheek to keep me close.

I adjust my position so I'm lying comfortably, and I let her hold me. I cling to her. Until her grasp weakens, and she falls asleep again.

I grab the chair from the desk, and I sit with her while she sleeps. I sit with her until she wakes. We hold hands. We stare at each other. We don't have to do anything else. Here, we can just be.

I tell her all the things she needs to know. About Nia and the ration cards and Sofia and Grace. About the survivors in Sam's

Throne and our strange, small community here. I tell her how at ease I feel in the kitchen.

"Maybe, on the other side of the plague, we'll find a way to be together and just live. That wouldn't be half bad, right? I'll find a job. I'll provide for us. I make a very decent raccoon stew. Though that may not be a very popular dish in a new world…"

I don't know if Leah can tell the signs from each other, if she can understand what I'm saying, but it doesn't matter. She's staring at me like she's drinking in my presence, and when I talk, she smiles.

"We survived so much, we'll keep surviving. Together. I'll make sure no one will ever attempt to separate us again."

Because if Leah trying to protect me is what brought us here, I will do—I have done—anything I can to protect Leah now. I learned how to fight, and I'll fight for what I want.

"Maybe Nia could stay with us too, if she has nowhere better to go. We could try out new recipes. We could hold on to each other. We could be home."

I already know how our lives will look. A small apartment with a dozen cats, like we dreamed of. It won't be anything like any of the houses I broke into, but quiet and colorful and safe.

It'll be at the edge of a small town, somewhere near the woods or hills or a creek, so I can go for long walks in the middle of the night.

And everyone who would happen by or come stay with us would hear the best sound in the world. The two of us, laughing.

thirty-four
GRACE

"IT HURTS, CASE."

"I know, Star Kid."

It's night again. I don't have to climb out of my window to see the stars, but in a cruel turn of fate, the sky is overcast. The clouds are fluffy and bright, like a blanket over all of us. Snow sky, Mr. Podolsky used to call this, though it rarely ever snowed.

I cough again. Every breath feels like I'm breathing in small shards of glass instead of oxygen, but every time I gasp for air, Casey counts with me. Hyperventilating now would only make things worse.

Not that it matters much.

I'm glad he's here. I'm glad Emerson is here too. They've stopped trying to convince me to come inside, and instead they've set up camp. Both of them have wrapped themselves in a blanket and are keeping quiet watch at a careful distance. They both have empty plates next to them, from food that Josie brought and left nearby. I didn't pay attention to what they ate. I can't quite remember. They each have a thermos with steaming-hot tea, the flasks stolen from the guard station and thoroughly cleaned. I have my water bottle. It's lying next to me, within reach but untouched.

"I really wish those aliens would have landed," I say, when the silence gets too deep and uncomfortable.

Casey pulls up the corner of his mouth into a crooked smile. "What was it again? We would all get eaten by giant penguins? Or hamsters? Face-huggers and chest-bursters."

"Squirrels."

"We should try to eat them instead, see how they like it," he muses.

"Maybe Sofia can—" I don't manage another whole sentence before my breath runs out. I gasp and cough until my entire body is trembling. My diaphragm feels like it's on fire, and my shoulders and back are aching. The cold air does not help either. "Maybe Sofia can—maybe she can set traps."

I try, I really do, but it's hard to lighten the mood when you're suffocating.

Casey and Emerson exchange a worried glance, and I groan. Not out of pain but out of frustration. "Don't treat me like I'm dying," I say, in between shallow breaths. "Treat me like I'm here."

Casey flinches at that word. *Dying*. Emerson merely tilts their head.

"Do you regret it?" Emerson asks, softly.

"What?"

"Going into town. Whatever it is that brought you here. Any of it."

I pull my knees up to my chest, making myself as small as possible. It does not make breathing easier, but it makes me feel less exposed. I consider the question. It may be the cold or the fatigue, or it may be the fever, but I struggle to formulate my thoughts.

"No. I don't regret it. Any of it."

I don't regret pulling Ian off that girl and helping her, because I wouldn't have been able to justify walking away from someone who needed help. I regret the consequences, but those are hardly my fault.

I don't regret going with the others into town. Not the first night. Not any night since.

And I absolutely don't regret breaking into that last house to get us the cards we needed, the cards that will—hopefully—allow the others to survive. It was necessary.

Although—

"I regret one thing."

Casey waits until I stop coughing to ask, "What do you regret?"

"I regret thinking that no one cares about us."

"*Who* cares?" Emerson scoffs, and they immediately turn bright red when I look at them.

I breathe in hard, and I somehow manage to pull up the corner of my mouth. "*I* do. I've always cared."

Casey turns away from me and rests his head on his knees. His hands tremble. He's pale with cold or pain too. "Fuck, Grace."

What a harsh night. I always imagined we'd stay in touch after Hope. You can't share your nightmares and night terrors with someone without forming a lifelong bond, and I liked the idea of both of us grown up and having it all figured out. Better.

I didn't imagine it would end like this.

"I don't want to die, Case," I tell him honestly. "I'm scared."

"I know, I am too." He reaches out a hand like he wants to hold mine, even though we're too far apart.

And even though we're too far apart, I do the same.

"People survive, Grace," he tries, not for the first time. His voice is as raw and ragged as mine, but I know it's grief, not plague.

I manage a weak smile. "I wouldn't mind that."

Eventually, my arm becomes too heavy, and I cannot hold it up any longer. I've never been as tired as I am now. My body is heavy and weak at the same time. Breathing is a struggle. I want to close my eyes.

"We'll be okay though, Grace," Emerson says, their words barely carrying through the garden. I force my eyes open again.

They're toying with their necklace. "We have food. We have coffee. We have each other. We'll make it through."

"You better," I manage. "I didn't go through all this trouble—"

"We *will*," Casey interrupts me. "I told you. We'll save ourselves."

I smile. Another bout of coughing racks through me. I double over and clutch my stomach. Everything hurts. If my bones could crawl out of my body, I'm certain they would. Is this how all the plague victims felt? I hate it.

"Good, because I want you to work at a hospital when you grow up," I say. I'd point at him, but I don't want to move too much. My voice isn't as strong as it was. "Be the coolest doctor or nurse on the block."

"And you." I turn slightly in Emerson's direction. "I want you to find a place where you belong. Where you find your place in the universe again."

"What about you?" Casey asks. He scrunches up his face and amends, "I mean, in an ideal situation?"

"Stop trying to make me laugh," I scold, though it's hard to sound stern when you're constantly coughing.

He winces, so I talk.

I tell them about Paris and the Podolskys and my father and the picture. I admit I dreamed about going back to school, even though I'm still not sure if that was ever for me.

"You'd make an excellent therapist," Emerson whispers.

I've always been more comfortable talking with others about their issues than admitting to my own worries and fears.

"Beyond that, I think…" I hesitate. I feel so fragile. "I'd want to create a home for kids like us. A place where they can feel safe and cared for and where they can grow." A home like this, where my heart is. With the outcasts and the rejects and the survivors.

If I can't find my roots, I'll plant new ones.

If I close my eyes, I can see it too. A house, like so many of the ones in Sam's Throne. With a dollhouse on the floor of the living room, and old, leather armchairs, and a vegetable patch in the backyard, and a whole line of persimmon trees. I'd teach every kid about the constellations and how to stand up against bullies and how to always protect your friends.

If I close my eyes, I can hear them call my name in the distance.

I don't know how much of that I say out loud to Casey and Emerson. Truth is, I don't know when I stopped talking and when I started dreaming, but I walk around in this house and feel at home here. I lie in a garden surrounded by carrots and kale and a raggedy shed and feel at home here.

When at last the stars appear, the cold takes over, and I don't even feel pain anymore, like the tension in my shoulders releases and my lungs stop their protesting.

I am watched over by my friends and feel like I belong. None of them will forget about me.

For an ending, it's not a bad way to go.

epilogue
EMERSON

THE WORLD CHANGES AND CHANGES again, but I'm growing used to it. One day, one step at a time.

When the sun comes up, we find a place for Grace to rest. Josie digs a grave between the roots of two trees. Next to the others, but with her own patch of clear sky above her. It's quiet and serene. It's fitting, but it doesn't make it easier.

Unlike with the others, where it was just me or Josie taking care of practicalities, everyone comes out to say goodbye. Sofia is pale and tense. She has her hands balled into fists and she taps rhythmically with one foot. Logan, Riley, and Nia stick to one side, while everyone else aside from Leah and Xavier huddles closely together on the other side. Eleven here. Thirteen in all.

Grace will be the last to die of the plague in Hope. For now. Forever.

None of us who went into town are showing symptoms of the plague. We'll take care for another couple of days, but I'm feeling hopeful.

Hopeful. What a novelty.

Perhaps it's faithful too, this belief in a better world to come. I try not to think about it too hard. I'll take that one step at a time as well. But for now, I know better times are ahead.

We'll remain healthy. We'll be able to go back to Sam's Throne for more food. We'll grow our vegetables and catch fish, and we'll do exactly what we promised Grace. We'll survive. We'll make it all the way to a vaccine or a cure, whichever comes first. And what happens after that… The world we knew is gone. It's up to us to build a new one.

I help Casey tenderly lower Grace into the grave. He said his goodbyes last night. Others have come by this morning or do so now. It's different for everyone. A word. A smile. A gesture. A silence.

I play my violin for her.

Perhaps we should have done this for everyone, but it seems to me we've only now found the space to breathe and consider. And the others are still here. We will remember them, like we will remember her.

I wait until everyone is gone. I sit next to the freshly filled grave and pull the medal I wore to town over my head. The silver shines a little brighter from contact with my skin, and it's warm against my fingers. I weave the fragile chain between my fingers and then sling it over the single white stone Josie placed on the overturned earth.

"You taught me to trust in us," I say. "You taught me to believe in the hopeless cases. Trust I'll find a place to belong."

I sit in silence, until the wind picks up around me and the scant leaves in the trees above me rustle and fall.

When this winter is over, we can plant new fruits and vegetables. We can plant seeds and our garden will flourish. Over time, the graves will be covered in flowers and green and all the stones we can find. It will be a part of us, like we will be a part of it. This place to grieve and dance. To doubt and love.

To heal.

I rock to my feet and stand there for another moment longer, letting the wind play with my hair and dry my tears.

Then I turn and walk to the garden, and from there—on.

Phone call between Emerson and their mother

EMERSON: Mom?

MRS. WARD: Em—

EMERSON: *Emerson*, Mom.

MRS. WARD: Emerson.

MRS. WARD: How—how are you?

EMERSON: Alive.

EMERSON: How are you and Dad?

MRS. WARD: We're...we're alive too. He got sick, but he made it through, by the grace of God.

EMERSON: Of course he did.

MRS. WARD: I'm glad you called. Your father and I had a lot of time to talk after you left. We regret a lot of things we said and did that day.

EMERSON: I didn't *leave*, Mom. You kicked me out.

MRS. WARD: Yes. Yes, of course.

EMERSON: And then you did it again when I got arrested.

MRS. WARD: ...

MRS. WARD: What's your point, Emerson?

EMERSON: I *really like* hearing you use my name. Absurd, isn't it? I know you don't care, but it still matters to me. That's all I ever wanted. For you to see me as I am. That's all I ever asked.

MRS. WARD: I—

EMERSON: My point is, I want you to know you don't have to worry about me, if you did at all.

MRS. WARD: I'm glad—

EMERSON: I don't forgive you.

EMERSON: Maybe I'll practice forgiveness somewhere in the future, like Dad always wanted me to. Maybe I won't. It doesn't concern you.

EMERSON: But I want you to know, I found a place of good earth.

EMERSON: And I'm alive.

This phone call has been disconnected.

Emerson's story is, unfortunately, that of too many young trans and nonbinary people. If you're a trans, nonbinary, or questioning reader and you're in need of support, please consider reaching out to the **Trans Lifeline**, a trans-led organization that connects trans people to the community, support, and resources they need to survive and thrive.

United States (877) 565-8860

Canada (877) 330-6366

translifeline.org

AUTHOR'S NOTE

The fictional Hope Juvenile Treatment Center is set near the equally fictional town of Sam's Throne. The details and makeup of the Hope Center, however, are as real and representative as I could make them. That includes the overwhelming racial inequalities in the juvenile justice system, the lack of support for disabled youth, and—though exaggerated for the purposes of this story—the way people in the justice system are often left forgotten in the wake of a pandemic. Mass incarceration is a human rights disaster, and criminal reform is sorely needed.

In spite of those overwhelming racial inequalities, I chose to make all three of the main characters in this book white. I did so because I do not want to take away space from a writer of color.

And because I don't believe the experience of teens of color in the U.S. criminal justice system is my story to tell.

So instead, I'd love to point you to other spectacular books. If you wish to continue reading about teens interacting with the criminal justice system, these YA titles are a fantastic place to start:

- *Monster* by Walter Dean Myers
- *Dear Martin* and *Dear Justyce* by Nic Stone
- *Allegedly* by Tiffany D. Jackson
- *This Is My America* by Kim Johnson
- *Punching the Air* by Ibi Zoboi and Yusef Salaam (based on a true story)

If you would like to know more about the history of mass incarceration, Michelle Alexander's *The New Jim Crow: Mass Incarceration in the Age of Colorblindness* is a necessary read.

In addition to the titles above, if you wish to keep educating yourself, I would also recommend:

- *Just Mercy: A True Story of the Fight for Justice* by Bryan Stevenson
- *Teen Incarceration: From Cell Bars to Ankle Bracelets* by Patrick Jones
- *Free Cyntoia: My Search for Redemption in the American Prison System* by Cyntoia Brown-Long

ACKNOWLEDGMENTS

I wrote this book while recovering from Covid-19, and during a time when we were (and are) all dealing with our loss of normal, learning to shape our lives around this new fear, and uncovering both the fault lines and the strongest links of our communities. While the virus may not discriminate, the response to the virus often did. So this one goes out to the essential workers, the researchers, the helpers, the teachers, the day-by-day survivors. Thank you.

I was incredibly lucky to work with two amazing agents while writing this book. Thank you to Jennifer Udden, for being such a supporter of this book and every single book of mine in the years we worked together. Thank you to Suzie Townsend and awesome assistant Dani Segelbaum for being there for the next steps. I'm thrilled to work with you and so excited for many more literary adventures on the horizon. And, of course, to everyone on Team New Leaf: you're the absolute best.

Thank you to Eliza Swift, whose wonderful notes and gif comments made this book shine, and the entire team at Sourcebooks, for their passion for stories and for continuously taking such good care of me and my books: Zeina Elhanbaly, Beth Oleniczak, Jackie Douglass, Cassie Gutman, Danielle McNaughton, Michelle Mayhall, Nicole Hower, Kelly Lawler, and Cristina Wilson.

Thank you to my early readers and my expert readers. Thank you for your wisdom and your insight, and for not hesitating to tell me when I messed things up. For the stories you shared with me. You made this story infinitely better, and any mistakes I made are squarely on me.

To you, dear reader, for picking up this book. I know this isn't always an easy story, but I think that's okay. I hope it won't just bring you heartache, but solace and some hope as well.

And finally, as always, to my family and friends, who keep me going when things are tough. Even in uncertain and difficult times, the best way to stand is together. My thanks. My love. Always.

ABOUT THE AUTHOR

Marieke Nijkamp (she/they/any) is the #1 *New York Times* bestselling author of *This Is Where It Ends, Before I Let Go*, and *Even If We Break*. In addition to novels, she writes comics and graphic novels, and her short stories can be found in several anthologies, including *Unbroken: 13 Stories Starring Disabled Teens*. She is a storyteller, dreamer, globe-trotter, geek. She lives in the Netherlands. Visit her at mariekenijkamp.com.

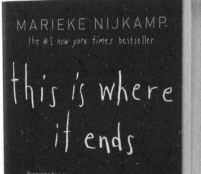